DANGEROUS LOVE

RILEY EDWARDS

Dangerous Love
Takeback Book 1

Cover design: Lori Jackson Designs

Written by: Riley Edwards

Published by: Riley Edwards/Rebels Romance

Edited by: Rebecca Hodgkins

Proofreader: Julie Deaton, Rebecca Kendall

Cover Image by: Golden Czermak- Furious Fotog

Dangerous Love

Ebook ISBN: 978-1-951567-15-6

Paperback ISBN: 978-1-951567-18-7

First edition: June 29, 2021

To my family - my team – my tribe.
This is for you.

1

Speech*less*.

Breath stolen.

Butterflies swarming.

Those were my thoughts when I glanced up from my laptop to find *the* most gorgeous man I'd ever seen in my life walk into the bar.

Now, some may think I was pretty lame sitting in a bar at eleven o'clock with my laptop in front of me. But I wasn't. My life was pretty damn awesome. And it really wasn't a bar-bar, it was a hotel bar and I'd only come down to work because I was starving and I'd learned the day before, the Park Lounge made the best cheeseburger I'd ever had. The bacon was extra crispy, they were generous with the condiments, and they used extra-sharp cheddar.

The cheeseburger was important to note—that was what had drawn me down to the bar. That, and my best friend Letty was in our room trying to sleep and I had work to do. So, I wasn't sitting in the corner all by myself because I was an introvert, boring, or didn't like to have a good time. I was just a hungry workaholic.

The man made his way to the table and that was when I noticed he wasn't alone. And I swear on all things holy—a sack of my favorite smut books, may they burn to ash, my ereader explode, and my ability to read to be stolen—three equally good-looking men followed the breath-stealing, butterfly inducing man.

Then they sat down at a high-top table right next to the booth I was sitting in. Right. Next. To. Me.

One could say I was a tad dramatic. I loved a good story and when I couldn't find one in real life, I read them. Luckily for me, reading books was my job. I was an audiobook narrator—I brought authors' words to life. I breathed life into their characters. Best job ever!

But right then, I didn't need to open a book or close my eyes and daydream. Oh, no, there was a real-life, walking, talking fantasy—or should I say, four fantasies come to life less than five feet away.

This was just too damn good to keep to myself.

I looked back down at my keyboard, saved the manuscript I'd been making notes on, and pulled up Messenger. I found Letty's contact and started typing.

Mayday. Mayday. Get dressed and come down to the bar.

Letty didn't answer.

Wake up. You have to come down here.

A minute that felt like an eternity later, she responded.

Sleeping.

Four of the hottest men I've ever seen are sitting five feet from me. Come quick.

No. Tired. And today, at least ten times you pointed out a hot male model you said was gonna be the father of your children. That's a lot of baby daddies, Brooklyn. A lot. Think about your poor va-jay-jay popping out all those babies and finish your burger and come to bed.

So, maybe Letty wasn't exaggerating. But, in my defense, we were at a book signing. Not any ol' regular book signing —a romance signing. And not a sweet, wholesome romance book signing. Nope. These authors had it going on; they wrote about over-the-top alpha men who took charge in the bedroom, knew their way around a woman's lady parts, were protective, bossy, but still sweet and respectful. In other words—totally fictional, not real, made up to give women like me something good to get lost in. And at this signing, there'd been cover models roaming the convention.

My day had been spent *swooning*. Models, authors, my reader friends. Great day.

My life revolved around books. Not only did I narrate them I also worked in Letty's book store aptly named, Smutties. The store was nirvana, solely dedicated to all things romance. Mostly she carried independent authors but in the last year, some of the big publishers had taken notice and wanted their books in Smutties. I had a small recording studio in the back so I could pull double-duty helping her in the store and recording when she didn't need me.

I was living my dream. It was awesome.

But life could always get better, as evidence five feet away suggested.

Like you weren't drooling. Get. Down. Here. And bring my phone so I can sneak a picture. P.S. thank you for thinking of my "poor" vagina.

I'm not bringing you your phone, you crazy stalker. Stop working and go to bed. You were up at five. I don't know how you're still awake.

You're missing out.

You're a crazy person. Leave me alone. I'm going back to sleep.

Fine.

I closed Messenger and sat as quietly as I could so I

could eavesdrop. I mean, what else was there to do? When four hot men sat close and you didn't have the gumption to approach, you listened to their conversation and filled in the blanks with your imagination. I could build a whole story around each of them.

By the looks of them, they were not businessmen. Three out of four had beards. Not straggly Grizzly Adams beards, not super-groomed either, somewhere in between. The one that had caught my attention had stubble but not full growth like the others. The color scheme of their clothes was interesting, too. Tan, olive drab, black, and plaid. Three of them were wearing a variation of the same color tan pants. Mr. Stubble was wearing olive drab pants and a plaid shirt with the sleeves rolled up. One wore a black tee, the other two also wore plaid long-sleeved shirts. Thank goodness the plaid pattern was different or they'd look like weirdos.

I was still in the process of my creepy perusal when I felt the hair on the back of my neck prickle. My gaze went back to Mr. Stubble and he was staring at me. No expression. Face blank. Just his eyes locked onto mine.

Nope, not a businessman. No way. Not even the savviest, most ambitious, cut-throat CEO could have a stare so intense. Law enforcement or military. And by the way they were dressed, the air of authority around them, I'd guess law enforcement. Further, we were in a hotel a few miles away from Dulles International Airport, just outside of D.C. so narrowing that down, it wouldn't be a stretch they were military, feds, or marshals.

Or perhaps I'd read too many books and they lived in the area, this bar was convenient, and they were meeting for a drink. Maybe they were mechanics. Which would be hot, too. Who doesn't love a man who has strong hands and can fix things? I'd bet Mr. Stubble could make my engine purr like a kitten.

Did I seriously just think that?

Letty was right. I needed sleep. My overactive imagination had been in hyperdrive all day. I was overworked and undersexed. I needed an orgasm that was not self-induced stat. As soon as I got back to Idaho I was getting on that.

But first I needed to tear my gaze away from the hottest man I'd ever seen. The problem with that was he was holding me captive. The butterflies had stopped fluttering their velvety soft wings and they'd started rioting. They were bumping into each other, making a ruckus that made my belly feel funny and gave me goose bumps.

One of his dark eyebrows quirked up and it felt like a question. No, it felt like a dare.

Now I couldn't look away. So I returned the brow lift and one-upped him with a smirk.

That earned me a smile that was so sexy my panties caught fire. Actually, they didn't burst into flames, they dampened.

Totally drenched from a smile.

What can I say, it was a really great smile that made his eyes crinkle at the corners. Eyes that were so dark from where I sat they looked black. *Everything* about him was dark. His hair, his eyebrows, his eyes, even the way he stared at me was dark.

Dark and decadent.

Panty-dropping-deliciously-dark.

His lips twitched. His jaw dipped. Then he looked over at his friend and I suddenly felt cold. I wanted his eyes back. I wanted his attention on me and only on me.

Feeling the loss of his gaze was ridiculous. In an effort to tamp down my urge to crawl into a stranger's lap and rub myself all over him, I glanced back at my screen and tried to focus.

I mean, who would do that? In this day and age what person in their right mind would even *think* about approaching a stranger in a bar?

Me. Right at this moment, I would do that.

Yep. Undersexed. That was what it had to be. It was official, I'd read too many books. And since any good Smut Bibliophile knew, there was no such thing. My life must've been coming to an end. There was no other reason for my reaction.

I was in lust with a stranger.

When my brain came back on station, I heard, "We'll meet the team in South Carolina and go from there."

"How many are they thinking?" The smooth, rich, silky voice washed over me and my gaze sliced back to the stranger. Sure enough, the voice belonged to him.

It was now one-hundred-percent certified Mr. Stubble was the sexiest man alive.

"Thirty. Maybe forty," one of the other men said.

"The locals have a location," another man put in.

Something else was murmured but I didn't catch it. I was in a lust-induced haze like I'd never experienced. My pulse pounded and all sorts of crazy thoughts galloped through my mind.

Me, Brooklyn Saunders—never having done it before—would absolutely follow this stranger to his room, participate in my very first one-night-stand-with-a-stranger, and bang his brains out. One hundred percent, I'd do it. I'd live out every fantasy, I'd feel no remorse, I'd feel no guilt, and then I'd tuck away the memory and relive it as often as I could.

That was if Mr. Stubble, Sexiest Man Alive, was good in

bed. And there was no way he wasn't; the universe wouldn't be so screwed up to give a man that good-looking a small wanker. Or a big one with no skill.

My gaze dropped from his profile to his hands. Oh, yeah, he had great fingers and nice forearms. I continued my perusal up to his biceps. Though he was wearing long sleeves I could still see the bulge. I was not a small woman but he'd have no problems hoisting me into his arms. Of course, I'd wrap my legs around his waist in an effort to assist with weight distribution. Oh, who the hell was I kidding? I'd wrap my legs around him so he could fuck me against the wall. Only after that was checked off the fantasy to-do list would I take him to the bed. I wondered if he'd let me ride him, or if he was the sort of man who would take charge and hold me prisoner while he did dirty, filthy things to my body. I'd be his willing captive or I'd ride him until I was breathless and exhausted. Either way, I wouldn't complain. I'd feel no shame begging him to take me harder. Though I doubted I'd need to beg or give instructions to a man like him.

He oozed confidence and masculinity. It lingered in the air. I inhaled it. It surrounded me. My body knew what it wanted. My mind was fully on board. I kept my heart carefully tucked away, understanding it had no place in this adventure.

"Would you like company?"

Smooth, like warm honey.

I blinked and lifted my gaze to find the stranger standing next to my booth. My eyes flicked to the now-empty table where he and his friends had been sitting.

How long have I been zoned out?

I didn't care how long. I was just hoping "company" was a euphuism for wild sex. I didn't ask for clarification, I just hoped I was reading the look on his face right or this would be awkward.

"I would love company."

I closed my laptop, slid it into my bag, made sure I'd signed the credit card slip, then started to scooch out of the booth.

The man's lips twitched and he held out his hand.

"Your room or mine?"

Yep. It was a euphuism, all right. Wild, fantasy-fueled sex, here I come.

"Yours."

I looked down at his hand, placed mine into his, and savored the warmth.

"You have great hands," I whispered.

I was tugged out of the booth to my feet, the man lowered his head, then a hair's breadth away from my ear he whispered, "You sure about this?"

A chill ran down my spine and my nipples tightened.

"I'm sure."

I guess he liked my answer because the next thing I knew he snatched my bag out of my hand and was pulling me through the bar. Holding my bag for me was a nice touch but unnecessary. So was the pulling part; I'd already decided I'd follow this man straight through the gates of hell if he was one iota as good as he looked.

Yes, I was lust drunk and willing to sell my soul to the devil to spend one night with a man I'd never see again.

He turned left, walked halfway down the hall, stopped in front of a door, and looked down at me with his dark eyes. Something stole over me. Lust, sex fantasies, wet panties, tingling nipples aside, he had beautiful eyes. And right then they were kind and gentle.

"You still sure?"

"Yes."

He inserted his key then pushed open the door but didn't go through.

"My name's—"

"No names," I rasped, totally unashamed.

He graced me with another panty-melting smile and gestured me through the door. After that, there was no more talking. He'd found better uses for his mouth. One could say, this beautiful stranger was an action man.

He was better than any fantasy.

He was as rough as he was gentle.

He kissed, caressed, and licked every inch of me. He nibbled, bit, and pinched. He fucked me against the wall, on the bed, in the shower, and on the floor. I sucked him off, rode him, and yanked his hair while his face was between my legs.

It was the wildest night of my life.

He was the best I'd ever had.

And in the morning when he kissed me goodbye I was having a hard time reminding my heart we couldn't keep him. I struggled not to ask him for a name. I fought back the temptation to ask for another night—or a week—or forever.

But in the end, my sensible side won out.

I wrapped my arms around him and told him I'd never forget a single second of our night together. He gave me a soft, slow sweet kiss that made my heart melt and cemented my decision never to see him again.

Truth be told, I was a romantic. I believed in love at first sight. I knew soul mates existed. One more night with this man and I'd tumble headfirst from lust to love. I was already halfway there. It was not the sex, it was the way his fingertips had softly traced the flowers tattooed up my arm. It was the way his face softened when I explained the meaning of each one. It was the way he'd kissed each blossom. It was the way he smiled and laughed. We'd had mind-bending sex, but we'd also connected.

"Ocean blue," he murmured and brushed his lips over my cheek.

I didn't know what he was talking about and I didn't ask.

I felt no shame walking out of his hotel room.

I felt no guilt taking what I wanted and living out my wildest dreams.

I felt no remorse.

And I didn't lie—I never forgot a single second. Not one. Every day I was reminded I'd had the best night of my life with a stranger.

But I did have one regret—I should've asked him his name.

2

Five years later

"Rhode, you're with Reese and Davis to secure the safe house," Wilson McCray, Takeback's team leader and federal liaison, told me as he started with assignments. "Cole, Jack, Asher, you're with me."

I stood in the shadows with my team and glanced around the bankrupt lumber mill. The area was awash with activity: police, fire, ambulances, passenger vans, and unmarked black SUVs surrounded the rescue site. Local and federal law enforcement out en masse.

This operation was three weeks in the making. Forty-one victims had been rescued. It wasn't the first time the team had recovered children—boys and girls as young as ten. Neither was this the first time I'd seen teenagers or young adults. The sixty-year-old woman who had her arms wrapped protectively around the three youngest didn't surprise me either.

Nothing did anymore.

I once thought I'd seen it all—ten years as a SEAL

deployed to the most war-torn countries, I'd done and seen shit nightmares were made of.

Nothing could prepare a person for this level of depravity.

Human trafficking knew no age, no race, no religion, no gender, no economic status.

It was the devil's work.

Period. The end.

"The families been called?" Davis asked, his voice low and angry.

"Yeah," Wilson answered. "The closest is thirty minutes away. Vic's name's Kiki Welsh. The rest will be a few hours."

I found the young woman in question amongst the other two victims who had family close. The three had already been separated from the rest of the group and paramedics looking them over. So far, none of them had injuries that would necessitate an ambulance ride or a medivac. But that didn't mean shit. The EMTs couldn't assess the real damage of the trauma they'd endured.

Weeks' worth of work, a successful rescue, yet my stomach still clenched. Victims but no one to arrest. Something wasn't right. Traffickers didn't leave their merchandise unattended.

Before the team could disperse, there was a loud commotion complete with a shrill scream.

"My daughter's over there."

"Shit," Wilson cursed.

Shit was right. Family at the rescue site was never good.

"Kiki!"

The young woman had no reaction to her name being shouted. I slowly turned and found a tall, slender, older woman with stick-straight black hair, beside her an older, taller man with salt-and-pepper hair and an olive complexion. And next to the older couple were two women. One of them was the spitting image of the older woman. I couldn't see the other woman's face but she, too, had dark hair.

Kiki Welsh was a ginger. A true redhead complete with green eyes, pale skin, and a face full of freckles.

"Wilson, you better go over there." I jerked my head toward the family. "And pray that girl's adopted."

Wilson looked from the redhead to the family calling out her name, then back to the redhead, and mumbled a string of expletives before he moved the few feet to the police barricade.

"Shit," Davis muttered, doing the same slow perusal Wilson had done. "This isn't going to end well."

"Ma'am, I'm Wilson McCray. If you give me a minute, I'll get you and your family cleared," he greeted the family.

"My daughter's been missing a week! I'm not waiting another second!" the woman shouted.

"Tallulah, Mama, he's going to help us. Let's give him a minute."

The sound of the soothing, lyrical voice hit me square in the chest. A pinprick of recognition washed over me. I turned and my eyes hit on the family. The last name Welsh didn't mean anything to me, and I never forgot a name or a face and none of them looked familiar, but that voice—I knew it. Hell, it had been years, and sometimes I still heard it in my dreams.

One night.

Six hours.

That was all we'd had. Yet letting her leave without getting her name was a regret.

A huge one.

I knew it when she'd slipped from my hotel bed. I'd felt my chest get tight when she'd walked out the door. It had been five years, and I still wondered what it was about her that to this day had me tied in knots. There were long stretches of time when I'd convinced myself it had been the sex. Other times I'd told myself it was her spontaneity. The woman had grabbed ahold of our night together like it was her last on earth. She'd taken my hand, followed me to my hotel room, then proceeded to live out a fantasy. And in doing so, rocked my world.

But it wasn't just the sex. It was the times between sessions when she smiled and laughed and teased that had clinched the deal. It was the way she got off on me taking charge, and she had no issue voicing how much she liked it. It was the way she'd turned the tables and tussled with me for dominance. Slow, drugging kisses. Hard, deep, wet ones. The woman was dynamite.

Beyond all of that—how good she was in bed, how sweet she tasted, the warm flowery perfume I could sometimes still smell, it was her eyes. So pretty, I couldn't stop staring into them while I was moving inside of her. So blue they looked like the Caribbean Sea. Big, blue, expressive eyes that held so much happiness and excitement they were intoxicating.

The kind of eyes you could get lost in. The kind that held you captive. The kind that made you smile just by looking into them.

So, fuck yeah, I regretted letting her go. It was one of the top five biggest mistakes I'd ever made.

"We should hit the road." Reese's suggestion pulled me from my thoughts.

I lifted my hand to curl it around the back of my neck and squeezed.

"Give me a minute."

Indecision weighed heavy. I was working a job and my

priority was the victims we'd rescued, but I couldn't get my brain on board. I knew that voice, was sure of it, and I wasn't making another mistake.

I started to make my way to the police line when I saw her.

Time stood still.

Those eyes.

Her hair was longer, but other than that, she looked the same. She held the older woman's hand, and her other arm was around the younger woman's shoulder.

Christ. Bad timing.

The worst.

My gaze went from the woman's arm back to her face. I heard her gasp right before her eyes went wide.

The young woman who was leaning into her looked up, her body jolted, and she muttered a very loud, "Oh my God."

"What? Do you see her? Where is she?" the mother asked and craned her neck. But when her gaze hit me she jerked as well.

What the fuck?

"Remington," the mother breathed.

"This is Rhode Daley. And like I said, my name's Wilson McCray," Wilson quickly corrected the woman. "We work for an organization called Takeback. We assist federal and local law enforcement."

When none of the women spoke, the man cleared his throat and pulled his wife closer.

"Michael Welsh. This is my wife Tallulah, our daughter Letty, and a family friend, Brooklyn Saunders. We'd be obliged you get a move on getting us to my daughter."

Brooklyn Saunders.

Finally, a name.

Brooklyn.

"Mr. Welsh, take a walk with me," Wilson started, then continued, "Rhode will stay here with your wife and daughter."

I peeled my gaze from the women and looked at my team leader. Hard-set jaw, eyes narrowed. Not at the man's tone or demand, but because there was a strong possibility Kiki Welsh was not there.

"I don't understand!" Mrs. Welsh screeched. "I want to—"

"Tally, stay with Letty and Brooklyn. I'll be right back," Mr. Welsh said.

"But—"

"Mom. Let Dad handle this. He'll be right back," Letty said, obviously catching on, like her dad, that something beyond the obvious wasn't right.

Wilson lifted the police tape, Michael ducked under, and together they walked in the direction of the ambulance.

Awkward silence ensued. This was not the time or place, but I wasn't letting the opportunity pass.

"Brooklyn?"

Her blue eyes skidded to mine and I didn't miss the wince.

Good Goddamn, that felt like a bullet to the chest.

I'd spent more time than I should've over the years thinking about her. She'd plagued my dreams. Seeing that wince, killed.

"You must be Dulles," Letty cut in.

"Come again?"

"Dulles. The airport." Letty turned to Brooklyn and bumped her shoulder. "This *is* Dulles, right?"

"Um, yeah," Brooklyn stuttered.

Before I could figure out what to say, the truth slammed

into me. Brooklyn had come with the Welshes—the family that lived thirty minutes away. My cabin in Sandpoint was a little over an hour from where they were in the Spokane Valley. Not that I spent much time in Idaho, but over the last five years, I'd been in the area several times a year.

Brooklyn had been close by the whole time.

"What's going on?" Mrs. Welsh demanded. "I want to see my daughter."

"Why would you do this?" Michael Welsh roared.

Fucking hell.

Tallulah pushed through the tape, Letty on her heels, Brooklyn a step behind.

My hand shot out and wrapped around Brooklyn's bicep.

"Get your friend and her mother back."

"What? Why? How bad is Kiki?"

"That's not Kiki, babe. I don't know who she is, but she gave a false name. Get Tallulah and Letty back. Let Mr. Welsh handle this."

"Oh my God." Brooklyn paled, then she yanked free and ran after her friend.

Bedlam ensued.

Brooklyn practically tackled Tallulah from behind and wrapped her arms around the woman. Michael Welsh was shouting. Davis ran to assist Wilson. Reese, Jack, and Asher rushed to form a barricade to keep the women back. Cole came to my side, and together we moved to flank the women.

"What's happening? Where's Kiki? Is she hurt? I want—"

"Mama, come with me," Letty pleaded and grabbed her mother's hand.

"No. I want—"

"Tallulah, Mama, please. Please come with us," Brooklyn tried.

It was then a mother's intuition kicked in. And when it did, I cringed. The pain was so great it pierced my vest and cut me to the core.

Tallulah Welsh's legs buckled, taking Brooklyn to the ground with her. Letty dropped to her knees in front of her mother. Then with Brooklyn and Letty bracketing her, a mother's wail of anguish rent through the air like a clap of thunder.

I closed my eyes, and when I opened them, they locked with ocean blue.

I'd waited five years to look into those eyes again.

Five years to right a monumental screw-up.

Bad timing. The worst.

But now that I'd found her, I wasn't walking away without a fight.

3

I'd messed up again.

A week ago I found him. Rhode Daley.

Rhode Daley. I rolled his name around in my head. I had a name. I'd thought about it a lot through the years—what his name was. John or Pete or Samuel. But those were too boring, so Letty had guessed his name had to be something cool like Bjorn, Magus, or Ragnar. When I'd reminded her the stranger wasn't a Viking, she'd smirked and reminded me he had pillaged, and she continued to come up with a bevy of Viking names for the stranger.

It wasn't until two months later the name-guessing and joking had stopped. Real life had smacked me in the face. I didn't know his name, and I really, *really* wished I had asked.

So in all of the guessing, I had never considered Rhode. Without a name to call him, I settled on Dulles. That would've been embarrassing if it wasn't so pathetic.

But now I knew his real name, and in the chaos and heartbreak of the day, I let him walk away again.

I had no choice. Tally and Michael had been beside

themselves. Letty was near broken. Kiki had been missing a week—now she'd been gone two weeks—but that horrible day, the Welshes thought a miracle had happened, and Kiki had been found.

But she hadn't been. Kiki's friend Desi Cunns had lied to the police and said she was Kiki.

And her excuse was piss poor, in my opinion. But seeing as Michael and Tallulah Welsh were good people—the best actually—once the shock had worn off, they'd forgiven her. And when Desi explained she was estranged from her family, scared, and knew the Welshes would help her, they'd done exactly that and had taken her in. Michael and Tally had been the ones to call her family and smooth things over. And yesterday, Michael and Tally sat next to Desi while she reconnected with her mom and dad.

Unfortunately, she was in a bad way. Fortunately, her family was committed to helping her heal and had checked her into a mental health facility. This was not done as a way to wash their hands of Desi; it was done out of great concern. The Cunns understood their daughter needed more help than they could provide, and they were getting her the help she needed.

All of that was good. What wasn't good was that Tally hearing what Desi had gone through sent her into a tailspin.

I could imagine on a small scale the terror Tally was going through. Not knowing where her child was, who had her, if she was being harmed, if she was already dead. The thoughts ran through my head on a constant loop and made me sick to my stomach. I'd known Kiki all her life. I moved in with the Welshes after my parents died when I was sixteen. But even before that, my parents were best friends with Tally and Michael. Our families had been close. Every holiday, every vacation, every special occasion we were with the Welshes. They had always been my second family. Letty and I had been best friends since forever. Kiki was like my little sister.

What those thoughts must be doing to Tally and Michael wrenched my gut. What Letty was going through, not knowing where her sister was—earth-shattering.

"Sorry we're late," Letty called out as soon as she entered the door.

It was Saturday. I was working the bookstore alone while Letty ran errands for her parents.

"Mommy! We brought you a milkshake!" the sweet little boy squealed and ran full speed across the store. Hearing my son's excitement never got old.

Remington. The real life that happened after my night with Rhode.

"Hey, there, buddy, did you have fun with Auntie Letty?"

I took in my boy's chocolate-stained shirt and I had my answer.

"Yup."

Remington popped the P and smiled big and bright. His dark brown eyes twinkled as he handed me the milkshake.

"I drank mine in the car," Remy informed me. "Auntie Letty said I could if I sat in the baby seat."

"Booster seat," I corrected. "Go wash your hands, would ya, bud?"

"It's a baby seat," Remy argued. "Pop says I'm big enough to ride a dirt bike."

"You're not," I told my son.

My gaze went to Letty and she shrugged.

"Don't look at me like that. We were—"

"Buddy, please go wash your hands," I cut Letty off and gave her squinty eyes.

Being as she was Letty, therefore not easily dissuaded,

she didn't take in my narrowed eyes and keep quiet. No, she pushed.

"You know Dad would never put him on a bike if he wasn't ready. He's almost five."

"He's not *almost* five. He's barely four and a half."

"Whatever, same thing."

It wasn't, but I wasn't going to argue. I also wasn't going to allow Remy to start riding dirt bikes, but that was a discussion for another day, so I changed the subject.

"A customer came in with a few requests. I wrote them down and put the list on your desk."

Letty glanced to the back of the store where a few customers were perusing the shelves and asked, "Have you been busy?"

"Steady stream all day."

"Awesome. And we're still on for tonight. Mom said she's good with Remy coming over."

"Letty—"

"It helps, Brook," Letty whispered. "You know her having Remy gives her something good. She and Dad both need this."

There was no doubt Tally and Michael needed all the goodness around them they could get, and Remington was a bright ray of sunshine in all of our lives. But Letty needed me, too. And tonight, she needed me by her side at this month's book club meeting.

"Okay, then I'm gonna take Remy home and clean him up. I'll be back in a few hours."

Letty's gaze dropped to my son, then her eyes came back to me, and I sucked in a breath when I saw her expression.

No one had brought it up.

There were more pressing issues.

But I'd known it was only a matter of time before the elephant in the room would be addressed.

"We need to talk about Rhode Daley."

"We will after Kiki's home."

"Brooklyn."

Letty glanced at Remy coming out of the backroom, and I knew what she saw. Dark hair, dark eyes, a beautiful face, tall for his age—a spitting image of his father.

A man I'd only been able to describe. A man that Letty had now seen.

"I can't talk about it yet."

"It's been a week. You need to talk about it."

"I will. As soon as Kiki's home, I'll find him. I have every intention of doing what's right. He needs to know. You know this. You know how much guilt I've carried. I just can't right now."

"Okay," she gave in.

Then she smiled and shook her head and lowered her voice. "I thought you were exaggerating."

"About what?"

"How hot he was. I mean, no one's that hot. But you weren't lying. Even in the middle of that shitshow and my mom coming apart, I didn't miss how good-looking he was."

"Told you so."

"And Remy looks just like him."

"Told you that, too."

"Thanks for being the best friend I could ever have and putting your life on hold."

The pain I heard in Letty's voice was precisely why I couldn't look for Rhode. I'd waited five years. A little more time wouldn't hurt. I owed the Welshes everything. But even if I didn't, there was no way I'd turn my back on my best friend. She needed me more than ever.

Guilt assailed me hard and fast, just like it always did. But this time, it was worse because I desperately wanted to look him up. Not only for Remington but for me. Five years was a long time to dream about a man you'd only had a few hours with. Sure, I couldn't forget him. We shared a son. But it was more than that—I could never forget the man himself.

"We're gonna find her, Lets. She'll be home soon."

"Mommy." Remy stopped next to me and tugged my hand. "If you're not gonna drink yours, can I have it?"

"No way, Jose, you already had one. Chocolate by the looks of what's on your shirt, and you know Grams and Pop will let you have a treat."

"That's because they love me," Remy proudly declared.

"They do."

"Don't you love me?"

Letty huffed, and the sadness was gone when she picked up her nephew and swung him around.

A ray of sunshine. That was Remy.

"You're a master manipulator. I think you're gonna be a lawyer when you grow up."

"No way. I'm gonna be an Army man and paint my face and crawl through mud and sneak up on bad guys."

"Jesus."

At the sound of a male voice, my head snapped to the door.

Jesus was right.

My time was up.

It was not Rhode who spoke—I'd know his voice anywhere. It was the man standing next to him who'd uttered the clipped statement.

Rhode's gaze was glued to Remington. His lips pinched together. His face tight.

My eyes drifted closed and my stomach clenched.
This was not how I wanted him to find out.

4

I'd warred with myself for a week.

Human decency warranted me to keep my distance.

But after seven days of not being able to concentrate on jack shit, I was done.

"You sure about this?" Davis asked as we approached the bookstore.

I glanced up at the sign above the door—a large piece of wood with the word Smutties curved into it at a diagonal. The hot-pink lettering wasn't what had my attention. It was the 1940s pin-up girl reading a book that made me smile. The store's tagline was: *I like my romance hot*. Seeing as I'd never read a romance book in my life, I didn't catch the meaning.

"Positive," I answered.

"What kinda books do they sell?" Davis asked, obviously catching the name.

"Romance."

"Damn, brother, you sure you're up for it?"

I was up for anything.

"Up for what?"

"Your woman works here, right?"

My friend was getting a little ahead of himself. But I didn't bother correcting him, seeing as Brooklyn would be my woman as soon as we found Kiki Welsh.

The moment I'd gotten back to my cabin after the raid, I'd dug into Brooklyn Saunders' life. At first, it was a cursory search. I was just looking for her address and phone number, but then I'd found that Brooklyn's life was intertwined with the Welsh family. And after I found why I'd talked to the team about approaching the Welshes and offering our assistance in locating Kiki. After all, that was what Takeback did. We found people.

Wilson had wasted no time contacting the feds and worked a deal. Now that it was official and Takeback had been assigned to the Welsh case, I wasn't delaying breaking the news to Letty Welsh.

And with any luck, Brooklyn would be at work.

"She does," I answered Davis.

"A woman who reads romance might have all sorts of ideas in her head." Davis whistled and shook his head. "Love and heroes. You sure you wanna tangle with that?"

I'd waited five years to find Brooklyn. I was more than ready to tangle with her, preferably in a bed, with her naked.

"Like I said, I'm positive."

Davis opened the door and a blast of perfumy air wafted around me. I hadn't recovered from the familiar scent of flowers when I spotted Letty holding a squirming little boy.

One who didn't look a thing like her.

One who looked a lot like I did when I was a kid.

So much so, I couldn't move.

The little boy wiggled free and as soon as Letty set him on his feet, he declared, "No way. I'm gonna be an Army man and paint my face and crawl through mud and sneak up on bad guys."

My heart constricted and my body went solid.

"Jesus," Davis muttered.

"Whoa. You're like huge," the little boy breathed and eyed me from my boots to the top of my head.

"Rhode?"

Brooklyn's panicked voice hit me square in the heart.

"Rhode? Is that your name?" the boy asked but didn't wait for an answer before he continued. "Hey, that's cool. My name's Remington."

Remington.

In warp speed, everything clicked into place. The flinch when Brooklyn saw me. Letty's weird reaction. Tallulah breathing Remington's name in shock.

What the fuck?

What in the actual hell?

"Remy, buddy, go with Auntie Letty to the office for a minute."

Auntie Letty.

Well, that confirmed the boy wasn't Letty's son. Not that I had much doubt. It hadn't been Letty I'd spent the night with. It hadn't been Letty I'd fucked. It hadn't been Letty I'd tasted. And it sure as hell wasn't Letty I'd thought about for five years.

"Come on, Remy." Letty tagged the boy's hand who still hadn't taken his eyes off me.

The kid's head tilted to the side, and with more awareness than any child should possess, Remy studied me.

The boy knew—maybe not the extent of it, but the kid knew something was going on.

All that was left was Brooklyn's confirmation, which

seemed pretty damn unnecessary since I knew without hesitation I was staring at my son.

"Letty, I'm Davis Wright. We met the other night. Why don't we switch it up and let Rhode and Brooklyn use the office to talk? I can help you out here."

"Yeah. Um. Actually, that sounds like a better plan. Remy, you can help me clean up the mess your mom made behind the counter."

Wordlessly Brooklyn handed Remy a to-go cup and smiled down at him. The boy beamed at his mom and put the straw to his mouth.

"I'll be right back, buddy." Then she turned those blue eyes to me and smiled. It was shaky and held a good amount of fear, and a part of me was pleased as fuck Brooklyn looked so nervous. "The office's back here."

My anger spiked as I started to follow when I realized I hadn't spoken to the boy.

I stopped and said, "Remington's a cool name. Much better than Rhode."

Remy's smile came quick. Pure and innocent.

He'd seen that same smile.

Identical.

Jesus.

Fuck, yes, I was pissed as fuck.

Not getting Brooklyn's name before she left my hotel room just got moved to the top of the list—biggest regret of my damn life.

I used the walk through the store to attempt to calm my racing thoughts. But when Brooklyn closed the office door, I was nowhere near calm. Calm was a memory. Irrational anger had taken root. I had a goddamn son I didn't know about.

I didn't get a chance to ask a single question before Brooklyn launched in.

"I tried to find you. I swear I did. I called the hotel and asked them for your name. Room one-ten. But they wouldn't tell me anything. I even tried to hire a private investigator, but they told me a room number at a hotel wasn't enough to go on. I didn't know anything else about you except what you looked like. I would've told you. I mean, I wanted to tell you. I mean, I was going to tell you. Now that I know your name, I was going to look you up so we could talk. But with everything happening with my family and Kiki, I had to wait. But I swear for Remington—for you—I was going to find you and tell you."

"So he's mine."

I wasn't asking.

I knew.

"Yes. But I understand if you need proof," Brooklyn said, then rushed on, "But I'm not asking for anything. That's not why I wanted to find you."

"You're not asking for anything?"

"Like money. That's not why I wanted you to know."

Brooklyn stopped, closed her eyes, and hung her head.

"God. I'm making a mess out of this. I'm nervous. I wanted this day to happen. You have no idea how many times I've thought about this. Meeting you. Running into you on the street, at an airport, bumping into you somewhere so I could tell you. But as many times as I've thought about it, as much as I'd hoped it would happen, I never thought it would. And now that you're standing in front of me, I don't know what to say."

She drew in a breath, lifted her gaze but not her chin, and when our eyes locked, some of the anger ebbed, but the hurt remained.

A hurt that dug so deep it turned to shame.

The shame I had a son I didn't know about hit so hard it was a miracle I didn't fall on my ass. The guilt hit harder. I'd knocked-up a stranger, and she'd carried my child and had been raising that child on her own.

My child without a father.

That anger came rushing back, and with it came frustration.

"Fuck," I bit out.

Brooklyn jolted and her eyes narrowed.

"I know this is a shock."

"You think?" I snarled, unable to check the agony that had coated my soul. "I have a son. I missed damn near five years with him. So, yeah, I'd say shocking is an understatement. More like a colossal fuck-up."

The woman in front of me turned to stone. Then she leaned forward, lifted her hand, and jabbed a finger in my direction.

"Not one single thing about Remington is a fuck-up, Rhode. Not one. I'm not asking you to be a part of his life. I'm not asking you for money. That's not why I wanted to find you. We've been doing fine on our own—no, better than fine—we're great. I wanted you to know because it's the right thing. But I won't let you near him if you're gonna be a jackass to my son. He's the best thing that's ever happened to me. He's a good boy. He's happy, and I won't let anyone near him who's gonna cause him hurt. And that includes you."

A lot was going on in my mind. The first being I liked the way Brooklyn loved my son. I really fucking liked that she'd keep him safe. I loved that she'd go toe-to-toe with me to ensure Remington's happiness. What I didn't fucking like was that she thought I would hurt my child.

"You think I'd be a jackass to my son?"

Brooklyn shrugged. "The truth is, I don't know you. I'd like to believe you wouldn't, but you referring to my boy as a colossal fuck-up doesn't give me warm and fuzzy feelings."

"*He's* not the fuck-up, Brooklyn. Me letting you walk away was the fuck-up. It was right there on the tip of my tongue to tell you my name, leave it up to you if you wanted to find me. I was so close to asking you to stay, asking you your name, but I didn't. That morning you were looking at me like you were struggling with something. I didn't want to push for more than you could give, so I let you leave. I've regretted that for five years. Now it's more than regret. I lost something I'll never get back."

"I don't know what to say," she whispered.

That was the screwed-up part about all of this. There was nothing *to* say. There was no one to be pissed at except myself. There was no one to blame, no one to yell at or rage at.

All of it, my fault.

All I'd needed to do was ask her name, give her mine, and I wouldn't have missed out on my son's life. I wouldn't have missed my child's birth. I wouldn't have missed his first breath. The list was endless—all of the firsts I had not been a part of.

The more I thought about all I'd missed, the angrier I became until it hurt to breathe.

"I need to go," I rapped out.

Those goddamn blue eyes I'd never been able to forget lifted and met mine. Tears brimmed, hurt shone, guilt clear.

None of those things began to touch what I was feeling.

"I understand."

"No, Brooklyn, you don't. And be very thankful you'll never understand what it feels like to miss your boy coming into this world. Hearing him cry as he draws his first lungful of oxygen. Be very fucking grateful you'll never understand because it hurts like a motherfucker."

I watched as pain carved straight through Brooklyn. Tears spilled down her pretty cheeks, making her eyes glimmer—not the way they did in my dreams—right then, they were shining and full of remorse.

Standing there in the office of a bookstore less than forty-five minutes from my cabin—a store I'd walked past a handful of times but never paid any mind—in front of a woman who was the mother of my son. A woman I knew really fucking well but at the same time didn't know at all. I felt my throat clog. I felt my skin start to tingle. I felt my soul yearn for a boy I didn't know.

"Fucking shit," I choked out. "I have to go."

I turned, took two steps, stopped, and looked back.

"I want to know my boy, but right now I need to...Christ, I don't know what I need. I don't know what to say to you or him. I don't know how to make this right. I know you don't know me, so promising you a bunch of shit right now won't mean anything to you, but straight up, Brooklyn, I'm a man of my word, and I'm going to be in Remington's life, and that's a guarantee."

I heard her suck in a breath and listened to the sob fill the room. With an ungodly amount of effort, I fought the need to pull her into my arms and instead walked out the door.

I needed to leave for a variety of reasons. The biggest being I needed to get a lock on my emotions before I said something I couldn't take back. I needed to plan, and I needed to come up with a good one and do it fast.

Remington.

Cool fucking name.

A name I hadn't helped pick out. But if I'd been around, I would've agreed, maybe even suggested it.

When I hit the big open space, I glanced around. My gaze landed on my son talking to Davis, and my heart pounded in my chest. Letty was next to Remy, her hand on his shoulder, standing sentry. She knew who I was but she didn't *know* me or Davis. Letty was playing nice, but she wasn't letting Remy out of her sight. I liked that, too; my boy had people in his life who loved and protected him.

That was to say, I loved my boy was protected, but I really fucking hated I wasn't the one doing the deed.

That shit was going to change.

I made my way across the room, taking in the bookshelves lining the walls, the smaller line of cases in the middle of the room, a sitting area in the back corner that right then had three people lounging, stacks of books on the coffee table in front of them as they talked quietly.

As soon as I was close, I heard my son's disbelieving question.

"You were?"

The disbelief also held a hit of excitement, and jealousy slammed into me with such a force I rocked to a halt.

"I was. Rhode was in the Navy with me."

"He was?"

"Yep," Davis returned.

"Did you paint your face and crawl through the mud and catch bad guys?"

"Sure did."

Davis glanced up and gave me a chin lift that did nothing to quell my urge to kick my friend in the balls for merely talking to Remy—something I had yet to do beyond complimenting his name.

Remington craned his neck, his dark brown eyes landed

on me, and I stood frozen, absorbing the pain of my son staring at me like the stranger I was.

Like a boy who doesn't know he's looking at his father.

Fuck.

I had to leave. Regroup. Get my head straight.

Davis being a close friend, a smart man—the kind who paid attention and didn't miss the tension in the room, broke the silence.

"Letty, I appreciate your hospitality. We'll see you tomorrow."

"Yeah, Davis. And thank you. My mom and dad will be grateful. We all are."

Davis must've used his time with Letty to explain Takeback's new role in the investigation of her sister's disappearance.

Letty's gaze came to me. Her arm slid around Remy's shoulders and she gave him a weak smile.

"It's really great to finally meet you, Rhode."

Her maneuver was defensive, curling Remy closer, but her statement was friendly. In other words, I was welcome to get to know my son, but I'd be doing it under a microscope. The boy had people who cared and loved him, and all of them, including Letty, would be watching me.

That pissed me right the fuck off. The unfairness of it. The mere thought that Letty knew my son better than I did, that she'd likely been at Brooklyn's side when Remy was born, was a punch to the gut.

"Remy, it was cool to meet you." Davis lifted his hand and tousled the boy's hair, and red-hot fury shot through me.

"Will you be back?"

I jolted when I realized Remy was talking to me.

Pain and pleasure seeped into my veins.

And with my attention riveted on my boy, I answered, "Yeah, bud, I'll be back soon."

It must be said that Remington Saunders—soon to be Remington Daley—didn't miss much if the way he sized me up was any indication.

Farewells were exchanged, and it wasn't until we were out the door and in my Jeep that Davis spoke.

"He's yours."

I didn't answer mainly because Davis wasn't asking. You'd have to be blind or stupid not to see Remington was mine.

"Christ, brother, I don't know what to say."

Neither did I, so I didn't say anything.

I drove in silence. The air trapped in the Jeep was so thick it nearly suffocated me, so heavy it filled my chest and constricted my heart.

Biggest fuck-up of my entire life.

5

The best part about having a best friend who was more like a sister and so deeply entrenched in your life was she knew when to give you quiet and when to dig in and make you talk.

Seeing as Letty Welsh was the best friend I ever had, more like a sister, and knew me better than anyone on the planet, she'd given me quiet. After she'd done a thorough yet silent assessment and came to the conclusion I was holding onto my sanity, she'd given me a tight hug and told me to go home, get Remy cleaned up, and she'd see me later. And later that night during the book club meeting, she treated me no differently.

She hadn't said a word about Rhode's visit to Smutties. She hadn't asked about what had transpired in her office. She'd done what she'd always done and, without words, offered me her unwavering support.

That was Letty. But like any good sister, she would only allow the quiet to stretch so long. I was sensing she'd given me fifteen hours to mull over Rhode's visit, and my time was up. This might've also had to do with the small fact Rhode would be showing up at any moment with a bevy of men.

This was something she'd just finished explaining. While Rhode and I were in the office, Davis Wright had gently—Letty's words—told her that he and Rhode worked with a group called Takeback. They specialized in human trafficking and assisted the feds with executing rescue operations—mostly the US Marshals—but they also worked independently with families. Davis had explained that Rhode had asked the team to take Kiki's case, something they all readily agreed to do. Now they—that was Rhode, Davis, and the rest of the team—were coming to the bookstore to talk about Kiki's disappearance. They were coming here and not to Michael and Tally's house because they wanted to meet someplace neutral.

I thought this was a mistake. Not the meeting with Takeback, but having it at the bookstore and not at their home. As one could imagine, Michael was struggling and Tally was even worse. Letty disagreed and said it was a good excuse to get them out of the house, something that was rare for either of them.

Letty finished setting out the donuts she'd picked up from the bakery and turned to face me. I heard her suck in a breath then she hit me with sisterly love.

"Before he gets here, I need to know if I hate him or if I'm giving him a chance to prove he's a good guy." She didn't have to say she was talking about Rhode. "I'm not asking for a full rundown right now, but I need to know if he was an asshole to you and what his intentions are."

"I've never seen someone in so much pain," I whispered.

"What?" Letty returned just as softly.

"Pain, Lets. He told me to be grateful I'd never know how badly it hurt to miss your boy coming into this world.

Hearing his cry as he draws his first lungful of oxygen. I'll never forget those words for as long as I live. He missed that, and it killed to see him in so much pain. He also told me he was a man of his word, and he was going to be in Remington's life."

I'd tossed and turned all night thinking over what Rhode said. I wanted my son to have his father in his life. I'd always hoped we'd find him. But now that day was here, and I was scared shitless. I'd had Remy all to myself for four and a half years. I hadn't had to share my time with my son unless I wanted to.

Now Rhode could demand time. He could take Remy…

"Oh, God," I breathed.

"What? What's wrong?"

"I don't know where he lives. What if he tries to take Remy? What if he lives—"

"Stop. First, no one is taking Remy from you. No one. Not ever. Secondly, one step at a time. Plenty of men say they're gonna do right, then they bail. *Hello* Jessica? She was with Douche Nozzle for six years. He acted so excited when Jessy got pregnant, swore up and down they were gonna get married, then he took off when Jeremy was three months old. Poof. Gone. Vanished. No one saw that coming. You don't know this guy. He might not even stick around."

Letty was wrong. Rhode was not Douche Nozzle. Not even close. The two men were very different, and I didn't need to know Rhode to know that. One night, six hours, five years ago. Ten minutes, one conversation, yesterday, and I knew with certainty Rhode would not walk away from Remington.

I didn't voice this because it would make me sound a little nutso. There was no way to know, yet I still did. I heard it in the ferocity of his tone, the way he froze when he saw

Remy, the way he looked at his son, and that was before I confirmed what Rhode had known *with a look*. No man looks at a child and instantly connects unless that man wants to be in his kid's life. Like Rhode. *One look, and he knew.* And he felt the pain of missing out on his child's life so acutely it filled the office. His pain had coated my skin and slithered down my throat.

The front door opened. I turned and watched Rhode prowl in. His gaze scanned the store, and if I needed further proof that Rhode was not the type of man who would leave his child, looking for Remy sealed it.

"Holy shit, he's hot," Letty whispered, then leaned close and continued to speak softly but did it in a rush since Rhode was prowling our way. "If he turns out to be a good guy and he sticks around, I'm still calling him Dulles."

"No, you're not."

"Um, yeah, I am. Rhode's a cool enough name, but I'm callin' him Dulles."

Rhode's eyes came to mine, and before I could stop myself, I was transported to the past.

Speech*less*.

Breath stolen.

Butterflies swarming.

Only this time, I wasn't sitting in a bar, single and alone, staring at the sexiest man I'd ever seen and shamelessly fantasizing about using him for a night of fun. I was now a single mother with responsibilities. I didn't fantasize about anything anymore. Well, that was a stretch. I did fantasize about a nameless stranger and all of the incredible things we'd done together in his hotel room. But that was only when I was in bed late at night and Remy was asleep in his room. I never acted out those fantasies—I'd lived them. So they weren't really fantasies as much as they were memories.

Really, *really* great memories.

I watched Rhode walk straight to me, and I couldn't stop thinking he had a great walk—the same as he had five years ago. Confident. Controlled. Dark and delicious. There was no doubt the man had swagger.

Unfortunately, I was still speechless when he stopped in front of me.

"I'll let you two talk." Letty flashed Rhode a sassy smile and she walked away.

She was a good friend and part of that was doing her duty to remind me of the possibility Rhode could split. But Letty was like me—a romantic through and through and wanted Rhode to be the hero in my story.

And, yes, all of that was conveyed in one sassy smile and declaration she was keeping the nickname we'd given him.

"Is Remy here?"

Reality sliced through me.

"No. He's in school. Well, preschool until noon."

Rhode nodded, his face perfectly blank when he asked, "When this is done, if you're not busy before you pick him up, I'd like to talk to you."

And so it begins.

I swallowed the lump that had wedged in my throat and nodded.

"Sure. There's a bakery two doors down. We can go there or if you'd prefer privacy, I live around the corner. We could go there."

"I'd prefer privacy."

Shit. Okay. I could do this—sit and have a conversation with the father of my child four years and a handful of months later than the conversation should've actually happened. The hard part was over, right? He knew Remington existed. All that was left was to hammer out the details.

Details that would mean Rhode spending time with Remy. Then a sick, nasty, vomit-inducing thought invaded my mind. One whose answer would crush me into dust even though it shouldn't.

"Are you...um...married?" I stuttered.

The absurdity of the situation was not lost on me. I had no claim to Rhode so his answer shouldn't be life-altering, yet it was. Then there was the small, teeny-tiny matter that I actually had to ask.

Never once had I imagined myself a slut for having a one-night stand. Not even after I got pregnant. Not even when Letty was with me when I had Remy. Not until I had to ask if my son's father was married because I didn't know. Not until I was faced with a visitation schedule and I didn't know where he lived. I didn't even know his phone number.

"No."

Weirdly, he didn't ask if I was.

"A girlfriend?" I pushed.

"No."

Again he didn't ask if I had someone special in my life. If the relief of his answers hadn't been thumping through my body I would've thought more about how strange it was he hadn't inquired about my relationship status. But I was too busy figuring out why I was so pleased to find out he didn't have a wife. I could've told myself it was because I was worried about Remy having a stepmother but that would've been a lie. My reaction was purely selfish. Seeing Rhode with another woman would've killed.

"Brooklyn?"

Gah! Hearing him say my name did crazy things to my insides.

"Yeah?"

"We're gonna work everything out."

I wanted to believe him. I really did. But I didn't. I couldn't. There was too much at stake. I wasn't the same fun, free-spirited woman I was when I met Rhode. I no longer lived in my head, in my books, in made-up stories. I had Remington and his happiness was more important than anything else.

"Okay," I agreed.

"I know you don't believe me. But you will."

With that, he turned and walked away.

Thankfully Tally and Michael came in the door before Letty could pounce. I knew she was doing what any good sister would do and had been standing close, listening in.

Everyone was exchanging greetings. It was time for me to set aside my personal life and concentrate on Kiki.

She'd been gone a little over two weeks. I was not stupid nor was I naïve, though I'd never say anything to the Welshes—not because they were stupid or naïve either but they didn't need the reminder Kiki was running out of time. Wherever she was, whatever was happening to her was not good—it was likely the worst. She needed to be found sooner rather than later.

Letty was sitting between her mom and dad on the small couch that was meant to accommodate two. I was perched on the armrest. Wilson McCray was seated directly across from us in one of Letty's overstuffed purple velvet chairs. Reese Turmel and Cole Keniston were sitting in antique highback chairs both upholstered mustard yellow twill. And to complete the huddle, Jack Donovan, Asher Noble, Davis, and Rhode stood.

I'd been introduced to all of them. Belatedly, I realized I recognized Wilson, Davis, and Asher from the night at the hotel bar.

Also belatedly things were starting to snap into place—my assessment had been semi-correct; they weren't businessmen, they weren't buds hanging out at the bar after doing some manly activity. They were all former military. Wilson had been a marshal and Asher had worked at the FBI.

It took a lot, but I shoved all thoughts of the bar out of my mind. Wilson repeated what Davis had told Letty. I felt Tally go stiff at my side the moment the words "human trafficking" were uttered. Michael made a disgruntled sound that was painful to hear. But Letty was stone-faced, the dutiful daughter who hid her anguish from her parents.

"Do you think Kiki's still in the area?" Michael asked.

"We don't know yet," Wilson gently told him. "Right now, we're going over the reports the local PD gave us. The feds started building a file so we're looking at that, too. Desi Cunns provided new information, including the bar they were taken from so we have a new lead."

My hand resting on Tally's shoulder slid down her arm. I bent and grabbed her hand and squeezed. She returned my squeeze but didn't release the pressure. Nothing would release the pressure building inside of her until her daughter was home.

Wilson went on to explain how the investigation was going to go from then on. Reese had added a few words, but my mind was on Tally—the way she remained stiff, holding on tight. And my heart was heavy with the weight of her pain, Michael's pain, Letty's pain, and lastly, mine. I was also thinking that if my parents were alive, they'd be devastated. Letty and Kiki were their goddaughters—an honor my parents had taken seriously. My mom and Tally were like me and Letty. Best friends. Sisters of the heart. She would know what to do, what to say, how to help Tally. And my dad and Michael were just as close. He would've been out on the search for Kiki. He would've followed up on the calls the Welshes had received from people who'd claimed to see Kiki. He would've kicked in everything we had, making the reward for Kiki's safe return even larger than it was.

I didn't have much but I'd given every penny to the reward fund. This was after much argument from Michael. I wasn't proud of my actions but I'd pulled out the big guns and used emotional manipulation, reminding Michael that he and Tally had taken me in. They'd financially supported me. My parents didn't have life insurance, and after the sale of my parents' home and cars and all the final bills were paid, there wasn't much left. Michael hadn't blinked an eye taking on another mouth to feed. Neither had Tally. She and Letty got me through the loss of my parents. I owed them everything and I didn't have the first clue how to help them now that they needed me.

"We interviewed a few of Kiki's friends. One of them mentioned Kiki had a boyfriend." Cole's declaration grabbed my attention. "Trevor?"

When in the world did Cole have time to interview Kiki's friends?

"Kiki didn't have a boyfriend," Tally incorrectly answered.

Shit.

Tally didn't know about Kiki's boyfriend because her head would spin and Michael would be homicidal.

Trevor Lawrence was bad news. The kind of bad news you didn't bring home to Mom and Dad. Hell, you didn't even bring him around your sister, who loved you and would take one look at the guy and lock you away in an attempt to dissuade you from ever seeing him again. Something that Letty and I had done when we saw Kiki with Trevor.

That had been an accidental run-in. Kiki had not brought Trevor around because even though Kiki had taken a turn deciding she wanted to take a walk on the wild side—doing this about-face three years ago when she turned into a party girl to the extreme—she knew Letty would lose her mind about Trevor.

Not only was he into drugs he was also a biker. Not a friendly biker. Not a rough-and-ready alpha book hero biker. Nope, not Trevor. He was not in a biker club, he was in a biker gang. Everyone in a thirty-mile radius knew who the Horsemen were. Everyone also knew to steer clear because they were gross. Seriously gross. Slimeballs into drugs and sleazy women.

Kiki Welsh was not sleazy. And as far as I knew she didn't do drugs. So seeing her with Trevor had been alarming. After seeing Kiki and Trevor together, Letty wasted no time enlisting me to help her extradite her sister's head from her ass.

Kiki was having none of it. She'd told us to mind our own business. After Kiki disappeared Letty and I did tell the detective about Trevor but we hadn't told Michael and Tallulah. Mainly because Michael would go off on a tear and the Horsemen were not men you fucked with. They weren't even men you politely attempted a conversation with. With Michael beside himself with grief, he was unpredictable, and a man who loved his wife and children. A man's man who wouldn't give a second thought about waltzing up to the Horsemen biker gang headquarters and demanding answers.

Thankfully Letty and I hadn't had to tell Tally and Michael about Trevor because the police said Trevor hadn't been in Idaho when Kiki disappeared.

Now, the tea had been spilled.

"Trevor Lawrence," Letty confirmed.

"Who's Trevor Lawrence?" Michael boomed.

"Dad—"

"Who, Letty?"

"He's one of the Horsemen," Letty whispered.

Michael sucked back so much oxygen it was a miracle the rest of us didn't pass out. Tally's hand squeezed mine so tightly her nails dug in and I winced.

"Are you kidding me?" Michael roared and jumped up.

"I told the police. They looked into him and he was in California when Kiki went missing."

"But you didn't tell *me*." Michael jabbed his thumb at his chest. "How could you not tell me Kiki was dating a Horsemen?"

"I didn't want you going to the clubhouse and asking questions. You know the Horsemen. You know their reputation. And I know you're not thinking straight. You would've gone down there and—"

"You're goddamn right I'm not thinking straight! Your sister's gone. Vanished. And she was..." Michael trailed off and dropped his chin to his chest and shook his head. "And she was going out with a *Horsemen*." The last word was spat in disgust.

"How long was she seeing him?" Asher asked.

"She wouldn't say," I joined the conversation. "Letty and I saw them together in Spokane. A place called Jimmy's. We didn't approach them but a few days later, we talked to Kiki. She told us to butt out, she knew what she was doing and they weren't serious. She was just having fun. When we reminded her about the Horsemen's reputation, she laughed and told us not to believe the rumors. That Trevor wasn't like that. After that, she stopped taking my calls and she only answered the phone for Letty occasionally. That was three months ago."

"Jimmy's?" Rhode drawled. "What were you doing in a biker bar?"

How did Rhode know Jimmy's was a biker bar? And why did he sound so irate?

"We were there for research," Letty said and waved her hand like it was no big deal.

It wasn't a big deal; it was also the truth. I'd gone for research and she'd gone with me because that was what best friends do.

"Research?" Rhode pushed.

"I'm a book narrator."

"Know that, Brooklyn. So I'm unclear why you'd go to a biker bar in a shit area as research."

Rhode knew I was a narrator?

Suddenly sick hit my stomach. He'd looked into me. Not that I had anything to hide but still he'd invaded my privacy. Of course, he'd run a background check on the woman who was his long-lost baby mama. *Oh, God, I'm a baby mama.* That thought made my stomach clench.

"I'm not happy with either of you. The two of you keeping this from me is unacceptable and we'll be talking about it later," Michael grunted then turned to look at Wilson. "We've put our savings into funding the reward for Kiki. Whatever your fee is, we'll cover it. I don't care the cost, just find my daughter."

"Mr. Welsh—" Wilson started but abruptly stopped when Michael's spine snapped straight and his face twisted into a grimace so full of sorrow that Tally whimpered.

I didn't suspect much made a man like Wilson clamp his mouth shut. Unless what he was witnessing was so gut-wrenching, it stole his words. And Michael Welsh's distress was so visible it hurt to see.

I dipped my chin and averted my gaze.

"Whatever you want, it's yours. Just please find her."

With that, Michael pulled Tally to her feet and they walked out the door. The moment it closed behind them, Wilson began issuing orders.

"Reese, Cole, follow them home. If Michael leaves, call it in and one of you stays on him. If he attempts to hit the clubhouse, cut him off. Jack, Asher, get me everything on Trevor Lawrence. Davis, I want you on the Horsemen, anything you can find. Rhode, when you're done meet me at the hotel."

The hotel.

He didn't live in Idaho.

Shit.

"The police said Trevor was in California. That was why we didn't tell my dad," Letty offered.

"We're gonna double-check," Wilson returned.

The guys started to move out and Letty turned to me, her expression grim.

"I stand behind our decision, Lets," I told her. "I know he's pissed at us but I'd rather him mad than hurt."

"Did you see his face?" she whispered.

There wasn't a person in that room who could've possibly missed how destroyed he was.

I walked to my best friend, my sister of the heart, the best auntie to my son, and wrapped my arms around her as tight as I could.

Letty wound her arms around me, rolled to her toes, and

murmured close to my ear, "Somthin's wrong, Brook. I can feel it."

"Lets, sweets, you're holding on by a thread, putting on a strong front for your parents," I returned. "You can't keep going like this. You gotta open up to me, let me help you. And it *feels* wrong because it *is* wrong."

"No," she denied and shook her head. "It's not Kiki being gone. Well, it is, but it's Desi, too. There was something off about her."

"Honey," I started gently. "Desi was rescued with about thirty other people. I don't know how to say this without causing you more pain, but I think coming out of that nightmare, she gets to react however she reacts and we don't get to question it."

Letty's body went stiff and I hated feeling that from my friend. I hated it, but I hated it more that I caused it.

"It's in my gut, Brook. I'm not being judgy and I hear you. But I'm telling you, something is not right."

Guilt assailed me. Letty was not judgmental—she had never been and I'd all but accused her of being such.

"Okay," I gave in. "We'll talk to Wilson."

"And tell him what? I have a feeling? He'll think I'm crazy."

"No, I won't," Wilson said from nearby. "Actually, I'd like to hear what you have to say."

Letty gave me big eyes and pressed her lips together.

I glanced at Rhode expecting him to look irritated or at the very least impatient our conversation would be further delayed. Instead, I found he was not irritated or impatient, but he did look thoughtful. He was staring at me and Letty and when he noticed I was staring back he gave me a tight grin and dipped his chin.

A million thoughts raced through my head. I didn't

know where this new fork in the road would take me, but I was positive Rhode showing up was going to turn my life upside down.

That thought didn't scare me—it terrified me.

It also made my heart beat wildly in my chest.

It had been five years but I was no less romantic. I still believed in love at first sight and soul mates and cosmic connections and star-crossed lovers.

I'd fallen in lust with a stranger with a look. Now that stranger was back, he had a name, we shared a child, and my heart would forever be connected to his.

So, yeah, my life was about to be turned upside down.

6

I couldn't take my eyes off Brooklyn.

There in the flesh. Right in front of me. After years of dreaming about her, she was finally within my reach.

Yet, she wasn't.

So close, so far away.

"Take a seat," Wilson directed then asked, "How much time do we have before the store opens?"

"Half hour," Letty muttered and shuffled to the loveseat, taking Brooklyn with her.

And still, I couldn't stop staring. She was a mirage or a miracle or a dream come to life and I was afraid to blink—afraid she'd disappear, afraid she'd slip past me again.

"Tell me why you think something's off," Wilson launched in.

Letty glanced at Brooklyn. Brooklyn nodded at her friend and picked up her hand, grasping it in both of hers, and didn't let go. It hadn't escaped my notice how nervous Brooklyn was. I hadn't missed the sidelong glances, the stiff posture, the worry in her eyes, and I knew it had to do with more than Kiki Welsh's disappearance. But she'd pulled herself together, and she'd supported the family and her friend.

I respected that kind of loyalty, and if Remington wasn't a factor, I would've backed off until we found Kiki. But Remington was not only a factor, he was a priority; I wouldn't set aside getting to know my son.

Letty drew in a deep breath and her attention went back to Wilson.

"My sister's on the rebellious side. She goes her own way and doesn't much care what my parents have to say. She's always been like this. When we were younger, her rebellion was more about breaking curfew and wearing clothes Dad didn't approve of. When we got older, it was about not going to college, carving her own path, and ignoring my parents' pleas to get her act together. As you know, she's thirty. She's my sister and I love her but she has yet to grow up."

"What do you mean she hasn't grown up?" Wilson inquired.

"She lived in my parents' basement apartment until two years ago. She lived there partly because she couldn't hold a job long enough to save money to get her own place and partly because the money she did have she blew on going out and partying. Drove my parents around the bend. There was a big blow-up and Kiki packed her bags and moved out. No plan, no money. Just rebellion and stubbornness. She crashed on her friends' couches until she'd shack up with a boyfriend. Then she'd dump the guy and she'd be back on a friend's couch.

"That brings me to Trevor Lawrence. She knows he's bad news. Everyone knows the Horsemen are bad news. Every. One. I'm not sure if getting together with him was supposed to be a big fuck you to me and my parents or if it was something else. She didn't bring him around or tell anyone she was with him. And we hadn't seen them in CDA, we caught them in Spokane. But as big as CDA is, it's still a small town. Someone would've seen them together and told one of us."

Letty was correct about Coeur d'Alene, Idaho. It was a small town, but not that small. And that thought reminded me how close Remington and Brooklyn had been. Sandpoint was not far from CDA. When I was in Idaho I'd spent time downtown.

How many times was I close to her and my son and didn't know it?

That question had plagued my mind and churned my stomach for days. Even before I knew Remy existed I'd wondered if she'd been in the same bar or restaurant I'd been in.

"I get what you're saying, Letty, but none of that explains what feels off."

Wilson's tone was gentle, his voice soft and soothing. The one he only used when talking to victims' families. It was a far cry from his normally gruff, no-nonsense clipped manner.

"Desi had just been rescued," Letty said quietly. "So I could be way off base and this is going to make me sound bitchy, but from the beginning, when the police questioned her she seemed like she was... I don't know—worried. But when we got back to my parents' house it got worse. She didn't look relieved. She didn't look scared. She was worried. I can't explain it. She guarded every word she said. She only answered questions with a few words and offered no more. I thought maybe it was because my parents offered her a place to stay even though she'd lied about her identity. That's their way. They're selfless, they'd give anyone anything. I went to visit and Desi was in the basement. I went down to see if she needed anything and she was lounging on the couch with her phone. She was so totally engrossed she didn't notice me. I watched her for a good two minutes. She was texting someone and from the way her thumbs were flying over the phone I'd say she was mad."

"She had a phone?" I interjected.

"Yeah. And later I asked my mom if she or my dad had given her one. She told me they hadn't. Desi had used my dad's to contact her parents but other than that they hadn't seen her with one."

"Why didn't you tell me this?" Brooklyn asked, positively affronted.

Letty jerked her head in my direction but offered no words.

"Seriously?" Brooklyn spat. "That's not an excuse, Lets. What did Desi say when you caught her with the phone?"

"She didn't catch me. I went back up the stairs without her seeing me. I knocked and when I went back down, I pretended I hadn't seen what I'd seen and she was curled into a ball on her side, no phone in sight. Now, again, this is going to make me sound like a total ass. But when Desi didn't know I was there, she was lounging around texting. The second time I went down, it was like she was putting on a show."

Brooklyn's gaze sliced to me and she asked, "Is that normal?"

I took in the woman's hopeful expression and it pained me to have to explain to her in all that I'd seen, all the victims I'd assisted there was no such thing as normal. Everyone reacted differently.

"Can't say, don't know Desi Cunns. But the phone is concerning and we definitely need to know who she called." I turned to Wilson. "I didn't see anything in the report about her having a phone, and if she did, why didn't she use it to call the police?"

Actually, the phone was more than concerning; it was a red flag and I didn't like red flags. I also didn't like loose ends. Wilson liked them less so. Therefore it was no surprise Wilson's face was carefully blank, but I knew my friend—his mind was working putting pieces together.

"What else?" Wilson pushed.

Gritting my teeth, I fought back the urge to tell my team leader we had enough to start with. I'd impatiently waited for what seemed like an eternity to talk to Brooklyn; now I wanted nothing more than to get her alone. There were things I needed to say, questions I needed to ask, plans to put into action. But I couldn't do any of that until I got to Brooklyn's house.

Which I was interested in seeing. I owned a cabin in the mountains, not easily accessible during the winter. I would need to get a house in town, a family home.

Slow your roll, the logical side of my brain warned.

The issue was I didn't want slow. I wanted warp speed. I didn't want to delay winning over the mother of my son. That was the one thing I'd decided last night. I'd lost years with Remington *and* Brooklyn. There was a reason I couldn't get her out of my head. A reason why I'd dreamed of her. A reason that bore contemplation. And the more I thought about it, I knew why. And being the sort of man who learned from his mistakes, I wasn't going to make another one with Brooklyn.

She was going to be mine.

She *and* Remington.

I wanted both and I'd pull out all the stops to get them.

"Listen, Letty," Wilson started. "I'm sure this is hard for you so don't make it harder. We're not going to judge you.

We're not going to think you're bitchy. All we're going to think is that you're a concerned sister and something's not sitting right. Go with your gut and just tell us what's making you uneasy."

"It was the way she was staring at my parents," Letty blurted out. "God, I don't know the right words. She was watching them—carefully. Again, not like she was scared of them, but like she was hiding something and was worried they'd figure it out. I swear every time I saw her I felt like she was acting like she *thought* she should act. I mean, not even a shiver when she told the police about the night she and Kiki were taken. Her tone wasn't dead or freaked out. It was like she was telling a well-rehearsed story."

Brooklyn's shoulders stiffened and she tilted her head before she nodded.

"Letty's right. I didn't think much of it. I figured Desi was in shock. I know I was, thinking Kiki had been found, then..." Brooklyn let that hang and shook her head. "It was a bad night. Tally and Michael were beside themselves but trying to be understanding. Desi answered all of the questions. But damn if she didn't say all the right things. She didn't stumble, she didn't hesitate. And she lied when the officer asked her if Kiki had a boyfriend. Desi and Kiki are roommates, or Kiki was staying on her couch, but they're close. Desi also would've known Kiki was seeing Trevor.

"At the time, I was grateful she hadn't said anything in front of Michael. But now, thinking on it, if someone kidnapped Letty, I'd be spilling my guts, every secret, anything that could help find her. But Desi flat-out lied."

I'd read the report Officer Sara Stan had submitted after she interviewed Desi Cunns. Victims were not asked to relive their time in captivity so soon after a rescue. The officer had gone gently, asking only about the night she and

Kiki were taken, and that was only because Kiki wasn't among the rescued.

"Desi is under a doctor's supervision," Wilson noted.

"She is," Letty confirmed. "Her parents picked her up. Which was strange considering she hasn't spoken to them in years. I don't know Desi, but from what Kiki told me Desi hates her parents; like hates them so much she left Seattle when she was twenty because she wanted away from them. I thought maybe being taken and held for a week against her will, having God knows what happen—and I'm not making light of that but I cannot let my mind wander there while my sister is missing— but I figured after that trauma it shook her and she wanted to repair her relationship with her family. But now looking on it, it feels like she was using that as an excuse to leave."

Letty stopped and hung her head, then whispered to her lap.

"God, what if I'm wrong about everything? What if Desi's telling the truth and she's just traumatized and acting strangely because of that? What kind of person does it make me to even say this about her?"

Brooklyn gathered her friend into her arms, the gesture natural, like she'd done it a hundred times, a testament to their friendship. And there was something about witnessing their closeness that eased some of the guilt I'd felt when I thought about Brooklyn raising Remy on her own. No parents, no siblings. But she'd had family around and I liked that for her and my boy. None of them were substitutes for all I could've given Remy but Brooklyn hadn't been all alone.

"It makes you exactly what Wilson said, a concerned sister. And I highly doubt Wilson or Rhode is gonna tell her what you said." Brooklyn paused and skewered Wilson with a scathing look that made me want to smile. "Right?"

"You're exactly right. This conversation won't be shared outside of the team. And, Letty? Always go with your gut. Especially when it's uncomfortable." Wilson waited until Letty nodded her uneasy acknowledgment then turned to me. "Walk me out."

Thank fuck.

I followed behind Wilson, and I did this not wanting Brooklyn out of my sight but I was happy to send my friend on his way if it meant I could get her back to her place so we could talk. Or more to the point, get her alone so I could set my plan in motion.

"I'm gonna call Shepard, see what he can dig up on Trevor and the Horsemen," Wilson said as soon as we stepped out the door. "I know you got a lot to go over with her, but while you have her away from Letty, it might be good if you ask her about Kiki. There might be more, something she doesn't want to say in front of her friend."

A surge of possessiveness brimmed inside me, a need to shield Brooklyn from any more hurt, protect her from the truth of a bad situation that was more than likely worse than we'd thought.

After hearing what Letty had to say, I had to agree there was more to Desi. And I hoped I was wrong, but my gut told me there was more to Kiki's disappearance, too.

I ignored Wilson's request and concentrated on Shepard.

"Shep will be all over this. He'll have what we need by nightfall."

"You're not gonna ask her, are you?"

It wasn't a question, but it still required an answer.

"Not gonna commit to talking to Brooklyn about Kiki. Besides, the way those two are, I doubt there's anything she'd tell me that she wouldn't say in front of Letty. But if she brings it up, I'll let you know."

Wilson held my gaze and nodded. "I hope you know what you're doing."

"I do."

"You're willing to give up Takeback? The team?"

"For my son? Fuck yeah."

There was no question in my mind I'd leave everything behind for my boy. My only uncertainty was Brooklyn, and that was not on my part. I knew what I wanted—knew I'd give it all up for a shot with her.

The only question I needed answered was if Brooklyn was ready for me. And if she wasn't, how long would it take to convince her she was.

7

"Go out to dinner with me."

Six words that made my body jolt, my legs tremble, and my heart lurch.

"Like a date?"

Rhode looked away from my favorite picture of Remy—which had pride of place on the bookshelf next to my TV—to me and smiled.

Jumping Josiah, that damn smile. I resisted the urge to ask him if he had braces growing up. If he hadn't, I hoped he'd passed down the perfect-teeth gene to Remy. I refrained from asking but barely. And the only reason I didn't ask was because when Rhode added a deep throaty chuckle to go along with that brilliantly white smile, I was mesmerized. I needed to keep my wits about me but it was damn hard when Rhode was in my home.

Alone without Remington, Letty, the Welshes, his friends.

Just us.

There were a thousand things I wanted to say to him. But at that moment I couldn't think of a single one.

"Yeah, babe, like a date."

Five words that were more powerful than the first six.

"Though," he went on and I watched his lips twitch. "Not lost on me, it's ludicrous I'm asking the mother of my child out on a date—that being our first."

I felt some of the tension ease. He was making a joke, cutting some of the uncomfortable anxiety.

"Yeah, we jumped ahead a little."

"A little?"

"Okay, a lot."

Rhode didn't smile again but his face remained friendly. His dark brown eyes stayed locked with mine; eyes I'd seen every day when my son looked at me. I never thought I'd see the original pair again.

God, how many times had I wished I'd asked his name?

"I'm really sorry," I whispered.

"You've already said that. And it's not your fault. We had our night and went our separate ways. I didn't ask for your name, you didn't ask for mine. Neither of us could've known how big of a mistake that was. But just to say, I've thought about you over the years."

I could not believe my ears. How could that even be possible?

"You did?"

"Yep. When we were at the door I was trying to think of a way to ask you to stay. But you looked uncomfortable and I didn't want to make you more so. At the very least I wanted to tell you my name, leave it up to you if you wanted to contact me. But the way you said goodbye sounded final so I let it go. I knew it was a mistake as soon as the door closed. A year later when I was still thinking about you, I was full of regret. Another year went by and I still couldn't forget you, I knew it was something I'd regret for the rest of my life. I'm not big on regrets—not big on making the same mistake twice. You hafta know; now that I found you again, I won't be walking away."

Right. We shared a child. He'd said before and he was making it clear now he wanted to know his son.

"Remington," I murmured.

"Straight up, I'm gonna be in Remington's life. I want him to know me. I want to be his dad—not part-time, not a once-a-month dad, not a holiday-dad. I want in the trenches, the day-to-day. But you need to know *before* I knew Remy existed, I wasn't walking away from *you*. And it fucks me, Brooklyn, you've been close for years and I didn't know. I can't say I've spent a lot of time in CDA, but I've been here. I've walked past that bookstore. I've been in the bars downtown. I've been to the grocery store not far from here. I've eaten in a variety of restaurants from here to Sandpoint and I have to wonder, how many times were you close and I didn't know."

The feeling was back—butterflies in my belly. They weren't fluttering, they weren't rioting. No, not this time. Their velvety wings ignited a sensation I'd only ever felt once before. Five years ago in a bar in Washington D.C. when a stranger wrapped his hand around mine. The feeling of the unknown. Excitement mixed with anticipation along with a healthy dose of eagerness.

My heart was at war with my mind. Common sense told me to tread cautiously. My soul begged me to jump straight into the fire and tell Rhode there hadn't been a single day I hadn't thought about him. Tell him that I wanted to find him not only for Remy but for myself. That I regretted walking out of that hotel room. Tell him the truth about why I left. Tell him I was a romantic and everything he'd said to me called to a place deep inside of me that had belonged to him and only him.

But I couldn't tell him any of that. Common sense won out. Remington's well-being was more important than my silly musings.

"Do you live in CDA?" I asked.

"I have a cabin in Sandpoint. I go up there whenever I can, normally between jobs."

Holy, *holy*, crap.

How was that possible? I mean, what were the chances that Rhode lived—albeit part-time—less than an hour away?

With a great deal of effort, I silenced the voice in the back of my head—a whisper, a hum, a satisfied undertone that I'd been right. I wasn't deluded or full of fanciful thoughts. That night I was meant to cross Rhode's path and I was meant to find him again when the time was right.

Only, the timing was all wrong.

That made the butterflies die and my stomach clench.

"Brooklyn?"

"Huh?"

"What's wrong?"

I couldn't tell Rhode where my thoughts had led me. I didn't know a whole lot about relationships, and I certainly had no experience with starting one with my son's long-lost father but I knew enough to know Rhode would run a mile if I told him the connection I felt to him lived in my soul.

"I'm just shocked you were so close all these years."

Before Rhode could respond, there was an obnoxious pounding on the door followed by, "Open the door, Brook."

Shocked, my heart stopped mid-beat. I sucked in a breath then I raced to the door as fast as my feet could take me. But Rhode got there faster. His arm hooked around my belly and he pulled me back.

"Wait," he murmured.

"That's Kiki."

Rhode held me tight. My back was pressed against his hard chest—and it must be noted his chest felt like a wall of sheer muscle—but when I shared who was at my door those muscles bunched and turned to stone.

"Rhode," I hissed. "Let me go."

"I know you're in there, bitch. Open up."

Okay, so I was wrong. Rhode hearing Kiki call me a bitch turned him to stone. Or maybe I was the one who'd gone stiff. Kiki could get nasty, but she'd never called me a bitch.

"You're behind me," Rhode clipped.

"But—"

"No lip, Brooklyn. You stay behind me."

Hm. I didn't like that. As in, not at all.

"First, don't snap at me. Second, I know Kiki, you don't. And third, don't tell me not to give you lip."

"We're not having this argument now. I need to see to Kiki, and while I'm doing that, you're behind me and that's for your safety. So, really, we're never having this argument. Or, we can, but it's one you'll lose when I feel you're in danger."

"Open the fuck up!" Kiki banged again.

It was a pisser, but perhaps Rhode was right. I'd never heard Kiki so mad. And I didn't want to have any argument —I needed to get Kiki in the house.

"Fine. I'll stay behind you until she calms down. But that's it, Rhode. She's family and she's been missing for two weeks. Open the door and get her in the house."

Rhode let me go and gently shuffled me to the side.

Once he had me positioned where he wanted, he lifted his shirt and unholstered his sidearm.

"Do you really think that's necessary? You're gonna scare the crap out of her."

"I think keeping you safe is more important than me worrying about scaring the shit out of Kiki Welsh. And just to say, the way she's shouting through the door, acting the way she's acting, I hope it does."

Hm. Something else I didn't like.

Rhode unlocked the door and barely opened it an inch when suddenly Kiki pushed it open and shoved in. Rhode moved me back and shuffled again so he could slam the door closed and throw the deadbolt.

"Who are *you*?" Kiki demanded angrily.

Who are you?

That was when the reality of the situation hit me. Something was not right. Kiki had pounded on my door and did it angrily, not afraid. She was not pounding and desperate to get inside to safety after she'd somehow managed to escape her captors. She was not pleading for me to open the door and help her. She was in clean clothes, hair and makeup done like she was getting ready to go to a bar.

And she was angry.

I peeked around Rhode and demanded back just as irately, "Where have *you* been?"

"Who is this guy?"

"Answer Brooklyn." Unsurprisingly, Rhode's demand held way more authority than mine did. And he didn't sound angry or irate—he sounded way the hell pissed-off.

"Is he a cop?"

That was it.

I was done.

I pushed to the side and scooted around Rhode the best I could while he was pushing me back.

"Does it matter if he's a cop? You've been missing for two weeks, Kiki. We've been worried sick. Are you okay? How'd you—"

"I'm not missing," she spat.

My breath caught in my throat and a lump so big formed I had to force sound to come out of my mouth. Only one word escaped, "What?"

"Just because I don't wanna talk to any of you doesn't mean I'm missing. And if I don't wanna talk to any of you, I certainly don't wanna see you."

I wasn't angry or irate or pissed off. I was devastated.

Totally wrecked.

Not for me. For Letty, for Michael, but mostly for Tally. A mother who had cried herself to sleep. Worried endlessly. Tortured herself with thoughts of what was happening to her daughter.

Not only had the Welshes been beside themselves with worry, they'd spent hours looking for her, they'd rallied half the city to search for her. They'd contacted the police and the FBI. Man-hours wasted that the authorities could've been using to solve crimes, find someone who was actually missing.

"You ran away?"

I felt Rhode slide his arm around my waist. He tucked me to his side. It was a damn shame I was in the middle of an epic drama because I really would've liked to savor the feel of his arm around me.

"I'm a grown-ass woman, Brook. I didn't run away. I took a vacation."

A vacation?

A *fucking* vacation?

"Des—"

"Babe," Rhode interrupted me and gave me a squeeze. He turned his attention back to Kiki. "The right thing to do would be to contact your parents and let them know you're safe."

Kiki cut her eyes to Rhode, the look so ugly I didn't even recognize the girl I'd grown up with. The girl I'd spent countless hours playing with. The girl who turned into a snotty teenager though she'd still have moments when the old Kiki would break through. The teenager who'd grown into a selfish woman, but still every once in a while the sweet Kiki would shine through and I'd get a glimmer of the girl I loved so much.

But right then, I didn't know who she was. Never in my wildest dreams would I guess she'd pull something so horrendous on her parents and sister.

"I don't know who you are and I don't really care," she said to Rhode, then to me, "I'm here to tell you to tell my parents to call off the search and leave me the fuck alone."

I was not going to relay that message to Michael and Tally but I didn't get a chance to deny Kiki's request.

"Brooklyn's not your go-between. You wanna cut ties with your family? As you said, you're a grown woman. So act it and call them yourself."

That was pretty much what I was going to say so I didn't add anything. I also didn't speak because I was at a loss for words. Or I was at a loss for nice words—I could think of a few things to say, all of them mean.

Kiki shrugged. "Whatever. I'm not calling them. Tell them, don't tell them, I don't give a shit."

Every muscle in my body seized.

They locked so tight it hurt.

"How can you be so hateful? What happened to you?"

"*You* happened, Brook. You. Everything was great. Then the perfect Brook moves in and I lose my sister and mom and dad. Everything's about your parents dying and helping *you*. You and Letty against the world. Best friends. Mom and Dad shoved so far up your ass they forget they have a real daughter. *Me*, not fucking you. Then *Remington* comes along and Mom and Dad are so happy to be grandparents they don't even say shit about the colossal slut you are. Hell, you don't even know who his father is, but they don't care. They act like you're the Virgin Mary birthing Jesus himself. What a fucking joke. You have a bastard child and you're still fucking perfect."

I found I was wrong again. So very wrong. My muscles seized and anger ricocheted through me. Kiki spitting out my son's name like a curse sent pain slicing through my body, chased by a furiousness I'd never felt. I couldn't care less she called me a slut or her snide comments about me needing compassion after my parents died, and Michael and Tally giving that to me in spades. Her jealousy meant nothing to me—but calling my son a bastard had me seeing red.

"Get the fuck out of my house before I claw your face off!" I shouted.

"Like you could," Kiki sneered.

"Get out or I put you out," Rhode rumbled.

He didn't wait for her to comply before he unlocked the door, opened it, and used the hand still holding his gun to wave Kiki on.

"What, are you gonna shoot me?"

At that juncture, I figured Kiki was a little bit stupid. The waves of hostility rolling off Rhode couldn't be missed. He was pissed and not hiding it. She didn't know who he was and he had a gun practically in her face.

"I'm considering it," he told her.

Kiki huffed out an obnoxious laugh.

Okay, there was no figuring anything. She wasn't a little stupid—she was seriously whacked.

"Tell them, Brook," Kiki said and walked to the door.

She'd barely cleared the threshold when Rhode's deep, hoarse voice halted her process.

"Just so you know, I'm Remington's father. I'm not a man you wanna fuck with so in the future, you better think twice about calling Brooklyn a slut. And if you want a future *at all,* I suggest you never call my son a bastard again."

Holy shit.

He was sticking up for me.

Me and Remy.

"You threatening me, big guy?"

Totally stupid.

"Yep."

"You don't know who I am—"

"I know who you are. You're a selfish bitch. Your parents put up their life savings to find you. They've been living in hell for weeks and you don't give the first fuck. Your sister's been living in that hell and so has Brooklyn. All of them, looking for you. Putting their lives on hold, giving it all to you. But you don't give a shit about that. They wasted their emotions on some spoiled brat throwing a temper tantrum, running away from home like a cowardly little girl. Which you coming here asking Brooklyn to do your dirty work proves it's true. And if you think you got the protection of the Horsemen, think again. They don't throw down for club ass."

Kiki's torso swung back and her face twisted into a snarl.

"They do for an old lady. And you just threatened one."

God, I wanted to vomit.

"Seriously? Old lady? Gross."

Kiki aimed her dirty look at me, cocked her hip, and placed her hand there.

"Yes, seriously. And Zeus is gonna hear about that, too."

Zeus? How unoriginal.

"As long as you're passing along messages, be sure to tell them Brooklyn's under the protection of Takeback. They got any questions about what that means, they should ask around. They still need clarification and I gotta take time out of my day to communicate what that encompasses I'll be displeased. Tallulah, Michael, and Letty fall under that umbrella and I think it goes without saying but I'm gonna make myself crystal clear. Remington is untouchable. Any of those assholes breathe in his direction they'll be put down. You get near my son and I'll put *you* down. We clear?"

By the time Rhode was done I was breathing heavily. I was panting so fast I was getting light-headed so it was a good thing Kiki was ready to leave.

"Yeah, asshole, we're clear."

I watched her stomp away, my heart shattering into a million jagged pieces.

8

I waited until Kiki Welsh hefted her bitch ass into a Nissan Pathfinder that had seen better days. I waited until she slammed the door and shot away from the curb like the hounds of hell were nipping at her heels. I memorized the plate number then turned, and when I did the breath in my lungs crystalized.

Brooklyn looked devastated.

The picture of heartbreak.

In the five years I had worked with Takeback, I'd never run into this type of situation. The people I'd searched for were victims of human trafficking. The people I'd rescued the same. Never had I run across a spoiled, selfish bitch who'd run away.

Which meant Desi Cunns had lied and that was something I needed to deal with. But first, I needed to see to Brooklyn.

"What chance do I have talking you into sitting on this information for twenty-four hours?"

Brooklyn jolted out of her stupor and answered, "Depends on if you're gonna spend that twenty-four hours hunting Kiki down, then finding a way to turn her back into a decent human being. Alternately, you use the twenty-four hours to figure out a way for me to tell Tally, Michael, and Letty...that...Kiki's...I don't know what she is. Not missing. That they've been living a parents' worst nightmare. That Letty's been sick about her sister and Kiki just..."

Tears hit Brooklyn's eyes and she choked out a string of jumbled words I couldn't understand.

I took in her pain-filled expression and just like that, my plan to slowly win Brooklyn went to shit.

I made short work of shutting the door, locking it, and walking to her. And once I was there I didn't hesitate to swing her up into my arms. She buried her face in my neck and I had to take a moment to control my body's reaction.

Five years I'd waited to touch her again. Feel her body close to mine. Breathe in her flowery scent. I did not however imagine the first time I held her in my arms she'd be crying. I certainly never imagined she'd be brought to tears of heartbreak because Kiki Welsh was alive and well. That thought made my neck muscles contract.

Something wasn't adding up. Desi straight-out said she was with Kiki when she was taken. The security footage inside and out of the bar confirmed they'd been together that night. Unfortunately, there were no cameras down the alley where Desi said they'd been snatched from. By the time I made it to Brooklyn's couch, sat down, and settled her on my lap, I was no closer to puzzling the pieces together.

"I never knew she hated me," Brooklyn whispered. "Growing up we fought and after I moved in with them we bickered. I thought it was because we were close like sisters. Like Letty and Kiki argued all the time. It's what sisters do. But I love her, Letty loves her. Tally and Michael love her like crazy. I just don't get it."

Neither did I. I didn't understand a lot of things people said or did. I'd long ago stopped trying to grasp why people were assholes who thought it was their God-given right to spout whatever hateful shit popped into their heads. I couldn't fathom why they were *thinking* hateful shit. So not understanding why people were dicks as a whole, I couldn't begin to comprehend how a daughter could do what Kiki had done to her family.

"They're gonna be crushed. Letty's gonna go through the roof. I don't know how I'm gonna tell them."

"Sucks, baby, but I still gotta ask. I need a day to get with my team before you tell them Kiki came by."

"Why?"

"Because Desi lied."

Brooklyn went stiff and as she lifted her head, her nose grazed my jaw and the familiar attraction sizzled to life.

Ocean blue brimmed with unshed tears.

Fuck. I'd never forgotten those eyes.

"She lied," Brooklyn repeated in a whisper. "Why would she lie?"

I could think of a few reasons. None of which I would share.

"Not sure, but I'm gonna find out. I know you wanna put the Welshes' minds at ease but before it gets out Kiki wasn't kidnapped and it gets back to Desi that we know, I need some time."

"They won't tell anyone," she argued.

They would and it was natural they'd want to share with family and friends that Kiki was safe. There were a lot of reasons why they'd spread the good news; one of the reasons would be to stop the search.

"Babe, something like this has a way of getting out. Michael and Tallulah are gonna want to tell their family and even if they ask them not to say anything, someone still will. They'll call a friend and confide in them. That friend will call someone else and swear them to secrecy. That's just the way this works. We can't risk it getting back to Desi before we get to her."

Brooklyn went silent. Her eyes became pleading and my gut tightened. That look didn't bode well for me. Those Caribbean eyes coupled with her brows pulled down and her lips puckered meant I didn't stand a chance of winning.

"At least let me tell Letty."

Shit, goddamn.

"I know you don't know her," Brooklyn rushed out. "Well, you don't know me either but I promise if you ask Letty not to tell her parents, she won't. She's a vault when it comes to secrets."

"That's a big secret to ask her to keep," I returned.

"As big as the one you're asking me to keep."

"Touché." Then just like I knew I would, I gave in. "I'll go back with you to the bookstore to tell Letty and I'll call Wilson on the way."

"Just like that?"

"It's not like you weren't gonna tell her anyway."

Brooklyn's eyes darted to the wall and she looked perfectly adorable trying to hide her grin.

"Not even gonna deny it?" I joked.

"I have a philosophy about lying."

"Oh, yeah? What's your philosophy?" I asked when she didn't continue.

"Not to do it." She shrugged.

I tried to fight it but I lost the battle and my body started to shake, then my amusement peaked and I belted out a laugh.

"Good philosophy to have," I said through a chuckle.

After a beat of silence, she smiled and I was reminded of the first time I saw her. She was staring at her laptop, typing something, with a sexy grin tipping up her lips. That was what had caught my attention—her alone, typing, smiling like she was totally comfortable in her own company. Then I'd sat with Wilson, Asher, and Davis at our table counting down the minutes until I could make my approach. I'd barely listened to Wilson's brief, all my attention riveted on the beautiful woman in the booth next to me stealing glances when she thought I wasn't watching.

"I'm really glad you found us," Brooklyn murmured.

The space around my heart constricted. Regret burned in my stomach. I tightened my arms around her.

"So am I."

"I promise—"

"You've already explained and apologized multiple times. I've explained I don't blame you. No more of that. Let's move on from here."

Brooklyn's chin dipped, her gaze held mine, and she studied me. She did this for a long time, long enough for me to slip back to the night I met her. The feel of her hand as it slipped into mine. I'd felt the spark before we'd made it back to my room. Ten minutes later, that spark had ignited into something surreal. The feel of her straddling my lap, taking my cock, pressing her body to mine had opened me to a whole new level of connection—then and now—that awoke a savagery I'd kept leashed. It wasn't a protective instinct—it went beyond that. It was barbaric, uncivilized, rude, and obscene.

And I felt the power of it again with her innocently sitting on my lap now.

I had planned to move slow, dig in until I was rooted in Brooklyn's life, in Remy's. But now I understood that wasn't going to work. I had a great deal of patience. I was good at the long game, silently hunting my prey until the time was right to strike.

Except now with Brooklyn, need overshadowed patience.

"Are you going to take Remington from me?" she whispered, and my body jerked, taking Brooklyn along for the ride.

"Fuck no!"

Her eyes flared at my violent response before she completely relaxed in my arms.

"You said you didn't want to be a part-time dad," Brooklyn reminded me.

The time was right to strike and I was really fucking glad she was still on my lap. I wanted her close, wanted to feel her body's reaction to what I was saying, but the bottom line was I simply liked touching her.

"I'm not gonna be a part-time dad. I'm also not going to take a boy away from his mom and family. I'm gonna stay in Idaho and be present in his life and in yours."

I waited for her to stiffen but instead, she sagged into me.

"What else is weighing heavy on your mind?" I continued.

"It was just that."

"Bullshit." At that, Brooklyn went solid. "As soon as we walked into your place you went wired. And when I started looking around you got antsy. So, tell me, Brooklyn, what else is on your mind? We've got a lot to catch up on and the only way we get past this is if both of us just let it hang out. All of it, babe. You can tell me anything and I'll repay the favor."

"There's not enough hours in a day for me to tell you all

the things that have been running through my head since I saw you again."

Brooklyn was right about there not being enough hours. We needed to get back to Smutties and talk to Letty before she had to go pick up Remington from school. And I had no idea what her work schedule was but I reckoned at some point in the day she needed to work.

"Fair enough. So how 'bout we start with something easy? Why were you nervous when we got here?"

Brooklyn let out a long exhale. Then she shocked the hell out of me and did exactly what I'd asked—she let it all hang out.

"Because this is beyond weird. You're a complete stranger...okay, not a *complete* stranger, but a stranger, and we have a kid. I'm worried about what you think about me. I'm nervous about what you think about my place because your son lives here and I don't want you to think I can't provide a good home for him. I do...provide a good home that is. I make a decent living and Remy has everything he needs. But maybe you're loaded and to you, my place looks like a hovel. I don't know. And I'm worried about what you think of my job. I work in a bookstore and I narrate romance books. I work hard, and Remy doesn't suffer because of it, but sometimes when I'm on a deadline, Tally or Letty will take Remy overnight so I can work in the studio. But that doesn't happen often. And my parents are dead, so Tally, Michael, Letty, and Kiki are our only family...scratch that, no Kiki. I'm also worried you think I'm slutty and I wouldn't blame you if you did, but you're my one and only one-night stand and I certainly haven't done anything like that since. It was a once-in-a-lifetime opportunity and I took it. So I'm nervous about all of that and more stuff I can't think of. But above all, I'm worried about Remington and how we tell him. I mean, what do we tell him, and when? I'm rambling, sorry."

Brooklyn pressed her lips together and sat perfectly stiff. *It was a once-in-a-lifetime opportunity and I took it.*

I liked that a helluva lot. I liked she cared what I thought. I liked she hadn't changed and just like our night together she hadn't held back. Yeah, I liked that.

But before I got into how much I liked all of that, we needed to get the rest squared away.

"That's a lot to be worried about, Sugar. We'll start with the easy stuff. Your job. I don't give the first fuck what you do for a living. Although you might care about what I do and I'll explain that later. You needing help with Remy so you can work and reaching out to people who you trust and who love him is a given. And I'm happy you have good people to help you. Soon you'll add me to that list and I'll kick in and spend time with him while you're working. Now, your house. You gotta sweet setup here. Close to work, nice neighborhood, it's warm and inviting, and I like seeing Remy's pictures on the wall and his toys scattered around. It says a kid lives here and he's comfortable playing where he wants and his mom's not uptight about where he leaves his stuff.

"As far as what I think of you, I've thought a lot about you over the years. I've thought about your smile, your voice, your pretty eyes. I've wondered where you lived, how you were doing, if you'd found a man and were married. I've thought about what would've happened if I'd asked you to stay. I've wondered about your name. And I've thought about the things I knew about you, none of which would help me find you. Never once in all the times I was thinking about the beautiful woman I spent one night with did it ever cross my mind to think you were slutty. That's total bullshit.

I was right there with you that night. I saw you and knew it was going to be a good night. Even if all I got to do was sit across from you and share a drink. How the night proceeded was outstanding. And not just the sex. All of it, Brooklyn. Every minute we shared is seared into my memory. I remember everything."

I stopped but only to lift my hand and cup her ruby cheek. The blush was something I'd never seen on her pretty face. The night we'd shared had been wild, and not once did I see her cheeks tinge pink. Not when I ordered her to sit on my face so I could eat her. Not when her lips were wrapped around my dick and I'd toyed with her pussy until she moaned her orgasm around my shaft. I'd fucked her every way I could fuck her in the limited time I'd had. I'd tasted every part of her and not once was she shy or embarrassed. The opposite actually. I'd never met a woman who sated my every need and still wanted more.

"Every second was phenomenal," I went on. "Straight up honesty; that wasn't my first and there were others after, but none came close to what I felt that night with you. Part of that is because you're seriously good in bed, you're gorgeous, and you have a fantastic body. But more importantly, it was the way you looked at me with those beautiful eyes. The way you felt pressed against me whispering about your life, shit that was so meaningless but really it was everything. In my life, in my job, I see shit so disturbing it's hard to turn it off. But for six hours with you, I felt a peace I'd never known. That was everything to me and that was what I wanted to explore. More honesty for you; I still wanna explore that connection. But before we do, we've gotta get you through what's going on with Kiki. I gotta get with my team and find out what game Desi's playing and if Kiki's involved. If she is, I've gotta help you get the Welshes through that. We've also got to come up with a plan about how we introduce me to Remy. That's something I don't want to delay but we gotta do it smart so that's gonna take time. And with that, I'm gonna have to follow your lead. You're his mom, you know him, and I trust you'll make the right plays to smooth our way and make this good for him. The last thing I want is Remington's life disrupted in a way that causes harm."

One of Brooklyn's hands came up to cover mine and then she leaned into my touch. And some of my lingering trepidation melted away. The rest of it was wiped clean when her other hand hit my chest and she gave me a gentle smile.

"Thank you," she said softly.

"Not sure why you're thanking me."

"You're really not mad." When I started to interrupt, Brooklyn's fingertips dug in. She rushed out, "I know you said you weren't, but I'm a mom and it's my job to worry. I want you to get to know Remy, I don't want to wait to start on that. From there we'll watch him and adjust accordingly. He's a smart kid, and I'm not just braggin' because he's mine. He's got this way of watching what's going on and he asks a lot of questions. After he saw you at Smutties he asked who you were. I told him you were a friend. He asked why he looked like you. I didn't know what to tell him so I changed the subject. Luckily for me, he's smart but easily distracted by the promise of his Gram's dessert. He might only be four but he won't let it go for long. I'm going to need to tell him sooner rather than later."

I wasn't surprised Remy had asked about me. I saw it in the kid's eyes. I knew, just like I had the moment we'd seen each other.

"He knows, Brooklyn. All you need to do is confirm it."

"What?"

"You might've missed it, but he knew just like I did. He doesn't just look like me—he's a carbon copy."

"I know. I was praising the Lord above when he came out with your dark eyes and a head full of black hair. Then he turned one and I started to see more of you in him. By the time he was three, he looked so much like you I knew God loved me. I couldn't have you but I had him. And like you said he's a carbon copy, so every day I got to look at my son and see you."

At Brooklyn's words, my breath left my lungs in a whoosh, my muscles tightened, and then I felt it—the warm peace I felt that first night. The rush of excitement mixed with calm forming the perfect storm inside my chest. A feeling I'd fight to keep.

"Fuck," I rasped.

"Rhode—"

"Fuck," I repeated. "You've got no clue, baby, but you'll learn."

"Learn what?"

"How much what you just said means to me. How hard it's been to do the right thing. Shit timing, everything going on. You're not at a place where I can take us where I want. And we got Remy in the mix, so I gotta go extra slow for him and for us. But warning you, Brooklyn, you say more shit like that, slow will be a memory."

"Maybe we should talk about us," she whispered.

"We will. But right now we gotta get to your girl and tell her what's going on so I can get to the hotel and talk to my team."

"But—"

"Up, baby." I didn't wait for her to follow my instructions. I stood with Brooklyn in my arms and kept my arms around her as I settled her on her feet. "We're running out of time before you gotta pick up Remy."

"Rhode, really, we need to talk about us. This isn't smart."

"You're right it isn't smart. It's fuckin' brilliant."

I leaned forward, brushed my lips across her forehead, down her temple, and let my mouth linger at her ear where I murmured, "I've waited a long damn time to find you. I've spent years dreaming about you. If you think now that I've found you I'm gonna let you go, you're crazy. If you think I'm gonna let this opportunity slip by, you're wrong. Seeing you was a shock. Finding out I had a son I didn't know I had, learning I'd missed four years of his life, was a blow so painful I felt that stab in my soul. It's gonna take time for that wound to heal. Time I'm gonna spend getting to know my son. Time I'm gonna spend getting to know you. Time I'm gonna spend getting me and you to a place where we're an *us*. So for now that's all that needs to be said."

"Rhode."

Christ.

Brooklyn saying my name breathy and sweet. I'd heard that before and hearing it again reminded me we were alone and I couldn't do what I wanted to do to her so we needed to leave.

"We gotta go," I reminded her.

"Before we do, I need you to promise me something."

"What's that?"

"Promise that if you get to know me and don't like what you find...that even if there's not an *us* there...there will still be a you and Remington."

I had no doubts, thus it was an easy promise, so I made it.

"I promise."

"Swear it, Rhode. Swear to me that you won't leave Remy."

I shifted one hand from her hip, glided it to the middle of her back, and put pressure there until Brooklyn was pressed tight against his chest.

"I swear it, Brooklyn. I won't leave Remy."

Her body sagged in relief and her arms wrapped around my back. I took a moment to soak in the feel of Brooklyn's arms around me and I let the healing begin.

9

I was sitting across from Letty.

Rhode was to my right and we were scrunched on the loveseat in the corner of Smutties. Not because there wasn't room for us to spread out a little but because Rhode insisted on sitting close. His thigh was pressed against mine and his arm was resting on the back of the couch. That meant I was mostly leaning into him.

This was good and bad.

The good part was obvious—I was leaning close to Rhode.

The bad was two-fold—I was leaning close to Rhode so my concentration was shot. I wanted to rub up against him or crawl into his lap again and hold on tight or maybe pinch him to make sure he was real. My thoughts were scattered and wandering.

The other bad part was; being so close I could feel the anger rolling off Rhode. It started when I told Letty that Kiki came to my house. The mix of relief and happiness on my best friend's face was painful to see. I know Rhode felt the same because he knew what would come next. And it happened in slow motion. Letty's smile faded, shock crept in, then sadness, and finally hurt turned into extreme fury.

Rhode's body tensed.

Letty's face was set to thunder.

And I was pissed right the fuck off.

"Please tell me that didn't happen," Letty whispered. "Please tell me my sister did *not* take a vacation." She added finger quotes and I pinched my lips together at my friend's jerky, irritated movements. "And put my parents through hell." She finished and flung her arms wide before they dropped in her lap.

Okay, so, I was incorrect. I wasn't pissed right the fuck off —I was nuclear. And Letty was so furious it decimated her.

In life, I'd tried and succeeded in never hating anyone. I disliked, I even loathed, but hate was off-limits. Hate felt like a place you went to die—where your insides rotted from bad feelings. But at that moment seeing my sister of the soul —my best friend, a woman who had stood by me through thick and thin, held me up after my parents died and held my hand when I pushed out my son—seeing that person crushed; hate filled my heart.

"Letty," I returned just as softly.

"No, hell to the no, Brook!" Letty flew off the couch.

I quickly stood and Rhode followed.

"Letty, please calm down and listen for a second," I pleaded.

"*Calm down*? My sister ran the fuck away like a toddler having a temper tantrum and you want me to calm down? I'm gonna wring her neck and this time I'm doing it for real. I'm gonna slap the shit out of her for what she put Mom and Dad through, then I'm gonna choke her for what she said to you. And after that, I'm gonna smack her again for putting *me* through this shit."

"Letty!" Rhode boomed. "Sorry to say but your smack-down's gonna have to wait a few days."

"And I'm sorry to inform *you*, big guy, but that's not gonna happen. I'm closing the bookstore and hunting her ass down right now, and when I find her I'm knocking some sense into her."

"Babe," Rhode growled.

I took a moment and let Rhode's rumble roll through me. I took another moment to think about how much I liked him calling me 'babe'. And I might've taken an extra second to wish I had more time to enjoy it. After I did that, I stepped in front of Letty to stop her from pacing.

"There's more, Lets, and you need to listen. Earlier you said something wasn't right with Desi, that you felt it in your gut."

"Oh my God. Right."

"You were right. Desi lied about Kiki being abducted. And if she lied about that, what else did she lie about?"

"I knew it!" Letty exclaimed.

"You're not gonna like this next part, but I promised Rhode if we told you Kiki came by you'd keep it a secret. Just until Rhode can look into Desi."

Letty's head tilted in confusion and she shrugged.

"Why wouldn't I like that?"

"You can't tell your mom and dad," I rushed out in a whisper. "Just a few days, maybe less."

Letty's eyes got big and her body jolted.

"What?" she screeched.

My gaze shot around the store, double-checking no patrons were perusing the shelves. Thankfully, it was early and Smutties was empty.

"Letty—"

"We need to get a man on Desi," Rhode cut in. "When

she finds out we know she lied, she'll bolt. Once we got what we need in place and the news spreads we know she lied, and she bails we'll be able to track her. She starts making calls, we'll be listening in. Part of that is so we can understand why she lied, who she's covering for, and what her part in that is. The bigger reason is for your family's protection and that includes your sister."

"But my parents wouldn't tell anyone."

"Shit like this has a way of leaking out. I get you wanna put your parents' minds at ease and I know you wanna do that now. But you wait until we got eyes and ears on Desi and you can do that with the added assurance you're all safe."

"Are we *not* safe?" Letty asked and gave me big eyes.

Rhode didn't hesitate.

"Earlier you laid it out. Your gut told you something wasn't right. And it's not. Now, my gut's telling me with all you shared, your sister hooking up not with just any member of the Horsemen but with the president of the club, her showing up, Desi lying about what happened, no, your family's not safe. But you have my word we'll make you that way. We just need a few hours to get everything in place."

"But—"

"Straight up, Letty, Brooklyn and Remington are caught up in this. Your sister stood in Brooklyn's yard and threatened not only her but *my* son. I don't think I need to remind you that I've yet to get to know my boy and no offense, but no one's taking that opportunity away from me. Not you, not your parents, not your sister, and certainly not some fuckin' MC and whoever Desi's running with. So, really, I'm not asking you to keep this under wraps—I'm telling you not to say a word about this to anyone until I have what I need in place to protect Brooklyn and Remy. Now, Brooklyn said she trusted you to keep this quiet. I know it sucks, but don't make her a liar."

I watched my best friend's face pale and her eyes close.

I wasn't sure if I wanted to kick Rhode in the shin for laying it out, or to strangle Kiki, or to find Desi and shake her until she told the truth. Further, what Rhode said hit me square in the chest. Remington was in this mess. At the time I hadn't taken what Kiki had said as a threat, but now thinking about it Kiki's snide comment about telling *Zeus*—again, stupid name—unnerved me. I didn't know exactly what I'd done beyond offending her but I suppose that was all it took for criminals to lash out. I didn't know jack about the ins and outs of MCs. What I did know was I didn't like Kiki going back to their sleazy hangout and mentioning my name or Remy's or Rhode's.

"Why would she do this? I don't understand how she *could* do this to Mom and Dad or to any of us."

"I don't know, Lets. She was standing right in front of me but it wasn't Kiki. Not the Kiki I grew up with. Not even the smart-mouthed, teenage-drama Kiki. She was so pissed and hateful I didn't recognize her."

Letty's gaze went to Rhode and she lifted her chin. I knew that look well; she was gearing up for a staredown—one that would go on a while because she was stubborn. I didn't think this would bode well for her. Rhode didn't strike me as a man who'd back down from a staredown, or at all.

So there I stood, waiting until the appropriate time to step in and end Letty's obstinance and Rhode's silent appraisal. However, before I could, Letty shocked the hell out of me and dipped her chin, Rhode jerked his, and in some weird, silent communication the two of them came to an agreement I didn't understand.

"You'll take care of them?" Letty asked.

"Absolutely."

Firm.

Resolute.

And I didn't think either of them was talking about the Kiki-slash-Desi-slash-Horsemen situation.

"I won't say anything to my parents," Letty acquiesced. "But please do what you've gotta do quickly. My mom's holding on by a thread. And my dad..."

Letty let that hang and my heart squeezed.

"You have my word. We'll get this done quickly."

Then Rhode turned his head and looked at me. No, he didn't just look at me; he pierced me with his warm, dark eyes.

"Gotta get back to the hotel and brief the team. You staying here?"

"Yeah. I have to work before I go pick up Remy."

Those dark eyes continued to take me in. And I'd swear Rhode was making me a thousand silent promises. That might've been my romantic side being wishful. Or I could've been an idealistic fool hoping Rhode lived up to the man I'd dreamt about. Or maybe I was plumb stupid and he was just looking at me.

"I'll be back before you have to go get Remy and I'll follow you to his school."

"What? Why?"

"Because this morning Kiki threw down and until I know what's going on with her, you and Remy will have someone following you. Today that someone's gonna be me."

"But—"

Rhode's expression blanked and he interrupted me. "Don't worry, Brooklyn, he won't see me."

I tensed at the unexpected harshness in his tone.

Now, I was a fairly calm person. I liked to think I could keep a lid on, keep cool and not overreact. But hearing Rhode's insinuation, I found the lid wasn't screwed on tight and it flew right off.

"What exactly are you accusing me of?" I snapped.

"Not a damn thing," he returned with the same heat.

"Then what's with the comment for me not to worry because he won't see you?" I asked and when Rhode didn't respond right away I continued. "That tells me *you* think *I* don't want him to see you."

"No, Brooklyn, that means I'm pissed as shit I gotta follow you and Remy and the timing of that sucks because he doesn't know me, and he's not gonna get to know me as the man playing bodyguard to him and his mom. When the time is right he's gonna get to know me as his dad. And I want that to happen now but the situation being as it is, priority one is keeping the two of you safe."

Crap.

I read that wrong.

"Sorry, I misunderstood," I grumbled and braced for him to rub it in.

"You did, you voiced it, I explained, and now you understand. That's over. I gotta get to the hotel. Do me a favor and don't leave the bookstore until I get back. Letty, you, too. I'm leaving my number, if either of you needs to leave, shoot me a text and I'll send someone over. If Kiki shows up here, text me. If anyone you don't like the look of shows up, you text me."

"Got it, boss," Letty quipped and my body jolted.

"Letty!"

"Jeeze, Brook. Calm down. I'm just joshin' with him. We'll text you if we need you."

That last part was aimed at Rhode.

"Be back."

Rhode was halfway across the store when Letty called out.

"Hey, Dulles!"

Rhode jerked to a stop and craned his neck.

"I appreciate what you're doing and I'm serious when I tell you we'll call if we need something. I'd never let anything happen to Brook or Remy. You've got my word on that."

"Plain to see you have their backs so I didn't need your word to trust you'd do your part. But I appreciate you giving it to me."

And with that, Rhode left.

"I like him," Letty declared.

"What?"

"I was planning on putting him to the test and making him jump through hoops before I gave my stamp of approval. But that'd be a waste of time."

I knew before I asked which meant I knew Letty Welsh, my best friend since forever, the one person who had never left my side would take one look at Rhode, know our history —that being that I fell in love with him on sight and had been dreaming about him for five years—and she'd want that dream for me so desperately that she, too, would fall for Rhode hard and fast.

But I still asked, "Why would it be a waste of time?"

Her gaze went to the front door Rhode had exited then back to me.

"Because he's your person."

"Lets—"

"Advice, Brook, don't fight this. Whatever's happening here, go with it. Take the chance. Throw your hands in the air, jump with both feet, and enjoy the ride. And not just the one he's gonna give you in the sack. All of it. Start to finish, that man's gonna sweep you off your feet and you'd be stupid to fight it."

"Remington—"

"He's gonna sweep up Remy, too. And my nephew's gonna soak up the love his father's gonna give him and he's gonna bask in that warmth. I was wrong and you were right, Rhode is nothing like Douche Nozzle. Rhode would sooner give up a limb than give up a boy he's spoken a handful of words to. It's plain to see. And before you ask how I know—I just do. It's in the way he looks at you. His mouth doesn't have to open for him to speak."

Holy crap, Letty saw it, too.

Though it was a toss-up which one of us was more starry-eyed. So her evaluation of the situation was probably more skewed than mine. And as much as I wanted to jump with both feet and take a ride that was sure to be crazy and wild, I had Remington to think about. I didn't know if I could take a wild ride with *anyone*, even if the conductor of the crazy train was my son's father.

But I could open the door—just a crack. Then I could dip my toe in the water and test it out. If I stayed in the shallow end I might be all right. I might be able to keep from drowning. The problem was I wanted to jump off the high board and dive straight into the deep end. And I wanted to take Remy there with me.

I wanted the dream. I wanted Rhode. And I wanted Remy to have a family.

I didn't tell any of this to Letty. She'd shove me straight off the edge and do it gleefully, that was how much she loved me.

Instead, I told her, "I'm getting to work. I have a book due tomorrow."

"No, you don't." She shook her head and caught my play. "The book's due next week. But I'll let you off the hook because I see you're freaked out. I also know you'll do the right thing for you and Remy—you always do."

That was classic Letty; she was my biggest cheerleader, my biggest supporter, the person who had faith in me when I had none in myself.

"Love you, Lets."

"I know you do, Brook. I also know you love Rhode so don't fuck this up and start thinking with your brain."

Thankfully, a chime rang out and Letty's attention went to the door. Three women walked in and I hightailed it to the back of the store.

Priority one is keeping the two of you safe.

What was I supposed to do with that?

My heart said *sprint full-speed ahead*.

My brain said *go cautious*.

Rhode had thought about me over the years. He regretted not asking my name. He thought I had beautiful eyes. He wanted to do what was right for Remy, demonstrating he wanted to be a good dad. He thought the two of us together wasn't smart—it was brilliant. He said it was shit timing and was having a mind to that, which meant he was showing he cared about what I was going through. He wanted me and Remy safe.

Priority one.

Remy and I were his priority.

That was the foundation I would use to build what we needed to build for Remy. And the excuse I was going to use to run full-speed ahead.

Hopefully, Rhode would be there to catch me.

10

I knocked twice then used my keycard to let myself into Wilson's suite. Once I was inside I took in the room.

Jack and Asher were at the small table, both working on their laptops. Wilson was out on the balcony pacing, his phone up to his ear. Davis was on the couch, his booted feet resting on the coffee table in front of him, computer on his lap, his phone to his ear. He nodded at whatever the person on the other end was saying.

Only Jack spared me a glance as I entered. I returned a chin lift and made my way across the hotel suite.

"Wilson's updating the feds," Jack started. I had called Wilson on the short drive from Brooklyn's house to the bookstore so it wasn't a surprise my team was already on the Desi Cunns situation.

"Davis is talking to Shep, and Asher's getting us access to the hospital's security feeds where Desi's a patient. Reese and Cole checked in; the Welches went straight home and so far Michael hasn't attempted to leave." Before I could respond Jack went on, "We ran Desi. The last twelve months she's been flush with cash—before that, struggling. Then suddenly she pays off her car, all her credit cards, rent's caught up then paid on time when she's normally late. She's also got thirty K in a checking account. All cash deposits."

"Shit," I grumbled. "That cash coming from Kiki?"

"Doubtful, she's broke. Unless Kiki's using Desi to funnel money for her. And in exchange for cleaning the money, Kiki felt generous and forked over about forty large to pay off Desi's debt. Not to mention, there'd have to be a level of trust there to give all your money to someone and have them hold it. And I mean *all* the money. Kiki's got twenty-three dollars in her checking account."

"Where's Desi work?"

"Bartender at Houlihan's—before and after the influx of cash. Asher pulled the employee records from the bar, checked the other employees' bank accounts, and no one else working there had a sudden windfall."

In other words, it wasn't that the bar suddenly became a hot spot and the bartenders benefited from that by making more money. The good news was, whatever racket Desi was pulling she hadn't recruited other bartenders or waiters to participate.

"Desi involved with the Horsemen, too?" I asked.

"Done with the feeds," Asher entered the conversation then added, "we haven't gotten that far."

"Anything on Trevor Lawrence?"

I looked between the two men and watched Jack's lips curl before he answered, "He's got a rap sheet that proves he's a dumb fuck. Being as he's stupid as shit, the cops cleared him quick when Letty Welsh reported he was dating her sister after Kiki was reported missing because Lawrence was indeed in Sacramento, California, enjoying a free night's stay in lock-up. Bar fight—drunk and disorderly, assault, and property damage. Charges were dropped,

Lawrence paid for the damage and the fine, and he was on his merry way forty-eight hours later."

"Was Kiki with him?"

"Unknown," Asher told me. "I'll see what I can find after we secure Desi. It'd be good we could alibi Kiki but it won't be enough to clear her."

Technically Kiki Welsh had done nothing wrong. No law prohibited her from behaving like a selfish twat and her parents had done what any parents would do when their child fell off the radar; they called it in thinking there was foul play. So, seeing as Kiki was of an age where she had no obligation to her family, being in California with her felonious boyfriend wasn't breaking the law but it was part of the scope of Takeback's new investigation.

Not to mention, I just plain wanted to know where Kiki had been, and that was to give the Welshes peace of mind.

My attention went to the balcony door and I watched Wilson walk through. Jaw set, eyes hard and narrowed—not on anyone in particular, that was just Wilson. A telling sign his phone conversation hadn't gone well.

"Feds want Desi brought in but they want it communicated to her she's a witness, not a suspect. They also want her doctor to sign off."

"Dotting their i's," Asher noted.

"More like covering their asses," Jack corrected. "What they'd say about the money?"

Wilson stopped three paces away and looked at Davis. "You still on with Shep?"

Davis jerked his chin in the affirmative and Wilson went on, "Tell Shep I need that money traced however he needs to do that but we have to know who's bankrolling Desi Cunns."

"You hear that?" Davis asked into his phone. There was a

pause then, "Right. I'll let you go. Thanks."

"Feds said they'll look into her tax returns, see if she claimed the cash," Wilson answered Jack's earlier question. "They can deal with the IRS which, even if she did claim the cash on her return it won't give them shit, just that she paid taxes. Shep will get us what we need. Fucks me to say this, but, Rhode, I need you to run the list of victims."

"What am I looking for?" I asked.

"Anything. Connection to Desi, to the Horsemen, to Kiki, an influx of money, arrest record, any change in the last year."

I felt unease slither up my spine until my shoulders went rigid.

"You think Desi was working on the inside."

"Would make sense," Wilson agreed.

"And Kiki? You think she's involved?"

"Wild card. I hope for your woman's sake and for the Welshes she's telling the truth."

This time when my body locked and my muscles tensed it had nothing to do with Kiki. And when the blood rushed to my head and the buzzing started, it had not a damn thing to do with the Welshes.

My woman.

Christ.

I wanted that.

It was insane but I'd wanted it five years ago.

I wanted it when I saw her huddled next to Letty behind yellow police tape.

And I wanted it even more when Brooklyn was sitting on my lap holding on tight, burrowing close.

Total insanity but I didn't care. I felt it, so I was going with it. Add in Remington and I was taking what I wanted.

So, yes, *my woman.*

There was no reason to deny it or correct Wilson so I didn't bother.

"I think Letty was right. There's something off about Desi and I think you're right, too, she's working for someone. The question is—was she supposed to get swept up in the rescue or did we take her off-guard when we went in?"

"Fuck," Wilson bit off.

The rest of the guys went on alert but it was Jack who started talking it out.

"Desi getting swept up on purpose means she could report back. Lots of shit inadvertently gets said in front of victims and if she's smart, she'd suss out what the cops just by what the cops were asking. But Desi givin' a fake name says desperation. Like she got caught off-guard and panicked."

"She knew where Kiki was, that she hadn't been in contact with her family, had no plans of getting in contact, and gave the fake name as part of the act. Gaining sympathy. Not from the Welshes, though that worked in her favor, too. But by lying about her name she was drawing attention to herself and at the same time cementing her status as a scared victim. She'd be questioned and released immediately," Asher offered.

"Maybe," Jack granted. "Or Desi *and* Kiki are *both* neck-deep in this shit and Kiki coming back at just the right time means her family's no longer looking. Desi's in Seattle thinking she's in the clear."

"Or," Davis grunted, "Kiki's telling the truth. Desi got tangled in something, lost control, and found herself hours away from being in the back of a train car up to Canada where she'd be sold and never seen again. And her head's so fucked-up she's confused or afraid so she's lying through her teeth."

All plausible.

All within the realm of the fucked-up world we lived in.

Theories—which meant we had dick-all.

And part of living in that fucked-up world, where humans were traded, sold, and used. My only hope was that Kiki Welsh wasn't on the inside of a trafficking ring. My hope was that Kiki was simply a bitch with shit taste in men and a chip on her shoulder.

I didn't know Letty. But I knew she loved my son. I knew Letty and Brooklyn were tight. I knew she was a good daughter. So I didn't want this for her just as much as I didn't want it for Brooklyn. I had a feeling with time both women would get over and move on from Kiki being a twat. I doubted they'd get over Kiki aiding in human trafficking.

By the time I left the hotel to go back to Smutties, my head was throbbing.

I'd gotten through a quarter of the forty-one victims we'd rescued. All of them clean. Nothing out of the ordinary. Everyday, normal citizens going about their daily lives until they weren't. Until they were snatched and their worlds became hell on earth.

But that wasn't why I had a stress headache. All morning my thoughts had drifted from Brooklyn to Remington back to Brooklyn. And self-doubt had crept in. I was all-in. I wanted mother and son, knew that to my soul. It was the manner in which I would imbed myself into their lives that I'd begun to doubt. No, not the manner—the speed. Seeing as I was all-in, I wanted what I wanted and I wanted it immediately. If it were just Brooklyn, I'd move in so fast her hair would be on fire. But there was a four-year-old to consider.

I had a ten-minute drive to the bookstore and I planned on using my time wisely. There were two men I knew who could help—Alec Hall and Holden Stanford. But Holden would have the answers I needed.

A tight ball formed in my gut just thinking about what Holden had gone through. The man's life had been torn apart only to be resurrected by the love of a woman he'd thought he'd lost forever. A woman and the daughter he didn't know was his. I had played a part in Holden learning the truth.

I grabbed my phone and at the same time was remembering how painful it had been to watch my friend learn he'd missed almost nine years of his child's life, when my stomach clenched. The knot in my gut tightened and my hand shook as I scrolled through my contacts, found Holden's name, and before I could puss out, I hit the icon to connect the call.

Three rings later Holden answered, "Yo, Rhode. Long time, brother."

"Yeah, work's been busy," I explained.

"What's wrong?"

"That obvious?" I huffed a chuckle.

"You sound like you've been force-fed your balls. Bad case?"

If someone at any point in my life had told me I'd be contemplating if I'd rather have my balls forcibly removed or be in the situation I'd found myself in, I would've called that person a dumbfuck. Yet, there I sat wondering which would be less painful—missing out on more of Remy's life or losing my balls.

"Need your advice. But just to say, you don't wanna talk

about what I gotta bring up I understand."

There was a beat of silence before Holden grunted, "Where are you?"

"In my Jeep driving—"

"No, asshole, what state? Do you need me to come to you?"

Holden's offer scored through me and burned my throat so my voice was gruff when I announced, "I got a son."

"Come again?"

That knot turned venomous and I prepared to remind Holden about a time my friend would likely not want to remember.

"Remember when I called you about the box of Paul's shit I found?"

"There a point to you bringing up that asshole?"

Paul was Charleigh's dead husband. Charleigh was Holden's wife. But before Charleigh had married Paul, she'd been Holden's girl. Holden had stupidly broken up with her. Paul had quickly moved in, then lied to get Charleigh to marry him, then continued to lie to keep her. And it wasn't until Paul had been dead a good long while that I discovered the truth. And as they say, the truth will set you free. In Holden's case, that truth had led him to the daughter he didn't know he had.

And that was what I needed to talk to Holden about.

"I wouldn't bring it up if it wasn't relevant to my story. I told you I found the box but I couldn't bring it to Maryland for a week. I was out of town in D.C. working a case with Takeback."

"It was five years ago but I remember," he confirmed.

"I met the guys in D.C. and that night I hooked up with a woman. The next morning she left, that afternoon the guys and I flew out west. Didn't get her name and she didn't have mine. Fast forward five years, I'm in Spokane at an abandoned lumber yard pulling vics out of containers and the woman shows up with a family thinking we'd rescued their loved one."

"Fuck," Holden rasped. "And you got a boy you didn't know you had with a woman you didn't know you knocked up."

"Yep."

This time the silence stretched more than a beat yet I was at a loss. I'd called Holden looking for answers but now that I had him on the phone I understood there might not be a right answer.

"Fucked-up twist," Holden said. "You were pulling me out of my misery, giving me Faith, and at the same time you were unknowingly losing something precious."

There it was, the reason the knot had grown so tight. Five years ago, I'd called Holden on my way to the hotel where I'd met Brooklyn to tell Holden about a box full of papers I'd found hidden in Paul's mother's house. Papers that included a letter from Paul admitting his lie. A letter that would give Holden his daughter. And a few short hours later I had created a child and unwittingly lost my son all in the same day.

Same but different.

Close enough that Holden would understand what I was feeling.

"I don't know what you need from me, brother," Holden went on. "But whatever it is you got it."

"I don't know how to do this," I admitted. "I've seen Remington once. I've said less than ten words to him but it's like something has snapped into place and that sounds corny as hell, but there it is. A month ago I didn't know I had a son, but now I cannot imagine not having him. And that's my problem. I want him—right now. I want to know everything about him. I want to see every picture Brooklyn's taken of him. I want to hear him talk, I want to make him dinner and take him to the movies. I wanna toss a ball with him, teach him to ride a bike, buy him everything he wants. I want to hug him and tuck him in at night. I want him living under my roof and I want that to start tonight."

"First, Remington? Cool as fuck name. And second, brother, sounds to me like you got a handle on this—you want him in your life—so I'm not sure what you mean when you say you don't know how to do it. Lastly, you said a whole lot about your boy but what about his mother? Is she—"

"She's mine," I growled. "Brooklyn's not the issue. I knew it was a mistake letting her leave my room without getting her name—regretted that for years. Never thought I'd see her again and that sucked because I knew I'd live out my days knowing I let *The One* get away. Seeing as I'm not stupid, I won't be letting that happen. But I gotta work that smart because she's got shit piling up around her that I gotta see her through. I didn't know where she was at, but earlier she gave me an indication she was open to exploring things with me. I'm not gonna waste that opportunity and I'm moving in fast with her. But with Remy, I got no clue how to play that. I'm impatient to get to know my boy, but I don't wanna freak him out or push him away. So what I need from you is for you to tell me how fast I should go."

"As the man who's been in your shoes, I get what you're saying. I know that feeling to want to rush, be all you can be, get back all you lost all at once. But speaking as a father, thinking about Remington, you need to go slow and steady. Let the steady guide the pace. Remington will clue you in on how fast you can go."

That was smart.

I thought I'd follow Brooklyn but taking cues from Remy was better. Then Brooklyn could decide when and how we were going to explain that I was Remy's dad.

"Not trying to piss you off but you're sure he's yours?"

"So sure I'm positive. She offered a DNA test but either she found the long-lost twin I never knew I had and fucked him or Remy's mine. He couldn't look any more like me if I'd made him all by myself."

"Then the last thing I have to tell you is something you actually don't need me to say but I'm gonna share it all the same. No better feeling. I love my Leigh-Leigh more than breath, I don't hide that from her or anyone. But Faith, Paisley, and Ian—they're my lifeblood. There is no better feeling than looking at those three and knowing that me and Leigh-Leigh created all that beauty. You got all that waiting for you; hold on to it and if need be fight to keep it."

I wasn't the sentimental type—never had been. But after everything Holden had been through I was pleased as fuck my friend had found happy. No, my friend had found, lost, then fought to have it all.

"I take it the kids are good."

"My kids are perfect. Or I should say Faith's fourteen and driving her mother around the bend with teenage-girl attitude. Paisley's a daddy's girl and at five she's smart enough to know how to manipulate me into giving her anything she wants which drives my wife further around the bend. But my boy loves his momma and clings to her which fills her with glee and makes her forget that Faith rolls her eyes twenty-seven times a day and Paisley gets whatever she wants."

More confirmation Holden Stanford had it all. Three perfect kids and a beautiful wife he adored.

But that didn't stop me from giving my friend shit,

"Damn, fourteen. Boys are gonna be—"

"If the boys are smart they'll stay the fuck away from my daughters. And the ones who aren't and come sniffing around will learn quick I go from friendly to pissed-off dad in a nanosecond."

"Just to say, you've never been described as friendly."

"True story," Holden muttered.

I seriously meant it when I said, "I appreciate you giving me your time and wisdom."

"I owe you more than time and wisdom and you know it. But even if I didn't I'm happy you called. I'm sure it will be a while before you're ready for a Gemini Group invasion but when you are, let us know and we'll come to you. Meet your woman and your boy."

At that, I smiled. Remington would be beside himself meeting Nixon, Alec, Weston, Chasin, Jonny, and Holden. As soon as Brooklyn and Remy were comfortable around me, Wilson, Davis, Reese, Cole, and Jack, I was bringing the guys from Maryland out to Idaho or I'd fly them out there and stay at Chasin and his wife Evie's house.

On that thought, I wondered if Brooklyn liked country music. Evie was a former country music sensation and the only reason why she was a *former* superstar was because she'd given it all up for her slice of heaven. Luckily for Chasin, she found that with him.

"As soon as they're ready I'll set it up," I returned. "Listen, I gotta run. I'm at Brooklyn's work. Thanks again."

"Any time and congratulations."

Holden disconnected which was a good thing because suddenly I was breathing funny.

Congratulations.

Fuck.

Congratulations were certainly in order.

11

"Oh, no, baby, spread 'em. I'm hungry."

I quickly locked the bathroom door and got to my knees. I draped her legs over my shoulders and pushed her panties to the side.

With the first lick, I was drunk with desire. She tasted so damn good. My tongue teased at her entrance, and my thumb lightly grazed her clit.

"Oh my God," she mumbled.

My last thought before I went to work devouring her pussy was I hoped she remembered the towel. Because I was going to tongue-fuck her like she'd never been before.

I cleared my throat, made a few notes on the manuscript I was narrating, and tried again.

I was on my second practice run and about to start recording when I heard shuffling behind me.

"Lets, I only have ten minutes until I have to leave. Shut the door, yeah?"

When she didn't answer, I craned my neck to look over my shoulder and froze.

Not Letty.

Rhode.

Shit.

My head whipped around, my gaze went back to the papers spread out in front of me, and my eyes scanned the words. This was unnecessary since I'd memorized the passage.

Hungry. Knees. Panties. Lick. Desire. Tasted. Tongue. Teased. Clit. Devouring. Pussy.

"Letty said if the door was open, you weren't recording."

Rhode's gruff voice filled the small space and heat hit my cheeks. I'd heard that gruffness, that rasp, that terse tone before. The way his voice deepened when he'd ordered me to *my* knees. The husky timbre when he'd commanded me to ride him. The sharp desire in his voice when he'd told me how sweet I tasted.

"I was practicing," I squeaked.

"Practicing?"

"Male point of view. I was testing...um...never mind. I wasn't recording."

"Think you got the male point of view down pat, babe."

Oh my God.

"So, how much did you hear?"

"My guess all of it since I heard you run through it twice. First time was hot as fuckall, the second time, you deepened your voice, which is probably what you were going for since you said male point of view. Though I might not be the best judge since my brain went offline when he pushed her panties to the side. I hope to fuck the dude knows what he's doing and gets her off."

My eyes drifted closed—not because I was embarrassed but because my mind was flooded with memories of all the glorious things Rhode could do with his mouth. All the ways he could get me off.

"It's romance." I shrugged. "Of course he gets her off."

"You say that like it only happens in romance books."

"You know what they say, the book's always better."

"Was it, Brooklyn?"

"Was it what?"

"Was the book better, baby?"

Oh, crapamoly. I'd opened the door and Rhode had walked right through it and he was dragging me with him down memory lane.

"Rhode—"

"Five years I've been thinking about that night. Year after year and I can't forget. Year after year I wonder if I'm making it more than it was. If I'm remembering it incorrectly, if I'm exaggerating in my mind how fucking phenomenal it was. Year after year, dreaming about how fucking gorgeous you were when you came apart, how good you felt wrapped around me. Nothing before, nothing after, has felt better. So, tell me, Brooklyn, those books you read—are they better than what we shared?"

I knew he'd thought about me over the years, but him saying it again, this time straight-out talking about sex, I felt strange things happening between my legs. Maybe the wetness I felt wasn't strange, it was simply unfamiliar since I hadn't felt it happen in five years. But then it wasn't all that unfamiliar either, since I'd used the memory of the night to fuel my solo sessions with my vibrator.

"Brooklyn?" he growled and a shiver raced up my spine.

"No, the books I read aren't better," I admitted.

I felt his heat hit my back and his arms went around my middle. One of his hands rested on my hip, the other pressed against my stomach and held me tight.

I hadn't fully recovered from Rhode touching me when his head dropped forward and his mouth went to my ear.

"Six hours, Sugar. That was how long I had you. That was all it took for me to drown in the promise of you. Looking forward to more. Looking forward to feeling you wrapped around me—all of you, Brooklyn. Fuckin' love the way you hold on. So fuckin' tight, like you never wanna let go. Love feeling your legs wrapped around my hips, your nails scratching down my back, how fuckin' wet you get. Goddamn, baby, so hot and tight and wet. Every time. From the first time to last, every time I sank inside you. Never could forget how good you felt. Holding on tight but at the same time letting go, giving me everything. And, baby, I want everything. I want it all. I want your beautiful eyes staring at me when you come. I want your hands and mouth on me. I want you falling asleep next to me, pressed close. I want to hear you whisper more secrets. And I want all of that right *now*. I tried to find it in me to give you slow. But I don't have it in me. I had you, then I lost you, and, Brooklyn? I'm not losing you again."

My body trembled. I wanted all of that, too. So damn much it went beyond crazy, straight to out-of-my-mind. The problem was Rhode had no idea my heart, hopes, and dreams were also wrapped around him. It sounded like he wanted more sex—which, hello, I would be crazy-stupid to turn down. He wanted to get to know his son. And he'd asked me out on a date but maybe it was a get-to-know-the-mother-of-my-child-date.

"You want that, too."

He wasn't asking, he knew. He was holding me close so he felt the full-on body quake.

"There are things you need to know," I whispered.

"Yeah, Sugar, there are. A lot we both need to learn about each other. And I plan on laying it out for you. I'll tell you everything about me. No bullshit. No games. I got no problems baring my soul to you. All I ask is you give it to me straight. Everything, Brooklyn. Total honesty."

"Total honesty?"

"Absolutely."

I took a deep breath and wondered how honest I should be. How badly would it freak him out if he knew he'd stolen my heart back in D.C.? Would he run a mile if he knew I'd give him everything if he promised to stay?

"Everything, Sugar," he whispered like he read my mind. "Give it to me."

"I want you to stay," I admitted.

"That all?"

No, that wasn't even the tip of the iceberg.

"I'm happy you never forgot me because I never stopped thinking about you. And not because of Remington. Not because you were my fantasy come to life. I never stopped thinking about you because from the moment you walked into that bar I knew my life would never be the same. I looked at you and I started to fall in love. I know it sounds crazy—"

"It's not crazy." Low, gruff, raspy. I shivered again. "I walked into the bar that night with my mind being pulled in a hundred different directions. Then I see this beautiful woman sitting in a booth by herself and the first thing I think is I'd never seen a woman more stunning. Then I watched you work for a few minutes while I waited for the guys to come down. Every couple of seconds, your lips curved up and I wanted to know what you were reading that was making you grin. The longer I watched, the more the noise in my head started to dissipate. All my thoughts narrowed to you and why you were alone in a bar smiling. When you noticed me and I saw your eyes widen you had me hooked. Don't know what it was because you looked away so quickly but in that single second I felt at ease—something I hadn't felt in a decade."

"Why hadn't you felt at ease for a decade?"

Rhode went stiff behind me and his hand on my belly pressed deep.

"You want that story, I'll give it to you. But we don't have the time right now."

Hm. I liked that he said he'd tell me, but something was wrong.

"Why'd you tense up?"

"Because I liked that you asked me something personal."

That didn't jibe.

"Why are you lying?"

Rhode's sharp jolt of laughter made me jump but I didn't get very far when his hand on my hip held me in place.

"That's it, Sugar; don't let me get away with deflecting. Now and always, you call me on my shit."

"Oh-kay."

"Total honesty?" he asked and I nodded. "I wasn't lying. I liked that you asked me something personal, but more I liked that you sound like you genuinely cared about my answer. I have a lot of good friends in my life. Men who are like brothers to me. Men who I can call and no matter where they are or what they're doing they'll drop everything to take my back. But I've never had a woman who asked, cared, or wanted anything from me."

How could that be true? Rhode was hot, surely there'd been a slew of girlfriends—women who'd cared about him. Women *he'd* cared about. My heart revolted at the thought of Rhode being in love with another woman. My silly-romantic heart couldn't bear the thought of him not feeling the same way I felt for him. I had never loved another man.

Not even a puppy-love. Not even a twinge of the makings of love.

"It's true, Brooklyn," he said, once again reading my thoughts. "I've never cared nor have I been cared for. I can't say it's because I've kept myself closed off but I wasn't looking for it either. Bottom line is, until I met you, there was never even a stir of emotion. I won't lie and say I fell in love with you but I felt something deep enough I couldn't forget you."

Damn. That stung my fool-heart. The irrational, starry-eyed dreamer side of me wished he had. The normal, rational side knew he was being honest. Not only that but reasonable, sane people didn't fall in love with a glance.

I wasn't going to tell him I was insane and I'd wished he'd seen me across a not-so-crowded bar and knew down to his soul I was the woman he was meant to share his life with. That wouldn't have him running; that would have him checking me into a mental institution, worried I was a crazy stalker.

So instead I settled on, "Twice you've read my mind."

"You're easy to read, Sugar."

For my peace of mind, I chose not to believe that. If I was easy to read that meant he'd see more than I was prepared for him to see.

Rhode chuckled again and I quickly snapped my eyes shut so I could concentrate on the rumble vibrating from his chest. I felt his warm breath fan over my neck right before his lips brushed the shell of my ear.

If he wasn't holding me vertical I would've hit the floor.

"Yeah, Brooklyn, I see you," he gently murmured. "I saw it that night, I saw it when you were leaving. Torn, wanting to stay, too scared to tell me what was on your mind. So I let you go. And part of the reason why was because I was scared, too. Another reason was that I wasn't ready to admit to myself that I might not have fallen with a look, but, Sugar, by the time you walked away I knew if I spent more time with you I would. And I was right—the more time that passed the further I fell. But I was also wrong because I didn't need you present for me to take that fall. I've learned to listen to my instincts. There is something undeniable between us. It was there five years ago and time apart hasn't changed a damn thing."

Rhode's words wrapped around me as surely as he was holding me. My heart rate ticked up and my heart shattered open.

Wide-open, with no chance of me closing it.

"Please be sure," I pleaded.

"I'm positive."

"Rhode, please honey, be very sure."

"Brooklyn—"

"You want honesty. All of it. Right now I'm not thinking about Remy and what this could mean for him. I'm coming to you as a woman who lost her heart in six hours. I'm coming to you as a woman who hasn't looked at another man in five years because no one could compare. No one could begin to erase the memory. So, I'm begging you to be careful with my heart because it belongs to you."

I heard the sharp inhale. I felt his body go solid. I held my breath and waited.

Thankfully, Rhode didn't make me wait long.

"You have my word I wouldn't be where I am right now if I wasn't a hundred percent positive I want you right where you are. And just so you don't have to guess I'm gonna spell it out. If I wasn't sure, I'd stay to be in Remy's life and I'd do that in a way where you and I would be friends so we could raise our son together. But that's not why you're in my arms after years of being in my heart."

I didn't doubt him, not for a second. And that wasn't me being starry-eyed; that was me knowing instinctually that Rhode was not a bullshitter and he wasn't a liar.

"Would you like to come over for dinner tonight? Something low-key so you can spend some time with Remy?"

"Yes."

No hesitation.

"I talked to a buddy of mine," Rhode went on. "He was in a similar situation. His advice was to go at Remy's pace. Introduce me slowly at first but do it frequently. Then we can move at his speed to something more consistent. But you're his mom, you know best, so you're in charge of reining me in when I wanna go full-speed."

"Can you be reined in?"

"For Remy, I can do anything. Even the impossible."

I sucked in a breath so painful I swayed. Pain so exquisite I reveled in it. My son was blessed; he had a lot of people in his life who loved him. But right then, hearing Rhode's fierce determination, I knew down to my soul none of them could possibly love him more than Rhode would.

12

I was out of my Jeep walking up to Brooklyn's house when the door swung open and Brooklyn appeared on the stoop.

"Mayday. Mayday. We have a problem," Brooklyn said then disappeared into the house.

I jogged the rest of the way up the walk, jumped the three steps leading to the porch, and rushed into the house. My hand went to my hip as my eyes scanned the room and took in the mess, then my eyes landed on Remy, smiling.

Smiling.

What the fuck?

"Momma's in there." Remy pointed to the hall.

I stood frozen, staring at my boy, and my heart pinched.

Never in my life had I ever wanted to touch another person the way I wanted to scoop my boy up and hug him. I had four years and a handful of months to make up for. And fuck, but I wanted to start right that very second.

"Remington!" Brooklyn shouted and Remy took off.

I followed, taking in the state of Brooklyn's living room.

Total disaster. Remy's toys were strewn from one side of the living room to the other.

Jesus. How was it possible for one little human to make that much of a mess in less than three hours?

The second thing I noticed was that there were towels all over the floor leading down a short hallway.

Wet towels.

Fuck.

"Baby, get Momma some more towels," Brooklyn requested.

Remy rushed past me just as I stepped into a small bathroom. Brooklyn was on the floor, on her right hip, half her body under the sink, and water was pouring out of the cabinet onto the already-soaked towel.

"Sugar, come out of there and let me—"

The rest of my instructions were cut off by a very loud, very high-pitched squeal.

Brooklyn sputtered and covered her face as water shot out of the broken pipe.

Soaked from head to toe, water now cascading, I moved quickly. I bent, hefted Brooklyn to her feet, scooted her out of the way, then got to my knees.

Cold water blasted me in the face as I shoved my shoulders under the sink and felt around for the shutoff valve. My wet hand hit the regulator and turned it. Once I didn't have water blasting me in the face I spotted a screwdriver and a pair of pliers.

"How did you do that?" Brooklyn asked.

I slid out and snagged the tools and held them up.

"What are these for?"

"Here." Remy came back into the small bathroom with an armful of folded towels and skidded to a halt. "You fixed it."

I took in my boy's wide-eyed wonder and I blinked. Then I thanked God I was already on my ass because I was having trouble finding my breath.

Dark brown eyes clashed with dark brown eyes.

Father and son.

My son.

Jesus Christ.

Without meaning to I lifted my hand and rubbed the area around my heart.

Remy dropped the towels then dropped to his knees and asked, "Will you show me?"

"Show you what, bud?"

"How you fixed it."

With a great deal of effort, I tore my gaze from Remy and looked up at Brooklyn. When I did I found her staring at us with a ghost of a smile on her lips and for some reason that felt really fucking good.

"Babe?" I held the tools out. "A screwdriver?"

Her lips curved up to a full-fledged smile and she shook her head. "What? Everything can be fixed with a screwdriver."

"And the pliers?"

"Just in case the screwdriver didn't work."

"Right." I chuckled. "C'mere, bud." I waited until Remy scooted closer. Then I waited another second to revel in my boy's nearness. After I was done but before I got the ache in my chest to subside I pointed to the back of the cabinet. "See those two knobs back there?"

"The plastic ones?" Remy asked and pushed closer.

Three deep inhales later I nodded and continued, "Those turn the water off."

Brooklyn was lucky and the break was below the turn-off valve or I would be at the curb turning off the main line.

"That's it?"

Remington sounded disappointed and I couldn't help my smile.

"Nope. That just stopped the water. Now we hafta crawl back in there and replace the pipe. But first, we need to clean up this mess and I need to go to the store."

"Can I go to the store with you?"

Jesus fuck, I wanted that almost as badly as I wanted to pull the boy into my arms and hug him for the first time. But reality crashed in quickly. I was not in charge, Brooklyn was.

"That's up to your momma after we clean up this mess."

Remy's face scrunched and he looked around the towel-covered floor. My gaze followed and something struck me.

"This is a lot of water. How long was this leaking?"

"A few days."

"A few days?"

Brooklyn sighed.

"It was just a trickle. So I had a bowl under there to catch the water. Today when I got home, I dumped the bowl like I always do then went about my business. Remy came back to go to the bathroom and the hall had water in it."

I was stuck back on the part where her pipe had been leaking water for a few days. It pissed me off badly that she and Remy lived alone and she was dumping buckets of water out for two days. How many other times in the last five years had Brooklyn had to go it alone? How many other things around her house had broken that she didn't know how to fix? My guess was a lot and that pissed me off, too. I should've been there to take care of them.

I tamped down the irrational anger and asked, "Do you own or rent?"

"Rent. I called my landlord and he's sending someone out to look at it. And just to say, if I knew about the knobs under there I would've turned off the water. And now that I know, I feel pretty stupid."

"Can't feel stupid about something you didn't know about. We'll mop up this water and I'll run to the store, get a new pipe, and fix it. You can call your landlord and tell him he doesn't need to send someone out."

"You don't have to."

Yes, I did.

"There another bathroom?"

Brooklyn rubbed her lips together and an inappropriate thought rushed front and center. Me on my back, Brooklyn naked on top of me, her lips wet from our kiss, and Brooklyn rubbing them together. She'd done that a lot when she was thinking about something. The night we'd shared, the wall she'd put up as soon as we'd walked into my room, I hadn't asked her what she was thinking. Now, I didn't want walls, I didn't want secrets between us, I didn't want her holding back.

"What's on your mind, Sugar?"

Brooklyn's eyes snapped to mine and I was lost in a sea of blue. So beautiful for a moment I wished Remington had inherited her eyes. A new thought flashed and I hoped we'd give Remy brothers and sisters.

I waited for my brain to kick in and remind me I was insane but no such thoughts arose. No panic, no hesitation, no remorse.

"This is the only bathroom," she told me.

"And?"

"And I rent. I don't want you wasting money fixing—"

"It'll cost ten bucks and you can give the receipt to your landlord."

A tiny hand landed on my forearm and I sucked in a breath at the contact.

"Can I go with you?" Remy asked again.

Brooklyn's gaze darted from me to Remy and that was when I saw it. She wasn't thinking about the bathroom situation, the pipe, or the cost of a six-inch PVC pipe and fitting.

"Hey, bud? Can you do me a favor and start soaking up some of this water in the hallway? Can't go to the store until the floor's dry."

Remy hesitated a moment before he pulled his hand back. I however felt no hesitation when I lost my son's touch —the pain of loss was immediate. I waited until Remy jumped to his feet and dashed out the door before I stood and faced Brooklyn.

"What's wrong, Sugar?"

"Nothing."

I stepped closer. My hand went to her hip and I gave her a squeeze. I released the pressure but didn't let go.

"Easy to read, remember?" I prompted.

"Nothing's *wrong*. Just watching you two together and hearing Remy ask if he can go with you to the store made me think about all he's missed, but at the same time I'm happy he hasn't missed the big stuff."

Fuck, that felt good.

"Big stuff?"

"He can ride a bike; he missed you teaching him that. But that was something I could handle. He wants to learn how to ride a dirt bike, something Michael's been wanting to teach him and I've been dragging my feet. He can throw a baseball but not well because I'm not big into sports. He's never picked up a football. He loves to draw and do puzzles and put together Legos—I can cover those things but there's so much I can't teach him and I was dreading him getting older and needing a dad and not having you that I felt guilty for all the ways I was going to fail him."

Brooklyn stopped, inhaled a deep breath, and settled her hand on top of mine before she finished. "So seeing him next to you asking you how to fix a sink—which obviously I have no idea how to fix—I was thinking how good it felt knowing you were here to give Remington all the things you can give him. Things that I can't."

No, that didn't feel good—that felt fucking great. So great, I couldn't vocalize how phenomenal it felt knowing that while I'd missed a lot I wouldn't be missing any more. Not another day, hour, or second.

"You good with me teaching him how to ride a dirt bike?"

Brooklyn frowned and pinched her lips.

"I'll take that as a no."

"He's four," she noted.

"Your call."

Brooklyn heaved a sigh and for once I couldn't read her. Which was unfortunate because that meant I was unprepared for her to rock my world.

"*Our* call. Mine and yours."

"Sugar—"

"I was dragging my feet coming up with excuses to put Michael off. My dad taught me how to ride. I remember every moment of it."

I didn't understand—if Brooklyn knew how to ride a dirt bike why hadn't she taught Remy?

"Not tracking. Why didn't you take Remy out?"

"I've never taken him to a movie at a movie theater. I've never taken him to Silverwood. I've never taken him out on the lake," she weirdly admitted.

"Baby, you say that like you've committed a mortal sin."

Brooklyn's head tipped back and with her eyes brimming with tears she whispered, "I was waiting for you."

Un-fucking-done.

My lungs seized and my body locked.

The atmosphere in the small bathroom charged when two words rasped from my throat.

"Come again?"

"I was waiting for you," she repeated. "Family memories. Stuff that I didn't want to do on my own with Remy. It was selfish not giving him—"

I didn't give her a chance to finish. Unpolite and unyielding, I slammed my mouth down onto hers. Brooklyn gasped, and not being the sort of man who missed an opportunity, my tongue pushed past her lips.

Good Goddamn.

Little feet pounded down the hall, ending a kiss that wasn't just a kiss but a welcome home. A glide of tongues. A sample of what was to come. The best thing I'd tasted in five fucking years.

"Done!"

Much to my shock, Brooklyn didn't jump away when Remy appeared in the doorway. She did back out of my embrace to take the sopping towels out of her son's hands.

"Thank you for helping." Then without missing a beat she smiled at Remy and continued. "If you want to go to the store, you need to change your clothes. You're all wet."

"Be back," Remy whooped. "Don't leave without me."

"You're wet, too."

The only thing that held back my retort was the pink that tinged Brooklyn's cheeks telling me she was thinking exactly what I was thinking and for now, that'd have to do.

"That I am," I agreed with a wink.

"I'm gonna...I'll just..." she stuttered and I smiled.

"Sugar?"

"Yeah?"

"Thank you."

"I didn't—"

"For thinking of me all these years. For giving me a chance—us a chance. And just so you know, you wantin' for our boy to have family memories doesn't make you selfish. It makes you a good mom. So mostly I'm thanking you for giving that to my boy. And when the time's right we're gonna start making those memories."

"I'm ready."

I paused to take her in. Whatever brought us back together—fate, the stars, the universe, I was grateful as fuck.

One step at a time, I reminded myself.

One. Damn. Step.

I wanted to charge ahead.

"We'll give it a week, then we'll introduce sleepovers." When Brooklyn didn't protest I went on. "We'll start by going up to the cabin. Neutral territory for him."

"Okay."

Thank fuck.

"Before that, you need me to leave after dinner so you can get him to bed, I'll leave and come back after he's asleep. I want all the time I can get with Remy. But that doesn't mean I don't want alone time with you."

"His bedtime's eight and he knocks out fast."

She was onboard.

Thank fuck.

"Go check on Remy, Sugar, so we can get to the store and get back."

Brooklyn didn't move—she stared.

And the longer she held my gaze the tighter the area around my heart constricted. One of her hands went to my chest, the other landed on my shoulder. Then she rolled up onto her toes and kissed me. After that, she dashed out of the bathroom leaving me in a daze.

Stunned stupid, I didn't move.

From a brush of her lips.

Brooklyn Saunders wasn't going to be the one that got away. She was the one I was going to keep.

13

"Is he ready?" Remy asked, bouncing from foot to foot.

"*He* has a name."

"Is *Rhode* ready?"

I was having second thoughts. Maybe I should go with them to the store. Remy could be a handful when he was excited and right then Remy wasn't excited—he was floating on cloud nine.

Still on my knees, I finished tying Remy's shoe and glanced up at him, and a pang of remorse hit. That was why I was going to let my son go with Rhode to the store without me. I didn't know if he was a good driver, had any accidents, DUIs, if he drove fast or slow yet I knew with Remy in the car he'd be safe. Deep-down I knew Rhode would never get behind the wheel of a car intoxicated because he'd think that was wrong in a way he'd probably punch someone and take their keys if they tried. It never crossed my mind that Rhode would take off with Remy and hide him from me. He'd said he didn't want to take Remy from me and wanted both of us. And Rhode was not a man you didn't believe.

"Momma," Remy whined and I shook away my thoughts.

"I'll go check. Start picking up some of these toys while you wait."

"But I'm playing with them."

"You won't be playing with them, you'll be at the store with your..." *Crap. Shit. Damn.* "With, um, Rhode."

My son stared at me in a way that would scare the hell out of me if he were ten years older. He'd caught my slip but was too young to understand. Thank the Lord for small favors.

"Go, bud. Clean up and I'll see if Rhode's ready."

"Is he—"

My heart slammed into my chest and I interrupted whatever question he was going to ask.

"Go on, Remy, so you'll be ready."

Remy wasn't buying what I was selling but he was a good boy and didn't argue. *Most of the time anyway*, I thought. I got to my feet and looked around my messy living room. Secretly, I loved seeing Remy's toys scattered around. What I didn't love were the towels still lining the hallway. Thank God, Rhode had showed up when he had or the disaster that was my bathroom and hall would've been so much worse. I was so grateful I didn't even have it in me to be embarrassed that I didn't know I could turn the water off under the sink. *And* I was grateful Rhode was willing to fix it —with Remy.

I didn't bother with the wet towels as I made my way to the bathroom. I stopped just outside the door and froze.

Then I blinked, and when the vision didn't vanish, I blinked again.

Nope.

Still there.

Rhode shirtless. Gloriously shirtless. The chiseled back that was seared into my memory was still cut and muscular. The scar he had on his right shoulder was still there. But that wasn't what caught my attention. Five years ago he'd been tattooless. Smooth, clean, uninked skin. Now, I could see lines and curls peeking up his left side from the waistband of his jeans all the way up to under his armpit. My gaze went to the mirror and I took in the front of him. And there was so much to take in. The hard chest I'd dreamt about running my hands over. The six-pack that was more pronounced than it was years ago—and I'd know because I'd spent a good amount of time running my tongue over those swells and valleys. I'd grazed my teeth down from his throat all the way to the prize between his muscular thighs. I'd kissed and licked every single inch of Rhode and I remember all of it. Every scar, every freckle, every hard ridge —all of it had been mine for the night.

And there had been no tattoo. Now there was and I was curious.

In the mirror, Rhode's gaze came to mine and he looked nervous. His eyes tipped down and I knew he was looking at the ink I couldn't see. Then his eyes came back to mine and they burned into me. Burned. Scorched. Ruthlessly held me captive and I didn't understand until his rumbling voice filled the room.

"Never forgot you."

With that, he turned, and without delay, my eyes dropped to the tattoo branding his left side.

My head swam.

Dogwood flowers.

I didn't have to look at my own arm to know his tattoo was damn near identical to mine.

Branches and vines and flowers sleeved my arm. Every bud held a special meaning. Red for passion, pink for love, white for hope. Only his were masculine whereas mine was feminine—bold whereas mine was soft.

"I didn't know your name or I would've inked that, too."

I felt the sting start in my throat until it felt like a lump so big I couldn't swallow had formed, making it impossible to speak. But Rhode didn't need me to respond as he continued.

"Devotion, safety, and passion. But also illusion."

He was telling me the meaning behind the dogwood tree. The very reasons I tattooed the flowers on my arm. Though he left out: desire and loyalty. The recipe my romantic heart held sacred. Desire and passion mixed with loyalty and devotion made for the perfect union. Add in safety and I had the hero I'd always dreamed about.

"Legend says a king sent his knight to Ireland to claim a bride and bring her back for the king. On the journey back the knight and the princess fell in love. The king had them killed and buried in separate graves. But death couldn't keep their souls apart and from each grave grew an ivy vine. The ivy meets and twines together—their eternal connection."

Rhode lifted his left arm and a riot of pink, red, and white dogwood blossoms intertwined with ivy. Some of the flowers were still on the branch, others were dotted in the deep green of the vine. Near the top of the tattoo one single, pristine, lavender rose still on its thorny stem jutted out, the petals brushing just over Rhode's heart.

A lavender rose.

Lavender.

"Love at first sight," I gasped.

"I saw it in your eyes and I fought against the very idea it was possible. Lavender also means enchantment. And it's safe to say I was enchanted—then and now."

There I was in the least-romantic setting, standing in my bathroom with wet towels littering the old and cracked linoleum floor, in front of the man who I'd loved for five years, the man who'd unknowingly fathered my child. I fought the urge to fist bump the air and dance a jig. I didn't want to weep tears of happiness, or fall into his arms and declare my undying love for him—I had a feeling he knew how deep my feelings for him went. No, I wanted to jump for joy. I wanted to whoop and sing and twirl around.

I wanted to shout that I'd been right. So right. After all of these years thinking I was a dreamy idiot—I was right. Not that there was such a thing as love at first sight or soul mates (Though I was obviously right about that, too.). No, I was right about something more important.

"You felt it too."

"I felt it," he confirmed.

"Whoa!" Remy stopped by my side and took in Rhode. "You're huge."

Rhode's startled gaze went to Remy and I wasn't sure what was more hilarious—the way Rhode's chest puffed out or the red that hit his face.

Was he blushing?

"Hey, why do you have the same flowers as Momma?" *See? Near identical.* "Do you have the other ones too?"

"Other ones?" Rhode inquired, ignoring Remy's first question.

Shit.

"The ones—"

"Remy, baby, are your toys picked up?"

"Yup. I'm ready." *Thank God, four year olds are easily distracted.* "Are you ready?"

Rhode untwisted his t-shirt and shook it over the sink before he pulled it over his head.

He turned to Remy, flashed him a smile I'd never seen before—well, that wasn't true, I saw that smile on my boy but never on Rhode—and he said, "All set."

Upon hearing this information, Remington returned Rhode's smile.

And my heart melted.

Right there on the spot, my knees went weak.

"Babe?"

"Oh, right. Sorry."

I jerked out of my trance and moved out of the bathroom and down the hall into the living room. My mind was filled with lavender roses and dogwood flowers when a strong hand wrapped around the back of my neck and warm breath fanned across my ear.

"You got more tattoos, Sugar?"

Without thinking I answered, "Yes."

"Looking forward to findin' them."

Rhode didn't wait for my response. His hand fell away and he followed Remy to the front door.

"Wait. Remy needs a booster."

"Momma."

The two syllables were dragged out into a whine.

"Rem—"

"Make you a deal, kid. You don't argue about the booster and I'll talk your mom into letting me take you fishing this weekend."

"Do you have a boat?"

This would be a deal-breaker for Remy. Michael took Remy fishing all the time, he loved it, but the Welshes didn't own a boat and Remy'd been asking about going out on the lake since last summer.

"Yep."

"You do?"

"I do, but it's up on Pend Oreille. Maybe I can talk your mom into you two spending the weekend up at the cabin. Would you like that?"

"Can we go bear hunting, too?"

My heart stopped. I'd lived in Idaho my whole life and had never run across a bear and I prayed I never did. The thought of my son traipsing through a national forest looking for a six-foot hairy beast gave me heart palpitations.

"No."

Thank God.

"But we can go out on the boat and fish?"

"Absolutely."

Remy's unhappy gaze cut to me and I reminded him, "You've been wanting to go out on a boat."

"Okay," he grumbled.

"Come on, short stuff, I'll walk you out."

"I'm not short. I'm the tallest in my class," he proudly told Rhode.

"Yeah?"

"My best friend Serafina is the next tallest."

Rhode's lips curved up into a grin as he ushered Remy to the front door.

"Serafina, huh?"

"I call her Fina and she doesn't punch me like she does the other boys when they call her that. And she likes to fish, and her dad lets her ride four-wheelers, and she's allowed to ride it by herself."

"Is that your way of telling me that your mom doesn't let you ride by yourself?" Rhode chuckled.

"Maybe?"

"So much cheek coming from such a little person," I said.

"No one says cheek," Remy told me for the five-millionth time.

"I do. You're a cheeky rascal. And I told you we'd talk about you riding four-wheelers when you're five."

Remington's chin lifted and his head tipped back as he fell in step next to Rhode.

"You're tall."

"Yep."

I held my breath and waited for more but Remy went silent.

Guilt gnawed at my insides. I had to tell my son who Rhode was, sooner rather than later.

Needing to get back into the house to clean up the mess, I quickly grabbed Remy's booster from my car and gave it to Rhode. For once Remy didn't complain and throw a fit about being buckled in. I waited for Rhode to pull away before I rushed back into the house.

I didn't clean up the mess. I called Letty.

It rang once and she picked up.

"Why are you calling me?"

"Nice," I snapped.

"Don't get your panties in a bunch, sister, it's a legitimate question. Hot guy baby daddy is over for a get-to-know-you dinner, and I hope for your sake some good ol' fashioned necking and groping."

"Don't call Rhode *baby daddy*."

"Sigh."

Yes, Letty muttered the word sigh and I rolled my eyes to the ceiling and took a breath.

"I need help."

"Okay, so first you tear open the foil. Then you pull out

the slimy rubber. After that, you pinch the tip as you roll it down his erect shaft."

"Letty!"

"Oh, sorry, I forgot it's been like twenty years since you've gotten the good stuff. I'll back up to—"

"I know how to use a condom."

"Hello...Remington. The walking, talking proof you don't actually know how to use a condom."

"It broke."

"Actually, now that I've seen him I think his swimmers are so powerful they penetrated the latex and swam upstream."

Usually, Letty being her normal funny self would make me laugh. But right then I wasn't finding anything funny. I had a crisis and I needed my best friend's input.

"I'm being serious."

"Just tell him you've been in love with him and I bet you all the books in Smutties he takes care of the rest."

She'd win that bet.

"I basically already told him that. And you're right, he's not shying away from telling me what he wants. If anything, I have a feeling he's holding back to give me time to adjust."

"You what?" Letty screeched. "We're breaking up. I cannot believe you didn't tell me you told him you fell madly in love with him while your best friend was upstairs in the hotel room sleeping. And for the record, I'm still pissed you let me sleep through you meeting your baby...I mean, you let me sleep through finding your One."

"I told you to come to the bar. I practically begged you. I also asked you to bring me my phone so I could covertly take pictures of him. To which you told me that was stalkerish and for me to let you sleep. So you don't get to break up with me—I'm breaking up with you for not bringing me my phone. That way we would've had a picture of him and we could've internet-stalked him and Remington would've had a daddy all these years. Which brings me to the point of this conversation: how do I tell Remy?"

Letty sucked in a breath and groused, "Take that back and I'll tell you."

"I'm not taking it back and stop acting like a five-year-old."

She mumbled something under her breath I couldn't make out then she finally got serious.

"Just tell him."

I closed my eyes and dropped my chin to my chest.

"It's not that easy," I told her.

"Sure it is."

"Okay, and what about all the questions after?"

"Brook, you're freaking out for no reason. You and Rhode tell Remington, then the two of you answer his questions together. The biggest one you're gonna face is where Rhode's been all these years. You're going to have to come up with a version of the truth that works for you and Rhode. My guess is Rhode will take the blame, wanting to protect you. You want to protect Rhode so he's got a clear shot with Remy. You two are gonna have to meet in the middle."

Meet in the middle.

That sounded smart. But I wasn't sure how to do that when I never, ever wanted my son to know his existence came about because of a one-night stand.

"And you might have to lie," Letty finished.

I never thought I'd agree with lying but right then lying sounded like the perfect thing to do. We could tell Remy we'd been madly in love when Rhode had been deployed to a faraway place. Then he was captured and held as a POW. He finally escaped and made his way home to us.

"Brook, I know you're in your head making up some crazy plot about Rhode being a prisoner of war in Siberia. But you need to reel it in. I'm talking about a small lie. Something like you lost touch with Rhode and didn't know how to find him to tell him you were pregnant. And Rhode can say he didn't know or he would've come to Idaho immediately, swept you off your feet, and married you."

"That's basically the truth," I reminded her. "Except the part about Rhode coming to Idaho to marry me."

"I said lie, but maybe I should've said stretch the truth a little, not come up with an entire season of a soap opera to explain his absence. You don't need to tell Remy you didn't know Rhode at the time of his conception. You can make it seem like you two were in a relationship and lost touch."

And...there was the problem with lying. It was never just one. Once the truth was stretched an inch, it might as well have been extended a mile.

At four, Remy wouldn't know what questions to ask, but at fifteen he would.

I was so fucked.

"I'm screwed."

"Obviously that's not true because you're on the phone with me. By the way, where is the sexy and handsome Dulles? And have I told you today how insanely hot he is?"

I told her about the pipe leaking and how it at the worst —or best, depending on how I looked at the situation— possible time, it finally burst. I also told her that Rhode had taken Remy to the store to get what he needed to fix the sink.

"You let him take Remy to the store alone?"

"He's Remy's father. I have to let the two of them spend time together without me. A trip to Lowes or wherever Rhode's going is the perfect opportunity."

"I agree."

"Then why do you sound so surprised?"

"Because you don't let Remy go with anyone you don't know. And by know I mean you grill them about speeding tickets before you let your kid in the car with them."

"Rhode would sooner die than do something to hurt Remington."

"Yeah, he would," Letty whispered. "And the fact that you know that says a lot, Brook. The two of you will do what's best for Remy. I'm sure of it." After she was done reassuring me she asked, "Would you hate me forever if I stole him from you?"

She wasn't talking about Remington. Letty adored her nephew but was all too happy to return him after she spent the day with him. That wasn't to say she wouldn't fight and die for my boy and if I kicked the bucket, I knew she'd take Remy and raise him as her own.

"I'd stab you."

"Violence coming from Brooklyn Saunders, now I know it's true love."

It was on the tip of my tongue to tell Letty about Rhode's tattoo. In all the years I'd known her I hadn't kept even one secret from her. She knew everything about me. But I wanted this for myself, just for a little while. At least until I could process the magnitude of what those flowers meant. And long enough for him to see the additions I'd made to my body.

"He loves you," Letty said softly.

"Rhode?"

"No. Well, he might but I was talking about Remington. That boy loves you. No matter what you tell him he won't stop loving you. And when he gets older and you can explain more he'll love you then, too. He's four, Brook; just tell him."

"Rhode wants us to go to his cabin in Sandpoint and spend the night. He also wants to take Remy out on his boat."

"That's good, honey. Remy will love it."

Yeah, Remington would absolutely love spending time out on the water.

"I'll talk to Rhode and see what he thinks. But if he's okay with it, we'll tell Remy then."

My plan was met with utter silence and when it stretched, nerves kicked in.

"Is that not a good idea?"

"So happy for you."

"Let—"

"Shh, Brook. Give me this and don't interject any of your rational thoughts."

The only person who'd ever accused me of being rational was Letty. Everyone else thought I lived with my head in the clouds. And Letty only thought I was rational because she was worse than me when it came to romanti-cizing life. Everything was a fairy tale to her.

"I was going to say thank you and tell you I was happy," I fibbed.

"No, you weren't. You were going to tell me not to get my hopes up about Dulles and you. Which is stupid because you're over-the-moon happy so you should let me be happy for you."

She was right, I was happy.

"If we're both happy then who's gonna be the sane one?"

"Um...hello...when have either of us ever worried about that?"

The answer to that was never.

"My heart's on the line," I reminded her.

"Your heart is where it's supposed to be."

I sucked in a breath.

Letty was right.

My heart was exactly where it was supposed to be—or more to the point, it was with the man who owned it.

"I'm hanging up now so I can finish closing for the night."

"You're the best."

"Remember that when you're eulogizing me."

God, Letty.

"You have a twisted sense of humor."

"Yet you still love me."

And with that, she hung up on me.

An hour later I had the water cleaned up and all the towels in the wash when Remy and Rhode got back.

My heart swelled as I watched father and son saunter through the door—something I never thought I'd see but prayed I would.

"Mommy! Guess what?" Remy shouted with more excitement than his normal level.

"What?"

"Rhode bought me a football. After dinner, we're gonna throw it in the backyard."

I glanced back and forth between Rhode and Remington. Identical smiles shone back and my heart melted.

"That's awesome. Then I better hurry up and get dinner started."

"What's for dinner?"

"Mac and cheese and hot dogs," I told Remy.

"That's my favorite," Remy whooped and turned to Rhode. "Do you like mac and cheese?"

"It's my favorite, too, bud."

Rhode lifted his gaze and for a moment he looked wounded and my heart sank. In the days and weeks to come there would be a lot of reminders of what he lost with Remington. It would take time for Rhode to learn Remy's likes and dislikes and I wasn't sure my heart could take the sadness in Rhode's eyes during his path of discovery.

It was on the tip of my tongue to apologize again. But before I could, Rhode shocked the shit out of me.

"You remembered?"

His tone clearly conveyed disbelief.

Then it hit me—*he* remembered. I took a moment to let the memory wash over me—warm and sweet—lying next to Rhode with my head resting on his chest, his hand sweeping over my bare back. At no time when I was with him had I felt self-conscious. He made me feel beautiful in word and deed. And there in his hotel bed, with only the dim light of the table lamp, he told me he loved homemade mac and cheese. I told him I loved tuna casserole. He told me when he was a kid, to impress his friends he'd eaten a worm— seriously disgusting—and for a nanosecond, I'd contemplated not kissing him again. Then I remembered how good he kissed and forgot all about the worm. I told him about the time I fell off my bike and the front wheel twisted, causing the handlebar to hit me in the solar plexus, knocking the wind out of me, and how after that, I was afraid to ride a bicycle and hadn't been on one since. Our six hours was about more than sex, more than whispered secrets. I'd connected with Rhode in a way I'd never connected with anyone. Not even Letty.

"I remember everything you told me," I confirmed.

"What do you remember, Mommy?"

"That Rhode liked mac and cheese."

"She makes it all the time. It's her specialty," Remy told Rhode proudly.

It was my specialty—I'd spent years perfecting the recipe.

14

Watching Remington beam at his mom with unadulterated love sliced through me. Watching Brooklyn give her son her full attention like what he had to say was the most important thing she'd heard all day had me contemplating my future.

Seeing that smile, suddenly our situation became clear. The knot that had taken up residence in my gut unraveled. More than anything I wanted Remington to look at me like he was looking at his mom.

Pure.

Uncomplicated.

Proud.

I wanted Brooklyn's attention and time, and I wanted that to include Remington. The three of us—a family. I wanted them in my cabin, on my boat, in my life and I wanted that starting now. No more delaying. Kiki Welsh had come forward, she wasn't missing—never had been. Once Michael and Tallulah were told and Jack and Asher secured Desi we'd be one step closer to closing the operation. But I wasn't waiting—Brooklyn and Remy were mine.

It wasn't that Brooklyn had remembered I loved home-made mac and cheese, yet it was.

It wasn't the way her gaze had lingered on my tattoo, yet it was.

It wasn't the way she'd laid it out open and honest, yet it was.

It wasn't the trust she'd shown allowing me to take Remy to the store, yet it was.

It was all of that and more. It was the past and what we'd shared. The connection I could never shake. The way her face softened when she saw her flowers inked onto my skin. It meant something to her and she hadn't hidden it. It was the way those eyes had haunted my dreams and now I had them back and I was never going to spend another day not looking into them.

It was also Remington. But I was smart enough to separate the two. I didn't need Brooklyn in my bed to have a relationship with my son—I'd have that no matter what. But the family I wanted included brothers and sisters for Remy. And for that, I did need Brooklyn in my life—that included my ring on her finger and her in my bed.

I ended my thoughts with a grin.

Fuck, yes, Brooklyn and her gorgeous eyes, pretty smile, her fierce protection of my son, her loyalty to a family who'd taken her in after her parents had died, her determination, and her honesty would be in my bed.

I'd give her until this weekend, then we were heading up to the cabin. And when we got back we'd be on an extended sleepover.

All of those thoughts flashed through my mind at warp speed.

Decision made, I turned to Remy.

"You ready to fix the sink, bud?"

"Yes!"

Remy rushed to the hall but skidded to a halt when Brooklyn called his name.

"Did you thank Rhode for buying you the football?"

A twinge of pain squeezed my heart at hearing Brooklyn call me by my name.

Soon, I reminded myself. Soon Remy would call me Dad. "I did."

And he had. I'd given him the choice of buying a football or baseball and bat. Remy picked the football, then thanked me three times between the store and my Jeep.

"Good," Brooklyn said softly. "Now go fix the sink so you can brush your teeth tonight before bed."

Remy puffed out his chest and took off down the hall, forgetting I had the water lines.

The whole shopping trip had opened my eyes. Remington was well-mannered and polite. He also asked a lot of questions. From the moment we'd entered Frank's Hardware store all the way to the checkout Remy had jabbered on, pointing to anything and everything we'd passed. He wanted to know what it was, how it worked, what it was used for, and so on. What should've taken five minutes tops took us almost forty by the time I happily answered all of his questions. The sporting goods store was a quick in and out but only because Remy didn't stop and ask questions—he'd asked while walking.

The rest of the time he'd asked about my boat and told me about the fish he'd caught with his pop. I'd had to remind myself I was happy Remington had good people in his life and Michael Welsh teaching him how to fish was just one example of that. But I was jealous as fuck I hadn't taught my son how to string a pole. I wasn't there to show him how to bait a hook and I didn't see him reel in his first catch.

So while Remy excitedly told me all about his adventures I silently vowed I wouldn't miss anything else. I'd all but given Wilson my official notice that I wouldn't be going back to Arizona where the Takeback headquarters was. I'd be selling my condo there and moving to Idaho full-time.

I would finish this case and from there I'd figure out what I'd do for work. Not that I needed the money. I had properties I could rent or sell and I had a healthy savings account but I wasn't the type of man to sit around, so I'd find something.

"Thank you for letting me take him," I said.

Brooklyn's head tilted slightly to the right and her blue eyes danced when she smiled.

"I didn't *let* you do anything, Rhode. He's yours, too."

Christ, that felt good.

"You know what I mean," I returned. "You've done a great job with him."

"Thanks."

There were a thousand things I wanted to say to her but Remy calling my name meant they'd have to wait. I had a four-year-old waiting to learn how to replace a water line.

Remy wasn't lying when he said mac and cheese was his favorite. The kid shoveled it in like he was scared someone was going to snatch his bowl away.

"Done," Remy announced. "May I please be excused so I can wash up?"

"No seconds?" Brooklyn chuckled.

Remy shook his head. "I want to be ready to play foot-ball with Rhode."

Pleasure and pain.

"Did you taste your food as you inhaled it?"

Remy looked at his mom in confusion. "What?"

"Nothing. You may be excused. Plate and silverware in the dishwasher and tonight you have the pot, it's already in the sink for you."

Without another word, Remy jumped off of his chair, snagged his dishes, and all but ran into the kitchen.

"Part of his chores," Brooklyn explained. "Every night he has to help clean up after dinner. I pick one pot or pan or something for him to wash. Saturdays he has to take out the bathroom trash and sort his laundry. Sundays he has to put his clean clothes in his dresser. We have a deal he gets three dollars a week if he completes all of his tasks. Two dollars if he misses one. And nothing if I have to remind him. If he saves fifteen dollars I'll match it and he can buy a toy."

Reality hit hard and fast. I'd been so caught up in all the fun stuff I'd missed in Remy's life that I'd forgotten about the actual parenting. Something I didn't know diddly-shit about. Growing up I didn't get an allowance. I had chores but it was about pulling my weight in the family, not money. And I had good parents; they'd been firm but didn't berate me when I messed up. When I joined the Navy my dad was proud and my mom was worried. I couldn't say I was close to them but the distance had more to do with geography than a falling out. They were busy enjoying their retirement and I was working so one day I could enjoy mine.

Thinking on it, I needed to reach out and tell them about Remington. Unfortunately, I'd have to do it through email, or I'd have to wait until they were home from their vacation. It was doubtful I'd reach them by phone while they were in Peru.

Misunderstanding my silence Brooklyn asked, "Do you think that's too harsh?"

"Too harsh?"

"That I don't pay him if I have to remind him. I struggled with it, but he has a whiteboard in his room with his chores written on it so he can see what he has to do. I want this to be a lesson in responsibility as much as it's teaching him how to manage money. I mean, I know he's too young to really understand. But my parents never taught me the importance of saving and I struggled in my early twenties with debt. I don't want Remy to blow all his money like I did."

There was a lot there I wanted to ask about. Her parents being one and money being another. Brooklyn has said she didn't want money from me, which was unacceptable, and I needed to suss out how big of an argument we'd have when I gave her a check. I also needed to figure out how much she'd let me get away with giving her.

I'd address those topics later.

"I think you're a good mom and teaching him all the right things. He might be four but it's never too early to teach a child the importance of hard work and responsibility. One day he'll be a teenager and want to hang with his buds. Take a girl out on a date. He'll need money to do that. And he'll want a car, something he needs to be prepared to earn."

"What did you do in the Navy?"

Her left-field question took me by surprise.

"How'd you know I was in the Navy?"

"Remy told me. I guess Davis told him while you and I were talking in the office. Remy's been obsessed with the military since I took him to the Memorial Day parade in Hayden last year."

My eyes drifted closed to block out the horrendous pain as it worked its way through my body.

"What's wrong?"

I opened my eyes, found Brooklyn leaning close, and fought back the urge to pluck her out of her chair and fist all of her long shiny brown hair while I kissed the ever-loving fuck out of her. I wanted her mouth on mine and her ass on my lap. With Remy in the kitchen, that option wasn't available to me. One day him seeing me kiss his mother, sans her on my lap and my hands in her hair, would be okay. But now, no way.

That fucking killed, too.

Both of them mine, but unable to publicly claim either was going to have to end, and fast.

"Rhode?"

"I was there." I stopped to clear my throat to dislodge the emotional boulder that had lodged itself there. "Last year at the parade."

Brooklyn's eyes widened before they crinkled at the corners and the same pain sliced through her.

"So close," she whispered.

"Yep."

"I wonder if it will get easier," she continued in a soft voice.

Easier? Maybe. But losing out on five years when I was so damn close? I wouldn't forget that.

"Good dinner, Sugar. Mac and cheese was excellent. But the hot dogs, outstanding."

"You're trying to change the topic and don't deny it. No one says hot dogs are outstanding."

"I am trying to move us past the hurts we can't change. I

doubt the parade was the only place where we've been close to each other and didn't know. And if I dwell on it, I'll drive myself crazy. Right now I just want to spend time with you and Remy. Get to know both of you and take us where we always should've been."

Everything about Brooklyn gentled. From her lips parting, her jaw going slack, her eyes boring into mine—almost the same way she looked at Remy but better. She liked what I said and she wasn't hiding it.

"But I was being serious about the hot dogs. Most people think I'm a little strange because I like mine extra well-done."

"The crispy burnt bits are the best."

I dropped my forehead against hers and chuckled. "I think I'm in love."

"If all it takes is a burnt wiener to make you fall in love I think I'm offended."

I tried to hold it back but it got to be too much so I didn't bother. My hand went to the back of her neck, my fingertips dug in, and I busted out laughing.

15

I was consumed by all things Rhode. The way his fingertips dented the back of my neck, his forehead pressed against mine, his body shaking with hilarity, his breath coming out in fast puffs fanning over my chest.

Memories came rushing back. The last time I'd felt Rhode surround me he'd been moving inside of me. He'd held the back of my neck, his forehead had rested on mine, I'd felt his breath on my bare breasts, and his big body shaking above mine. Not from laughter, from exertion, fighting his nature and attempting to be gentle. All it had taken was wrapping my legs around his hips, silently begging for more, for him to give in and lose control.

I wasn't sure which I liked better, the rough or the gentle. I was glad with Rhode, I didn't have to choose.

"You have a great laugh," I told him.

He had one back in the day, too. We hadn't done a lot of laughing while we were curled together in his hotel bed, we'd used our time together wisely. But the between times when we were talking he'd laughed. He'd also made me laugh. And thinking on it, everything about that night was natural. At no time did it feel like we were two strangers who didn't know each other's names. In fact, it felt warm and familiar yet new and exciting. That was the reason I'd hightailed my ass out of his life. He had heartbreak written all over him. I knew I was in too deep. I was conjuring up dreams of forever and he was...not. I was nothing more than a one-night stand. A woman he'd met in a bar and taken back to his room. But weirdly at no time had he made me feel like I was mindless, faceless sex. That was just me, projecting my insecurities.

"If memory serves, you do, too." Then he dropped his voice to a near whisper. "Though when you did it I had you in my arms naked with your tits pressed against my ribs and your hands on me. So I'd say your laugh's far better than mine."

I felt those words in secret places and my nipples hardened.

"Looking forward to hearing you laugh again, Sugar."

At that moment I was fully prepared to strip naked, hop into bed, and find a Jim Carrey comedy.

Before I could tell Rhode this a loud clatter came from the kitchen highlighting we weren't alone.

Damn.

"I better check—"

"I'll do it. You finish your dinner."

With a squeeze Rhode let me go, but before he stood his head dropped to the side and he brushed his lips over the corner of my mouth, bringing on a fresh wave of memories both old and new. Our kiss in the bathroom had been a tease, a quick taste, a slow glide of his tongue that left me hungry for more. Just now the whisper-soft lip touch was a reminder of how gentle he could be.

I watched Rhode walk into the kitchen with my heart

pounding in my chest and I knew despite what I'd said to him about us getting romantically involved not being a good idea that I wasn't going to fight it. I'd made that mistake once. I was scared and I let my fear get the best of me. This time, I was holding on no matter what. This time, I was going to be honest and trust Rhode to see us through. All three of us.

My phone rang in the other room. I had a strict no phone at the table rule—that decree was obviously for my benefit seeing as Remy didn't have a phone. Table time was special, Remy and me with no interruptions. It was the one part of our day when I had my son's full attention with no distractions—no toys, TV, games—and he deserved my full attention right back. Just he and I and conversation. Sometimes Letty was a part of that if she came over for dinner. Sometimes if Remy and I were at the Welshes I shared my special time with them. Wherever we sat down to eat there was never a phone at the table.

"Mommy!" Remy shouted. "It's Gram. Can I answer?"

Shit.

I didn't want to talk to Tally. Which was crazy because I always loved talking to her. But I had a secret and I sucked at lying. She'd suss it out in two-point-five seconds. But if I didn't answer she'd know something was amiss because I'd never declined a call from her.

Shit.

"Hi, Gram," Remy greeted.

Welp, too late.

Damn.

"Guess what?" Remy asked but didn't give Tally time to respond before he rushed out. "A pipe broke. There was water everywhere. It was even in the living room. But I fixed it." There was a brief pause then Remy started again.

"Rhode showed me how. We went to the store and Rhode showed me what to get...hey, what was it?"

"Three-eighths inch stainless steel supply line," Rhode answered.

"Did you hear that, Gram? Three-eighths inch stainless steel supply line. I got to put it in and everything. Now the sink works. Me and Rhode are cleaning up the kitchen so we can go play football. Rhode said he's gonna teach me how to play." There was a beat of silence then, "I don't know, let me ask. Do you know how to play football?"

"Yep. Started playing flag football when I was your age. Played all the way through high school."

"Yeah, Rhode can play. He's gonna teach me. I wanna be the quarterback so Rhode said I need to learn how to throw the ball."

Much like me, Remy loved Tally. He was four and easily excitable but I'd never heard that kind of exuberance coming from my son. Not even when he went fishing with Michael. Not even when last Christmas Letty bought him a new handheld videogame I wasn't happy about but Remy had loved it.

Never.

I let the knowledge that my son was happy wrap around me and vowed not to screw this up for us. I wanted my son to be this excited all the time. Rhode deserved these moments with Remy after everything he missed. And for once in my life, I was going to admit I deserved something good, too. I wanted Rhode in my life and if I hadn't gotten pregnant with Remy I'd still want Rhode in my life.

I heard little-boy feet running out of the kitchen then Remy stopped by the table and held my phone out.

"Here. Gram wants to talk to you."

"Thanks, bud." I took the phone and before I had it to my ear Remy was out of the room.

Shit.

"Hey, Tally. Everything okay?"

"I don't know, sweet girl. You tell me."

Tally was using her mom voice. This was good. She was going to scold me for not talking to her about Rhode and I wouldn't have to worry about not telling her that Kiki was alive and well but acting like a monumental selfish bitch. Obviously, I'd never call Kiki selfish or a bitch to Tally or Michael. And while I'd agree with Letty right now—*she* called her sister that—I would never utter the words out loud to any of the Welshes. Though I allowed myself to think it after what Kiki had put everyone through.

"Everything's great."

"Why don't I believe that?"

Because I'm lying to you and I know where your daughter is.

Guilt struck full force. To dislodge the uncomfortable feeling I told her the truth as far as what I could disclose.

"You should believe that because everything is great. Well, the pipe under the bathroom sink wasn't great and I looked like a total fool for not knowing I could turn off the water before my hallway flooded. But I got it all cleaned up and Remy was excited to go with Rhode to the store and help fix the broken pipe. So it ended well."

I took a breath, but before I could tell Tally about dinner she launched in.

"I've given you time and I know you've given me space because of what's going on with Kiki."

God, I was such a freaking cow. A horrible, mean, cow. I wanted to tell her so badly that Kiki was safe. Ease her pain and her worry. I wanted to confess so badly I was seriously contemplating breaking my promise. The only thing that stopped me was Desi. But as soon as the guys got to her I was spilling the beans. I had to. And hearing Tally's sweet concern about how I was doing made it worse. So much worse.

"Tally—"

"Listen to me for a second. I love you, Brooklyn. I've loved you since the day you were born. I promised your momma I'd always look out for you. I'm sorry I haven't been doing such a good job lately. Remington's father showing up is a big deal. Letty says she likes him. Remy sounds excited and happy. But I'd like to meet him."

Tally was killing me. Killing. Me.

"You've met him, Tally. And just to say, you've always taken care of me. And I'm grateful for all that you and Michael gave me after Mom and Dad died. But I'm also grateful for what you gave me when they were still alive."

All the mean, nasty shit Kiki had spewed filled my heart. After my parents died I was devastated. I could barely function. One minute I had a great family, the next they were gone. I didn't know what would have been worse—watching them slowly waste away from sickness or the way they went. Head-on collision, both of them gone in a flash. Neither of them had made it to the hospital.

"And that right there tells me something's wrong, Brooklyn."

There was a reason Letty was so observant and in tune with those around her. My best friend had learned from her mother. Both Welsh women were thoughtful. And they both had a keen bullshit radar with the people they loved.

What was interesting was how Kiki had slipped past their notice. That was probably my fault, too. If Tally and Letty hadn't been so focused on helping me pick up the pieces of my shattered life, Kiki wouldn't have been jealous in the first place.

"I swear nothing's wrong."

Lies. There was so much wrong.

Remy came bouncing back into the dining room vibrating with excitement. "All done!" he shouted and ran past me.

My gaze followed my son through the living room to the sliding glass door and I watched him open it with more force than necessary before he hopped—yes, my child hopped—out the door, leaving it open.

"Babe?"

"Excuse me one second, Tally," I said into the phone and tipped my head back to look at Rhode.

"Kitchen's clean but I didn't know where the dishes went so I left them in the strainer."

"Oh, my," Tally breathed in my ear.

"You didn't have to do that," I told him, ignoring Tally's comment.

"Great dinner, Sugar."

It was Rhode's turn to ignore my comment. But he did it better because when he bent down and kissed my temple I forgot what I'd said.

"Thanks."

"We'll be out back."

And with that, Rhode took the same path Remy did, only he wasn't skipping. Nope, Rhode moved with long, confident strides. My eyes zeroed in on his backside and I knew from personal experience how fine his ass looked bare. How muscular it was. How it flexed under my palms when he drove his dick inside of me.

"Brooklyn?"

Oh, God.

"Sorry, I'm back."

"He's got your brain scrambled," she noted.

"Yep."

Tally sighed, but unlike her daughter, she didn't enunciate the word; she made the sound.

"How's Remington?"

"In heaven. Though he doesn't know Rhode's his dad. We're going up to Sandpoint with him this weekend. A mini-vacation complete with a boat ride and fishing. I think we'll tell him then."

"Good plan. That boy loves to fish."

"Do you really think it's a good plan or are you humoring me?"

"I think you've spent the last five years dwelling on that man. I think you've been heartbroken. I think you've been dreaming of the day you found him."

She was correct on all accounts but that didn't answer my question.

"I was asking about when to tell Remington."

There was a beat of silence and my stomach clenched. Crap. Tally was a great mom; if she thought I was making a mistake telling Remy so soon I'd have to talk to Rhode and reevaluate the situation.

"You know, Diane would be so proud of you," Tally said, and my throat clogged. "She'd be proud of the woman you've become. You've always known your mind and your heart—she gave that to you. She was fearless. Growing up with your mom was like a rollercoaster. There was never a time she wasn't having a good time. She also was the best person to go to when you needed advice. She always knew the right thing to say. I miss her so damn much and if she were here she'd know exactly what to tell you, what you needed to hear so you'd know with all your heart how good of a mother you are.

"For four years you've been mom and dad for Remy. For four years you've raised him all on your own and you've done an amazing job. Remington is smart, he's polite, he's always happy, and he adores you. What I'm saying is, don't second-guess yourself. However you've decided to tell Remington about Rhode is the right way. Trust your judgment. And the last thing I have to say is, kids are as resilient as they are fragile. They'll roll with the changes as long as their foundation is solid. You've given Remington solid parenting, so he'll roll with this change. I believe in you and I know you wouldn't've allowed Rhode to come over to your house if you didn't trust him and you certainly never would've allowed him to start to bond with your son if you didn't know that Rhode was in it for the long haul."

I missed my parents every day. But there were times when I missed my mom more. Times like these when I needed her advice. During my pregnancy, when all I wanted was my mom to hold my hand. When I gave birth and more than anything in the entire world I wanted my mom with me. I wanted to see her hold her grandson and smile at him and cuddle him. And there were times when I missed my dad more than I missed my mom. When I needed his steady strength and his compassion. When Remy caught his first fish and held it up for Michael to see—I wanted my dad there. I wanted my dad to praise his grandson and encourage him.

But with all the ways I missed my mom and dad, Tallulah and Michael weren't second best. They were *the* best. All of my memories were bittersweet. My childhood spent with my parents and the Welshes. All of the good times we shared, all the fun times we had. After my parents were gone, all the great experiences still involved Tally and Michael; it was just that my parents were absent.

"You're the best person I know," I croaked. "You were missing your best friend but you still took care of me. I'm so sorry I needed you so much. I was so lost I couldn't see how much pain you were in."

"Brooklyn Tallulah Saunders, you listen to me and listen good, child. Losing your mom the way we did broke me. She was everything to me. More than my best friend, she was my soul sister. I will miss her for the rest of my life. But you coming to live with us filled a hole in me that was so deep I never thought it would be possible to stop the pain. I lost your momma but I got you. And you filled that hole for Michael, too. He'll never tell you because he's a man and men don't talk about grief but Ronny was to Michael what your momma was to me. And you, my sweet girl, are the very best parts of Diane and Ronny. We needed you more than you needed us. So don't you ever apologize to me again. You've got nothing to be sorry for. It was our honor, Brook, to have you living with us."

"I want to do right by Remington and Rhode."

"Then follow in your momma's footsteps. Jump on the ride, lift your arms, and be fearless."

"And telling Remy—"

"Fearless, Brooklyn. Don't second-guess yourself."

"Okay," I breathed out and straightened my spine. "We're telling Remy this weekend."

"Good. And I expect Rhode Daley at my table sooner rather than later."

"Yes, Tally."

"Such sass. And you wonder where your son gets it from. The apple didn't fall off the tree to roll away from it."

My lips twitched because she was correct about that, too.

"Thank you."

"You can thank me by bringing your boys over for dinner."

My boys.

I wasn't sure Rhode could be described as a boy, but I didn't bother correcting her.

"You got it."

"And thank him for sending Reese and Cole to the house. Michael's in a fit and wanted to go to that biker hangout. He got in the car but didn't even make it out of the driveway before Reese was at his car door talking him down. Now they're in the garage talking or doing whatever it is men do."

Oh, man. Shit. I didn't know what to say to that. The Horsemen were bad news and Kiki was dating the president.

"You girls were right keeping that a secret," Tally told me. "Michael would've gone there and he would've gotten hurt. He's not thinking straight."

"Understandable, Tally."

"I've been thinking on things and I didn't want to say anything but maybe I should talk to Mr. McCray. When Desi was staying here I saw her with a cell phone. And she said something about Kiki that didn't make sense."

Danger. *Danger*. Danger.

"Tally—"

"I asked Desi if Kiki was still working at Houlihan's. Desi said Kiki quit before she left. When I asked her what left meant she corrected herself and told me Kiki quit and was looking for a new job right before they were taken. Then she started sobbing and I felt bad for bringing it up after everything she's gone through."

Not only was I a bad liar I was bad under stress. High-stress situations were not my thing. Some people thrived under pressure—not me. I froze then panicked. I was still at the frozen part but the panic was quickly seeping in. I needed off the phone before I blurted out everything I wasn't supposed to say.

"I'll tell Rhode. He'll know what to do."

"I think Desi's lying. I don't think Kiki was with her."

Please God, let Remy throw that football at the sliding glass door and shatter it.

"Tally—"

"And a mother never wants to think this about her child but thinking back to the last time I talked to Kiki we had a huge blowout. She wanted a loan and I told her no. She told me she hated me and I was dead to her. That conversation's been eating me up. The last thing my baby said to me was she hated me then she was gone. What if that's the last—"

"No, Tallulah momma, listen to me. Don't let your mind go there. Kiki is not dead. You know her, she blows up then comes around."

Kiki was alive and well and as bitter as I'd ever seen her. But once she burned herself or ran out of money or ran out of places to crash she'd have no choice but to make things right with her parents.

I heard background noise through the phone and Michael's booming voice before Tally said, "Sorry to cut this short. Michael needs to talk to me."

Thank sweet Jesus.

"Okay, Tally. Love you."

"Love you, sweet girl."

I hung up the phone and closed my eyes. I loved hearing Tally call me sweet girl. I just prayed when she found out I not only lied to her about Kiki's boyfriend but I also lied about Kiki coming out to see me she'd forgive me.

16

Something was wrong.

I'd left Brooklyn in the house smiling. Now she was sitting on a plastic deck chair, an oversized sweater-thing wrapped around her shoulders, watching me and Remy toss a ball and she hadn't said a word in the five minutes she'd been watching.

"What's the biggest fish you've ever caught?" Remy asked.

"Thirty-pound rainbow. You?"

"Twenty-pound lake trout."

I tamped down the pang of jealousy and asked, "On Lake Coeur d'Alene?"

"No, Priest. Pop mostly likes to fish there. He says they've got the best trout in Idaho. Why is your name Rhode?"

Remy's question came so far out of left field I jerked in surprise and fumbled the ball.

I bent to retrieve it and asked, "Why's your name Remington?"

"Mom named me Remington because she thought it was a cool name. Remington Steel." Remy proudly finished.

Cool as shit name.

"My mom named me Preston Rhodes. The story goes that my dad snuck to the nurses' station and asked for my birth certificate and changed my name without my mom knowing. He didn't want his son being named Preston."

"Preston's not a cool name," Remy interjected.

"No bud, it's not. Lucky for me my dad changed my name to Rhode. He dropped the S on Rhodes because he said a man only needs one road to travel when it's righteous."

"Your dad sounds smart."

"He is."

"Do you look like him?"

As casually as I could with my heart slamming in my chest, I lobbed the ball to Remy.

"I look more like my mom," I told him the truth. "She's got dark hair and dark eyes. But I'm tall like my dad."

"Where are they?"

"Right now they're in Peru. Before that, they were in India and before that Paris."

"Is that in Idaho?"

"No, buddy. Peru's in South America and..." I didn't get to finish my answer before my phone started ringing. "Hang on, Remy. I wouldn't answer the phone while we're playing but I'm expecting an important call."

I pulled my phone out and sure enough, it was Wilson. I glanced at Brooklyn, lifted my chin and she read my gesture.

"Remy, go grab an ice pop while Rhode takes his call."

"Yes!" The kid dropped the football and ran toward the door.

"Hey."

"You still at Brooklyn's?"

My body tensed and my gaze went around Brooklyn's fenced-in backyard.

"Yeah, what's up?"

"Desi ran."

Fuck. That didn't say good things.

"Was she tipped off?"

"Doubtful. But there's something else. Davis had a run-in with Lawrence and two of his crew. Davis made it clear Remy and Brooklyn were off-limits. Lawrence didn't agree. He said he's got a problem with the way you spoke to his old lady."

Fury rushed to the surface fast.

"Wilson, I'm telling you that motherfucker breathes in my woman's direction I'm taking that as a declaration of war. He looks at my son I'm putting him down."

"That's been communicated. Unfortunately, Lawrence isn't the brightest bulb, as in he's fucking dim. It's gonna take some time to convince him to stand down. I'm not sure what Kiki told him exactly but my guess is she made up whatever she could think of to get him riled up and in her corner."

Stupid woman.

"Not a safe place for her to put herself."

"I requested a meet," Wilson said in my ear but my attention had gone to the beauty standing next to me. When her hand grabbed mine and she laced her fingers between mine I was so fully engrossed in how good she felt—all of it, her coming to my side, her reaching out, her holding my hand—I forgot how angry I was.

"You there?" Wilson called.

"Yeah, sorry. When's your meet? I wanna be there."

"Lawrence declined."

Stupid fucker, playing stupid games.

"I'll track him down."

"Think it's a better idea you takin' your family up to your cabin and letting us handle this. Jack and Asher are on their way back. No sense them continuing to Seattle when Desi's taken off. Reese and Cole are breaking the news to the Welshes now. Shep's doing his thing and Davis and I will sit down with Lawrence."

Goddamn, I wish Wilson would've called to warn me before Reese and Cole told the Welshes about Kiki.

"And Letty?"

Brooklyn's fingers flexed and I squeezed back just as automatic gunfire rang out.

"Was that—"

"Need backup," I barked.

"Rem—" Brooklyn started.

"Get down on your belly, crawl to the far corner. Do not get up until I'm back." I shoved my phone in her hand, reached around and pulled my Sig out of the holster, and without checking to make sure Brooklyn complied I ran to the sliding glass door and threw it open.

"Remy!" I shouted then thought better of calling a four year old's name and having him run out in the open. "Stay where you are and get down on the floor. I'll come to you."

Methodically but quickly I made my way through the dining room, stopping only for a moment to check the living room. The huge picture window was shattered, glass everywhere. The couch was shredded, the coffee table riddled with bullets, and the puzzle that Remy was putting together scattered.

If we'd been in the living room, we would've been hit. My son would've been filled with bullets. My woman the same.

Red-hot fear slithered up my spine.

A fear I'd never felt.

One that was bigger than anything I'd felt on the battlefield.

A fear that started in my soul and burned as I exhaled it out.

Shuffling in the kitchen caught my attention but the whimper was what had my ass moving.

There, crawling on the floor, was Remy. Eyes wide, tears falling, terror easy to read.

Oh, yeah, someone was going to die for putting that look on my son's face. The gunshots had been loud; inside the house, with glass shattering and wood splintering, they were ear-piercing. And for a four-year-old alone while bullets ripped through the house—downright terrifying.

With my free hand, I plucked Remy off the floor then lifted him to my chest.

"I got you. Keep your head down."

His head barely nodded before his arms circled my neck, his long legs wrapped around my waist, and he shoved his face into my neck. Every single part of his little body was shaking. Someone was paying for that shit, too.

My son scared and traumatized in his own home. That shit wasn't going to fly.

With no good options and Brooklyn still in the backyard, I took off in a sprint. All was quiet, no more gunshots, no sound of motorcycle pipes, no car's squealing tires. An eerie silence filled the yard as I scanned for targets. The perimeter of Brooklyn's yard was fenced, but the white vinyl planks wouldn't stop a bullet or someone from jumping over it.

I found Brooklyn in the corner of her yard partially hidden behind a cluster of trees. As soon as she saw me she was up out of her squat. I was shifting Remington, prepared to hand him off to his mother when Brooklyn shocked the fuck out of me. She wrapped her arms around me, covering Remy's back, plastering herself to us.

As good as that felt—and it felt fucking phenomenal, another reason I was going to inflict bodily harm—I couldn't enjoy the moment our family locked in its first embrace.

"Sugar, I need you to take Remy so I can check the front."

Brooklyn jolted and her arms went tight.

"Don't go."

"Baby, I'll make sure you and Remy are safe, but I have to check the front."

The screeching of tires had me unlocking Remington's death-grip around my neck and transferring him to Brooklyn.

"On the ground," I barked.

My phone rang just as Brooklyn grabbed Remington. She immediately got to her knees, tucked Remy close, and lowered herself to her stomach, covering Remy's body with hers.

Covering his body with hers.

Protecting him.

Fury and fear mingled when I bent to pick up my phone, which Brooklyn had dropped in the grass.

"Yeah?"

"Don't shoot, that's us in the front."

Wilson. Thank fuck.

"We're in the east corner of the backyard."

"Copy that. Stay there, we're surrounding the house now. Neighbor called in the gunshots. Police ETA two minutes. Hang tight."

Wilson disconnected and I shoved my phone in my back pocket and relayed the message.

"My team's securing the house. It's all good, Sugar."

"Mommy!" Remy sobbed and my heart seized.

"It's okay, buddy, Rhode's here."

Jesus Christ.

"Clear!" Davis called as he entered the backyard. "Grab 'em and go out the side gate, Wilson's waiting."

"Come on, Sugar."

Brooklyn rolled and struggled to sit.

"Take him."

Fuck, that felt good, too, yet once again the situation being what it was, I didn't have time to process the feeling or the trust she was literally handing me.

I scooped up Remy and Brooklyn scrambled to her feet. I was at war with what to do. I didn't want to be unarmed, but with my left arm around Remy and my Sig still in my right, I couldn't hold onto Brooklyn like I wanted. Ultimately Brooklyn made the decision by tucking herself next to Remy and sliding an arm around my back.

Tactically, this was the worst position for her to be in. She should've been holding Remington and both of them should've been behind me. But fuck if I could let go of Remy. Putting all of my trust in Wilson and Davis I moved along the fence to the side gate. Brooklyn kept in step beside me.

"You're doing good, Sugar."

She didn't answer. Remy didn't make a peep. Both of them held onto me like I was their lifeline.

Fuck, yeah, that felt good even if the reason they were doing it pissed me off.

Wilson was at the gate waiting. His expression set to

granite, he did a quick sweep of Brooklyn then Remy. Then his cold, hard gaze came to mine.

"Take the SUV. Head north. Stay alert."

"Copy."

I took one step but my progress was halted when Brooklyn didn't move.

"Wait."

"Babe—"

"I need my purse and my phone. And if someone could spare a minute, my laptop. It's in my room."

Wait. What?

Her purse, phone, and laptop?

She hadn't asked where I was taking them. Not how long we'd be gone. If they'd be safe or any of the hundred other questions she could've asked.

Another boon. More trust.

Christ.

"Take them to the Tahoe. I'll grab her stuff," Wilson instructed.

Remy lifted his face out of my neck to demand, "My football."

"Bud, we'll get a new one."

"My football!" Remy shouted in my face.

"Okay, Remington. Wilson will get your ball. Anything else?"

"No."

He lowered his head back to my shoulder and nuzzled in.

Brooklyn's startled blue eyes met mine and instead of looking freaked the fuck out we'd been involved in a drive-by shooting her face gentled.

"If you can, his blanket's folded on his bed. It has trains on it."

"Got it. Get to the car."

As a unit, we moved to the black Tahoe parked on the street.

Brooklyn climbed into the back seat and I handed Remy off. As I was rounding the back of the SUV I took in the front of her house—riddled with bullets. Bullets that could've easily taken out my family. My gaze landed on my Jeep and my jaw clenched. All of the windows were blown out, holes punched through the side panel and the door, two tires flat. Total loss. Not that I gave two shits about the Jeep but the more damage I came across the harder it was to keep my anger in check.

I didn't enter the vehicle until Wilson opened the back hatch and deposited the only personal effects Remy and Brooklyn were taking. He slammed the liftgate closed and jerked his head.

"Go."

"You know with this shit, we've moved past a declaration of war."

"I know," Wilson sighed.

"Lawrence just bought himself hell."

"Get your family out of here."

"Wilson—"

"I get this is new for you. But starting now, your priorities have shifted. Those two," he jabbed his finger at the car, "are all you worry about. Get them the fuck out of here and let *me* handle the rest."

Something moved over my friend's features, but before I could gauge whether it was pain or anger, his expression blanked.

There was a story there, something Wilson had kept hidden. Or more like buried if the fierce assertion was anything to go by.

With our eyes locked I gave him the only thing I could.

My gratitude.

"Appreciate it."

"Just keep your family safe."

That was a given, therefore it didn't require a response so I didn't bother giving one as I got into the SUV.

17

Remington was shaking and I was doing my best not to look at my house.

Did that just happen?

I had Remy unharmed in the back of a black SUV with tinted windows, speeding away from the scene of the crime with Rhode behind the wheel driving like he was the king of the road and everyone should yield to him. I must've been in shock because now I wasn't scared or freaking out.

I was in total disbelief.

Not denial—*disbelief*.

Someone executed a drive-by.

A freaking drive-by shooting. On my house.

When does that actually happen other than in the movies?

I lived in a quiet neighborhood. A family neighborhood. Peaceful. Nice houses. Drive-by shootings didn't happen on my block.

Until today.

And since I was in shock I didn't know what to say. Not to my son, not to Rhode. Weirdly I didn't give a rat's ass

where Rhode was taking us. Wilson had said "up north" —
that could mean Canada and I was a-okay with that. Rhode
could continue to drive us up to Alaska and I wouldn't
complain. As long as Remington was far, *far* away from the
insanity that just occurred and Rhode was with us he could
take us anywhere and I wouldn't utter a complaint.

Rhode's phone rang and Remington startled.

"Remy, baby, we're safe." I pulled him closer and asked,
"Are you hurt anywhere?"

Remy answered with a shake of his head.

"That was pretty scary." I noted the understatement of
the year.

All I got was a nod.

"We should talk about it, bud."

That got me another shake of his head, this one more
forceful than the first.

"Your mom's right, that was scary," Rhode interjected
after he silenced the call.

Remy lifted his head off of my chest and asked, "You
were scared?"

"Oh, yeah," Rhode returned. "You were in the house and
I didn't know where you were. That scared me. I needed to
find you which meant I had to leave your mom unprotected
in the backyard and that scared me, too."

What was interesting was what Rhode *wasn't* scared of.
He was scared of not knowing where Remington was but
not of getting filled with bullets when he'd rushed into the
house. He was scared to leave me unprotected but not
scared for his safety. That made me wonder, unhappily, how
many times Rhode had been shot at and if that would
happen again in the future.

"But you're big," Remy argued.

"I can be as big as a giant, buddy, but that's not gonna

help me not be scared when I don't know where you are or if you're safe."

Rhode changed lanes and turned onto 95 north, then wove between two cars, not slowing down. I might've been in shock but I wasn't so far gone that Rhode's erratic driving made me wonder if someone was following us. But I also couldn't ask without scaring Remington. I also was too afraid to look behind us and find out.

"Are you still scared?"

"No. Now that I know you and your mom are safe I'm not scared."

Firm. Unyielding.

Remington snuggled back in and said, "Then I'm not scared either."

I wasn't sure if that was healthy. He was four and had been alone in the house during a drive-by shooting. I wasn't four and I was still scared shitless. However, I didn't think it would be a good idea to announce I wanted Rhode to take us to a secure underground bunker with armed guards to protect us until the police caught whoever tried to kill us.

On that thought, I asked, "What about the police?"

"Wilson will handle them."

"Shouldn't we have stayed to talk to them?" I pushed.

Thankfully, I'd never been involved in a shooting, nor had I ever been the target of a drive-by. Actually, I'd never been involved in any criminal activity of any kind—that was if you didn't count the one time I went skinny-dipping in the lake on a dare. But I hadn't been caught, and Letty was the only witness and she'd never tell. So, seeing as I was an upstanding citizen who didn't have run-ins with the police I didn't know for a fact but I was fairly certain they'd want to question me and Rhode.

"Wilson will facilitate communication. But it will be

after we're settled and he's had a chance to speak with the authorities to explain that you and Remington have been taken into protective custody."

Protective custody.

"Do you know—"

"Sugar, let's worry about that later."

Um. I didn't want to worry about anything later. The shock was wearing off and I didn't like being left in the dark.

"I'd like to know."

"And you'll know everything but I can't tell you something *I* don't know. Right now my only concern is getting you and Remy up to the cabin and settled."

Rhode's cabin.

Not an underground bunker with armed guards.

Then I remembered Rhode running into the house hell-bent to get to Remy with zero concern for his personal safety.

That was when I realized we didn't need armed guards —we had Rhode. We also didn't need a bunker. We had Rhode and he would protect us—with his life if it came to it.

So I settled back and cuddled my son close. I also decided not to think about my house or bullet holes or anything except that we were *safe*.

"Are you sure they're safe?"

We were at Rhode's cabin. Remy had fallen asleep on the drive up and he was now snoozing on the couch. Rhode had just finished telling me about his conversation with Wilson.

I was also freaking the fuck out.

Smutties had been hit by a drive-by, too.

Which if I thought about it made sense—the bookstore would be a target instead of Letty's apartment seeing as she lived on the fifth floor. Michael and Tallulah's had not been hit but according to Wilson that was probably due to the police presence. After what had happened at my place, Wilson had demanded protection for the Welshes. Thankfully when Wilson made demands it seemed the police listened and Michael and Tally now had protection from the local PD, and Reese and Cole, as well.

But I was still worried.

"Letty's staying with her parents," Rhode told me something I knew since we'd been over this. "Wilson arranged for a car to sit out front of the house and Reese and Cole have been assigned to security detail. They're safe and will be safer when Wilson talks them into going to a safe house."

Now that Michael and Tally knew Kiki had not been kidnapped and she wasn't being held by some ominous, shadowy figure, Wilson had reported Michael was furious and being stubborn. He wanted to speak to his youngest daughter and he wasn't leaving CDA until that happened. And he was insistent that he go with Wilson to the Horsemen clubhouse and yank his daughter out of there— his exact words according to Wilson.

I didn't doubt Michael would do just that. I also didn't doubt Michael had dug in and wouldn't be leaving until he saw Kiki.

"I need to call Tally."

"Sugar—"

"You don't understand, Rhode. By now she knows I lied to her. I need to explain and I need to talk to Michael."

"That's not a good idea," Rhode murmured.

The way he'd gently uttered the words made my heart sink.

"They're mad at me," I whispered, and in two quick strides, Rhode was in front of me.

His hand went to my hip and pulled me forward, bringing me close. His face dipped and with our noses almost touching he gave me more gentle.

"No, baby, they're not mad at you. They're mad at Kiki and trying to reconcile how an hour ago they were scared their child was missing and what horrors she was living, to now being angry she'd essentially thrown a tantrum because her mother wouldn't loan her money. They're embarrassed because when Kiki hadn't answered their calls, wasn't at her last known residence, hadn't shown up for work, and when they asked around no one had talked to her, they did what any parent would do and called the police. That led to a missing persons report and a search. With all of that, they're hurt, relieved, angry, and mortified.

"But there's more. They're feeling guilt you and Remy are in danger and Letty's business is affected. And lastly, Michael is a father whose daughter is in a new kind of danger. She's hooked up with a Horsemen. That's bad in and of itself, but, baby, Kiki went all or nothing and hooked up with the president. She now has his ear and told him a bunch of bullshit about you and me. And if she lied about us it's safe to assume she lied about her parents and Letty, too. Give Wilson time to talk to Michael and get him to leave Idaho. Let them process all that has happened and then you can talk to them."

It sucked but Rhode was right. But that didn't stop me from wanting to reach out.

"You still wanna call," Rhode sighed and dipped his chin, bringing us even closer together.

So close all I had to do was tilt my head back and his lips

would be on mine. And I really wanted his lips on mine. And his hands. And other parts besides.

"Baby," he groaned, and when he did I inched closer. "You're killing me."

"How's that?"

"You have no idea what you're asking for."

Oh, yes, I did. There wasn't a second of our time together I didn't remember. I knew exactly what I was asking for and if I didn't remember it from years ago I hadn't forgotten from earlier when he'd given me a refresher. One that was too brief, and now I wanted another taste. I didn't care if it was from the adrenaline, from the near-death experience, or from the twinge of excitement I felt every time I was in his presence.

I felt like I did when I first saw him in D.C. I was willing to take what I wanted and feel no shame after.

"I do," I said confidently. Then because I was feeling extra sassy I added, "I've had you, Rhode, so I don't know how you can say that."

As it turned out, my cockiness unleashed Rhode's.

And it must be said, he did it so much better.

"No, baby," he rasped and trailed his hand from my hip and up my back until he gathered my hair in his fist and twisted it until tingles radiated over my scalp. "Who you had was a man who saw a gorgeous woman in a bar and knew instantly he wanted to take her back to his room and spend the rest of the night fucking her. Now, Sugar, you got a new man standing in front of you—one that's not gonna let you walk away. So like I said, you have no clue what you're asking for. I was clear where I wanted us to go, the relationship I want us to build, the one I want with Remy, and finally the one I want the three of us to have. I saw some hesitation and wanted to take this slow. But, baby, you keep looking at me like you're looking at me, you're gonna find yourself in my bed and under me a whole lot quicker than you think."

At some point during his soliloquy, I'd shivered. At another, I'd trembled. But from the moment he'd said 'baby' in that deep, rumbly voice my nipples had pebbled and my panties had dampened. I wanted under him and on top of him. Further, I didn't want him to let me go.

"You misread the hesitation, honey. I don't want you to let me go and I'm all for moving this along. The quicker the better, if you ask me."

We stood there unmoving, locked in a moment that was five years in the making. Five long years I waited, hoped, prayed, longed for the man standing in front of me. Now, the wait was over and I wasn't going to waste more time on stupid stuff like indecision. I knew what I wanted and Rhode clearly knew what he wanted so I didn't see the point in slow.

Slow sounded horrible.

Slow sounded like torture.

In other words, I wasn't going to squander my good fortune.

My hands went to the hem on his tee. They dipped under the fabric, hit warm, smooth skin, and my eyes closed.

"That night I remember lying next to you feeling your heartbeat." My right hand skimmed over his abs to his ribs and I paused there to trace the tattoo I couldn't see. "There was something about the beat of your heart that soothed me. That's why I left in the morning. I was scared." I rested my palm over his heart and sure enough, the steady rhythm calmed my nerves and excited me all at once. It emboldened me and it scared the ever-loving shit out of me. "I knew I wanted to feel your heartbeat forever. I never wanted to leave your side. I wanted your strength and all you could give me. I wanted that so badly I had no choice but to protect myself from the hurt losing you was going to cause."

Rhode let go of my hair but only to slide his hand around and cup my cheek. Soft and gentle and so sweetly his thumb brushed over my lips.

"You're not scared now?"

"Oh, I'm terrified. But that's how I know this is right. I'm petrified of losing you a second time. So scared that I know I'll do everything in my power to keep you with me."

With nothing but Rhode's handsome face filling my vision, the steady beat of his heart under my palm, and his hand on my cheek, I started envisioning the rest of our life. Days and moments played out in my mind. Family time, alone time. Waking up and going to sleep with Rhode next to me. I wanted it so badly I could see it—I could *feel* it.

Then I could really feel it when Rhode dropped his mouth on mine. I opened and our tongues met. A slow glide that sent shivers racing up my spine. Wanting more, I leaned into Rhode and he gave me what I wanted. The kiss deepened and turned desperate. I whimpered my approval then suddenly I was up. I hadn't felt his hand leave my face nor had I felt his hands go to my hips. Thankfully I had just enough cognizant thought to wrap my legs around his waist because Rhode was on the move. I was so enthralled with the taste of him, the way he dominated my mouth, the experience fresh and new but familiar and extraordinary, I didn't open my eyes to see where he was taking us. Not that it mattered; I'd go anywhere with Rhode.

We stopped moving. My bottom landed on something hard—the only reason this registered was because now that

Rhode was no longer carrying me, his hands were free to roam—and roam they did.

Work-rough and warm, his fingertips abraded the bare skin on my back. His palms skimmed my ribs and moved around front to graze my stomach and didn't stop until his thumbs hooked the lace of my bra and pulled both cups down simultaneously.

Yes!

And he did all of this without breaking our kiss. His tongue continued to assault my mouth, leaving me mindless with need. I arched my back asking for more—no, silently *begging* for him to hurry. My pulse was pounding, my core aching, my emotions ran the gamut from turned on to pissed off it was taking so long. Finally, his thumbs swiped my nipples and I groaned. Rhode obviously liked my response and went for more. This time he rolled my nipples and my back bowed in an offering. Rhode groaned and he tasted so freaking good my pussy spasmed and clit throbbed. Feeling left out, the lower half of my body got with the program and ground down on his erection.

Yes!

Unfortunately, that was all I got before Rhode halted the festivities. He broke the kiss and rested his forehead against mine.

"Fuck," he rasped.

Yes, fucking sounds like a great idea.

I wasn't so brazen I could say that out loud so instead I panted, "More."

"Oh, you're gonna get more, Sugar. But the first time I have you is gonna be in a bed where I can take my time."

I felt that in my pussy, too. I knew what Rhode could do when he had time and the results were mind-blowingly spectacular so I groaned.

Rhode's head lifted only to drop to my neck and kiss his way up to my ear, sending mini shockwaves through me.

"You remember."

It wasn't a question but I still answered.

"Yes."

"Been five years, baby, but I still taste you on my tongue. Sweet like sugar. Tonight, Brooklyn, I'm claiming it back. All that you gave me that night and more." Rhode palmed my breasts—not hard, not gentle, somewhere in between. A show of possession. "Been mine all this time."

Again a statement proving my thoughts true—he owned every inch of me.

"Yes."

"Tonight, Brooklyn," he growled those words against my neck like a threat.

"Tonight, Rhode."

My retort wasn't growled and it was far too breathy to sound like a threat but I hoped it came out sounding like a promise.

Rhode slowly removed his hands from my breasts, fixed my bra, and pulled my shirt down. He did all of this with his lips on the sensitive skin below my ear and my hands still under his tee, resting on his chest.

"I missed you, Sugar."

Rhode's declaration pierced my heart and my fingers curled into his flesh.

"I missed you, too."

I only had a few hours until Remy's bedtime and I could show Rhode exactly how much.

On that thought, I said, "We should wake up Remy or he'll be up all night."

That turned out to be a horrible idea.

Five hours later it was just after midnight and Remington had finally knocked off, but not before he'd demanded Rhode come upstairs and get into bed with us. Seeing as the guest bed was a full and barely fit me and Remy, Rhode moved us to the master bedroom.

The king-sized bed that dominated the room accommodated the three of us and then some. Being as Rhode's cabin was indeed a true log cabin, not a house with faux wood on the outside, the two exterior walls were hand-hewed logs. The interior walls were drywall therefore they were painted an earthy brown. The bed was covered in deep blue bedclothes giving the entire room a warm cozy feel which, considering the size of the room, was impressive.

The room was totally Rhode Daley. He fit in this log cabin on the top of a mountain with a scary-as-shit road complete with switchbacks. He fit in this room full of heavy, masculine furniture with a kickass attached bathroom. Even the jetted tub and stone shower fit him. He was comfortable in his home, he looked like he belonged on his mountain. Where he didn't belong was in my cookie-cutter house in a neighborhood with postage stamp-size backyards, and while clean and tidy still had traffic, noise, and nosy neighbors.

"Sugar?" he called. I looked over the top of Remy's head to find Rhode staring down at me.

I was on my side, Remy tucked into the curve of my body. Rhode was on the other side of Remy sitting with his back to the headboard. The last time I'd glanced at Rhode he'd been reading a book; now he was looking at me with his brows pulled together.

"Yeah?"

"You two are safe, yeah?"

"Huh?"

"You're frowning."

I was?

"To be expected." Rhode dipped his chin toward Remy. "We'll bring it up again tomorrow and work from there."

Yes, Remy being restless was to be expected and I felt like shit for not thinking of it while I was behaving like a bitch in heat rubbing all over Rhode in his laundry room.

"He's with his mom, he's safe, and tomorrow's a new day," Rhode continued.

He was right, of course. But what freaked me out was that Rhode didn't seem to be freaked out. Like living through a drive-by was normal—just like it was any ol' day and bullets hadn't been flying.

I wanted to ask why he was so calm but I didn't dare. Remy might be asleep but I figured he'd sleep lightly and if he woke up I didn't want him overhearing Rhode's explanation, which was likely to scare the pants off me.

"I like your cabin," I blurted out. "It suits you."

Rhode's head twitched at my abrupt change of topics.

"It should. I built it."

"Built it or had it built?"

Rhode set his book on the nightstand and switched off the light. In the darkness, I heard sheets rustling and when the bed stopped moving he started talking.

"I had a friend in the Navy, Casper. All he talked about was when he got out he was moving his family here. He had the land, he had the house plans. Totally off-grid, mountain retreat for him, his wife, and two kids. Surprisingly his wife was on board. Not many women wanna move to the top of a mountain with crap cell reception and internet so slow it makes dial-up seem fast. But Lucy was all for it."

I had a feeling I wasn't going to like how this story ended considering I wasn't too keen on any story starting with 'I *had* a friend'—they typically indicated the friendship was no more.

"Casper never made it to Idaho. But he loved this place so much I wanted to give him his dream. I asked Lucy for the house plans and got to work. I needed a crane and a crew to build the structure but I worked alongside them. I hired a well digger, someone to put in the septic, and subbed out the plumbing but I did the rest. Took years to finish. I was still in the Navy, took every bit of leave I had to come up here and work. And every time I came I fell in love with the mountain. When I was here I felt different. I could breathe. Building this house was the most painful experience of my life until I found out about Remington. It was here, in this house, bone-tired from working all day I allowed myself to feel loss. Not only Casper but all the men I served with who didn't make it home, the wives who lost their husbands, the moms and dads, children. This was the only place I could allow it. The rest of the time all those emotions had to be locked away. I couldn't let them encroach. I had a job to do that included more marks on my soul, more killing, more death, more loss.

"After I finished the house Lucy and the kids came up here to scatter Casper's ashes on his mountain. The place he'd intended to bring his family. They stayed for two days. The day they were leaving Lucy asked me to take the kids down the mountain. She wanted a few hours to be alone with her husband. I hated leaving her up here alone to grieve but I knew this mountain had the power to heal and I was hoping she'd find what she needed to ease some of the pain."

Needing the connection I reached over Remy, felt

around until my hand skimmed Rhode's arm, then I found his hand and laced my fingers through his. Rhode didn't move, he didn't curl in his fingers, he didn't tighten his grip, he gave no acknowledgment I was holding his hand. But that was okay. I was simply content to touch him. I was honored he was sharing something deeply personal. But that didn't mean my heart didn't hurt for him because it did. I knew loss. I knew the pain that hit at the oddest of times. Something mundane would trigger the reminder you were never going to see the person you loved again and fresh grief would consume you. I lost two of the most important people in my life and I'd barely survived. I couldn't imagine Rhode going through that over and over.

"Before they left for the airport Lucy told me she left something for me up at the cabin. When I got back up here there were three envelopes. I opened the first." Rhode paused and cleared his throat. "A letter Casper wrote to Lucy that I'd never seen with his final wishes that I oversee the cabin being built. He left her detailed instructions to give me. The second letter was from Lucy explaining why she'd never told me what Casper wanted. Lucy said she never needed to tell me because I'd done it on my own. She went on to tell me she was giving me the land and the cabin —that Casper would want me on his mountain. I opened the third envelope and it was the deed to the land and the house.

"So this place suits me because here is where my brother lives on. Here is where Lucy brings his children every year to spend time with their dad. Here is where I became whole. And here is where I want you and Remington."

I'd never pictured myself living on top of a mountain, off-grid, up a scary road that in the winter would be death-defying to pass. But suddenly I wanted Remington to grow up in this cabin. I wanted to fill this house with happy memories to balance out the grief. I wanted to give Rhode what he wanted and I wanted this for me, too.

"This mountain is magic," I whispered.

"It is," he confirmed.

Rhode didn't need my praise. He didn't need me to tell him he'd given his friend a beautiful gift. He knew what he'd given and in the process what he'd gained—not the house and land—peace, resolution, and hopefully he'd found grace.

"Sugar—"

"I want to tell Remy tomorrow."

Rhode's hand in mine spasmed then tightened.

"You sure?"

"Positive. No better place to tell him than up here on your mountain."

Rhode muttered a whispered curse.

He wanted that. He wanted to tell his son the truth, I knew that, but it was more that he wanted the bond to begin up here in this cabin, on this mountain.

It took a while. I had a hundred different scenarios of how we were going to tell Remy playing out in my head but I finally found sleep.

Holding Rhode's hand, in his big bed, in his beautiful cabin, with our son between us.

Dream come true.

The magic of the mountain.

18

I wasn't lying when I told Brooklyn cell service was shit up here. That was why at the butt crack of dawn I was standing out on the back patio on the phone with Wilson.

"Any news?" I asked.

"First things first, I secured Brooklyn's house. Davis and I debated then decided her and your son didn't need to go home to a couch full of holes so we junked the couch and coffee table. Glass is swept up and the broken window's boarded up."

"Appreciate that."

"Got word late last night. It wasn't the Horsemen," Wilson groused.

It was just after five in the morning and I doubted Wilson had been to bed. His irritation practically leaked through the phone and his clipped statement held the same disappointment I felt. I wanted Lawrence neutralized—as in put to ground—but I'd take behind bars if it meant my family was safe.

"You sure?"

"As sure as I can be if I trust a DEA agent who's been

undercover for two years. He says all patched members were in a meeting at the clubhouse discussing Kiki. He also says Lawrence would never trust a hit to be carried out by a recruit but further, no such hit was put out. So, we're working on other angles tied back to the trafficking."

My jaw clenched and anger seeped into my tone. "You're telling me the DEA has an inside man and he didn't come forward with Lawrence's whereabouts when he was under investigation for the disappearance of Kiki Welsh?"

"That's what I'm telling you and it'll piss you off the same as it pissed me off but you'll come around to understand—this guy knew where Kiki was because he was with her and Lawrence in California. He explained he knew she was safe so it wasn't worth the risk of blowing his cover to report in she wasn't missing."

I bet that Brooklyn and the Welshes would disagree with that. And unfortunately, as much as I wanted to be pissed on their behalf Wilson was right; I did understand operational integrity and it was always a risk when an undercover agent reached out. They had to pick and choose what they reported. A spoiled, nasty bitch running away from home, no matter the pain she was putting her family through, wasn't worth blowing a two-year investigation.

"What's he under for?"

"The usual, drugs and guns. The good news is he confirmed the Horsemen don't run women. No stable of whores, no transport, and they don't provide security for anyone who does. They stick with what's easy and if they're caught they're not going down on trafficking charges."

"Why'd he come forward about the drive-by?"

"When he heard whose house was hit he got worried we'd blow his investigation."

Smart man.

"Something else," Wilson continued. "And I'm not sure how we play this. Kiki's running her mouth, working Lawrence up into a lather. Straight up, she told Lawrence you threatened him direct and called the Horsemen pussies. She also told them that Brooklyn threatened to go to the police. Our inside man doesn't know what Brooklyn was supposedly going to the police about, just that Lawrence for obvious reasons doesn't like the cops and wants Brooklyn silenced."

Silenced.

That meant dead.

Fuck yeah, I felt a headache coming on. I also felt my trigger finger getting itchy.

"That fucker's not getting near Brooklyn."

"You're right, he's not. But now we gotta figure out how we're gonna spin this. Did you know Brooklyn has a Ring camera?"

I didn't know; the first time I went to Brooklyn's I'd been nervous as hell and hadn't been paying attention, the second time the bathroom had been flooding, and the third time I'd entered her house I was with Remington who'd been rambling about football and again I wasn't looking around her front porch.

"I didn't. Audio?"

"Yep. We have the whole conversation. Now, we turn this over to Lawrence, he finds out the bitch is lying and Kiki goes missing, and this time it's for real and with no hope of ever finding her, but your problem's solved. The Welshes, however..."

Wilson let that hang. I didn't need him to explain what the Welshes would endure. Kiki would be gone in a very permanent way and it was unlikely they'd find a body to bury. Michael and Tallulah would live out the rest of their lives never knowing what happened to their child. Letty would always wonder where her sister was, and Brooklyn would live with that bullshit argument being her last memory of Kiki.

Fuck.

I wanted Kiki exposed but I didn't want her death or the Welshes' grief on my conscience.

Needing to think on the Kiki situation, I tabled the discussion and went back to Brooklyn's doorbell camera.

"Did the Ring catch the shooting?"

"Not anything useful. The range is the porch and the walkway, doesn't capture the street at all."

I figured that was the case. If the camera had captured the car Wilson would've led with that.

"And Desi?"

"In the wind. Jack and Asher are leaving in about an hour to go hunting. Shep's working multiple angles but so far nothing. Think on how you wanna play Kiki and call me later. I'm gonna try to get some shuteye before the next trauma hits. But before I go, how are Brooklyn and Remington holding up?"

Wilson's question made my gut tighten. Remington was struggling but at four he couldn't process what had happened in a way where he could pinpoint what had scared him the most—the shooting, being in the house alone, or both. He was afraid and didn't want to be alone, that wasn't surprising but what had shocked me was the way he'd clung to me. His mom, absolutely but I was still a stranger to him and he hadn't wanted me out of his sight. I'd be lying if I said that didn't feel good. But I hated the reason why my son wanted me close. Silver lining was he did, and I was all too happy to spend time with him.

Brooklyn was holding on but doing it because

Remington needed her to. If she wasn't distracted by Remy she was in her head thinking. And the woman couldn't mask a thought; her facial expressions gave her away, especially when she frowned or wrinkled her forehead. But seeing as Remy wanted us both close I hadn't been able to have a real discussion about what was on her mind.

"They're both freaked. Brooklyn's worried Michael and Tallulah are pissed at her for withholding her visit with Kiki. She's worried about their safety. She's scared and worried about Remy and his state of mind, which is fucked because he was huddled on the floor in his kitchen while bullets tore through his home. And I think it's sinking in how screwed up Kiki is and she's feeling guilty thinking it's her fault since the selfish bitch straight out blamed Brooklyn for all of her problems."

"You gotta see her through that, brother, before that shit digs in and festers. Women take on shit that is not theirs to bear and they do it quietly until the weight's so heavy they can't see their way out of it. Give her something good to focus on."

Again with the sage advice that sounded a lot like Wilson was drawing from personal experience, which again made me wonder what the man was hiding. He'd never mentioned a woman in his life.

"You say that like you got experience with a woman holding on to something that wasn't hers."

There was a beat of silence that led into five and I didn't think he was going to answer so when he did I was unprepared.

"More than you know," he rumbled. "And trust me, the results of not unburdening your soul, not trusting your partner to take on the pain and walk you through it is downright disturbing. So, when I tell you to not let Brooklyn internalize this shit I mean dig that cancer out now before it's too late."

A chill washed over me and goose bumps rose on my arms.

"You need to unburden your soul, brother?"

Wilson huffed out a humorless, bitter laugh.

"When you come home and find your wife hanging in your bedroom with a suicide note laying on the bed you shared with her and the note lists your transgressions like a grocery list you immediately find a way to process that tragedy and move the fuck on, or the pain doesn't eat at you —it devours you until there's nothing left."

"Jesus fuck."

"Long time ago. Also found out after the fact Barb had suffered from depression since childhood. But no one told me. Not her parents, not her. They hid it like mental illness was some dark and dirty secret instead of telling me, her husband, so I could fucking help her. At least watch for signs it was taking her under. And that was something she blamed me for in her note. Not knowing, not taking care of her, me leaving on deployments, her going dark and me not being there. So seeing my wife the way I saw her, I dealt with it and after that, I turned into a cold motherfucker who firmly put the blame on the people who should've fucking told me.

"Now, I'm not saying your situation's the same, not even close, but the fact remains most women, they're nurturers, they're fixers, they're emotional. And when you find a woman who means something to you, you better bust your ass to give her a safe place to land when it gets to be too much. Take it from a man who fucked up huge and didn't handle his woman with the care she needed."

That was bullshit.

"Sounds to me like you haven't given the blame to anyone, Wilson. You're holding on tight when it clearly wasn't your fault."

"Not to be a dick and I appreciate what you're saying but she was my wife, my responsibility and I missed something important. I'd be even less of a man if I didn't acknowledge that. Now I'm ending this fucked-up conversation because I'm done talking about this and also because I haven't slept in forty-eight hours which has obviously loosened my tongue. So before I tell you more about my fucked-up past, I'm hanging up."

And hang up is what he did.

I stood outside watching the sunrise wondering how I'd known Wilson for years and had never known he'd been married. What the hell else was the man hiding? Out of the six of us, Wilson was the most closed off but he'd never even hinted at trouble in his past. Or had he and I'd missed it?

Before I could go over years of friendship and try to remember if Wilson had let something slip, the door behind me opened.

Brooklyn and Remy.

Christ, how was it possible she looked more beautiful than I'd ever seen her? First thing in the morning wearing one of my shirts that hit mid-thigh and holding Remington. His long frame in front of her, his legs wrapped around her middle, his head resting on her shoulder, but his eyes were on me and he was frowning.

"You left," Remy accused.

"I didn't leave, bud. I'm right here."

"You left," he repeated.

"I told you, baby, Rhode didn't leave us, he just came downstairs," Brooklyn explained.

"You. Left."

Brooklyn jolted, my stomach clenched, and the muscles in my neck tightened at the ferocity of his little boy tone.

"Okay, Remy, I hear you, son. I did leave. I woke up early and wanted to let you and your mom sleep so I came down here so I didn't wake you. But now that you're up why don't you help me find something to make for breakfast?"

Brooklyn's eyes had gone round and I wasn't tracking the panic I saw there. I offered to have Remy help me make breakfast, not set bear traps.

"You all right, Sugar?"

"Why do you call my mom sugar?"

"Because she's sweet like sugar."

Remington smiled. Big and bright. So damn bright it was blinding. But it was his giggle that stole my heart.

I didn't need a reason to fall in love with my son. That had happened instantaneously. From the second I laid eyes on him a switch flipped on and I knew with a certainty that I'd never suspected existed, not only was Remington mine but that I would do anything to make him happy. So it wasn't that I fell in love with my son because he giggled, it was just that the small part I'd been holding back for self-preservation until we told Remy I was his dad and he accepted me was ripped clean away. I was totally defenseless against the onslaught of love I felt.

"Will you give me a nickname, too?"

Son.

"Hm..." I tapped my chin and shook my head. "A nickname is earned, not given."

"Earned?"

"Yep. Your mom earned hers by being sweet."

"Do you have a nickname?"

"I do."

"What is it?"

"How 'bout I tell you over breakfast?" I suggested in an effort to come up with a plausible nickname because there was no way in hell I was telling my four-year-old what nickname my team had given me and why.

Remington wiggled until Brooklyn set him down on his bare feet. He was still in his clothes from yesterday. That would have to be remedied and Brooklyn needed clothes as well.

A football and blanket were all my son had.

The thought pissed me right the fuck off.

I also doubted I had much in the cabin by way of breakfast food. I'd been staying in CDA at the hotel with my team. Canned ravioli probably wasn't what Brooklyn would consider a breakfast of champions.

"When are we going fishing?" Remy asked.

Fucking shit.

The hopeful, happy expression on my kid's face was a knife to the gut. I didn't want either of them leaving the mountain but seeing the shine in Remy's dark brown eyes I knew I wouldn't deny him. And while I hadn't promised I'd take him out on the boat, I had told him I would and that was as good as a promise and I wasn't breaking my word with my son ever. So I was going to risk taking them down the mountain.

Fuck.

"After breakfast, we'll get ready."

Remington smiled again and I knew I was so totally fucked for years to come I didn't bother thinking about how fucked I was right then. I just knew I would give him whatever he wanted if it meant he smiled at me like that.

"Is that wise?" Brooklyn asked.

Hell no.

But what she was actually asking was if it was safe.

"We'll be fine out on the boat."

More questions were dancing behind her eyes. Ones she wouldn't ask in front of Remy. As predictable as ever—not to mention transparent—I couldn't stop my smile when she turned to Remy and said, "Why don't you go snoop around the kitchen and see if you find something you want me to make for breakfast?"

"Okay, *Sugar*," Remy quipped.

Right or wrong I couldn't hold back my laughter. And when Remington joined in his high-pitched little boy laugh I sobered, not wanting to miss a single second of the sound.

"Okay, *popsicle*," Brooklyn returned.

"Popsicle?" Remy shouted. "No way."

"You love popsicles. But if you don't like that, what about lollipop?"

"No way. My nickname's bulldog because that's my favorite dog."

Good breed. I could get on board with having a bulldog. I'd prefer a shepherd or a Doberman but a bulldog would do.

"All right, bulldog, go find breakfast. I need to talk to your—" Brooklyn clamped her mouth shut, swallowed, and started again, "I need to talk to Rhode."

That was the second time she'd almost slipped up. The second time my heart had lurched, desperately wanting her to finish her sentence the way she intended. The second time she'd caught herself and called me by name. And finally, it was the second time Remington had looked at her funny when she did it.

The boy wasn't dumb; he sensed something was going on. I knew it by the way he looked at me. It was like he wanted to ask who I was, if I was his dad. If he were a few years older I had no doubt he would've already presented the question.

"I'll be in to help in a minute, bud," I told Remy.

With one more look between me and his mom, he took off into the house.

"Shit," Brooklyn grumbled as soon as the door was closed. "It's like I want to tell him so bad I keep slipping up."

Goddamn, that felt good.

"We'll tell him out on the lake."

"No," she insisted. "Here. I want to tell him on your mountain. Either before or after we go fishing. If I have a say, I think it should be before. Give him his first memory after we tell him he's going fishing with his dad."

If she had a say?

Christ, Brooklyn was killing me.

"Baby, you have all the say. I'm following you on this, remember?"

"And I've reminded you he's ours, not mine, and we make the decisions together."

Oh, yeah, she was killing me.

"Okay, then I agree; we'll tell him during breakfast. But warning, baby, we might be having canned SpaghettiOs."

"Remington will be in heaven." Brooklyn smiled.

And it sucked that smile was so radiant because I had shit to tell her that was going to steal her happiness. But it needed to be said and before we went down the mountain.

"Talked to Wilson this morning." As expected, her smile faded. "He got intel on the Horsemen. They were all accounted for during the time of the shooting."

"So it wasn't them?"

"No. Wilson's source is solid; the Horsemen are cleared. But later we need to talk about Kiki."

"What about her?"

Fuck, not only had Brooklyn lost her smile, she'd lost all remnants of happy.

"Come here, Sugar."

I waited until Brooklyn got close then tagged her around the waist and hauled her to my chest. Since she was in my arms in nothing but my tee and looking beautiful, I dipped my chin and kissed her. Unfortunately, with Remy running around it was closed mouth and quick but it was better than what I got yesterday morning, which was nothing.

"First, we're gonna rewind. Mornin', baby."

Brooklyn's lips curved up. It pained me to know we weren't done talking about the shit that was gonna make her unhappy now that I had that smile back.

"Mornin', honey."

"Wanna wake up to that every morning, Brooklyn. And just sayin', you give me that I swear you won't regret it."

Those blue eyes got watery when she replied, "You keep this up and I'll have to start calling *you* Sugar, and you look more like a Bruiser than a sweet treat. But lucky for you you're big enough no one will make fun of you when they hear your new nickname."

"No one would believe you if you told them I was sweet." I chuckled.

"Really?"

"Really," I confirmed. "Can't recall anyone in my life thinking that."

Her smile turned sly then sad. But when her hands came up and rested on either side of my neck I forgot about her smile and starting wondering how a touch so innocent could make my blood run hot and my dick jump to attention. Then I concluded I didn't give a shit and just enjoyed it.

"Well, I think you're sweet, and since you're mine my opinion's the only one that matters."

You're mine.

Good Goddamn.

"Sugar, I am most definitely yours. But you cannot say shit like that to me when Remy's snooping in the kitchen and you're in nothing but my tee and all I've been thinking about for the last twenty-four hours is searching that beautiful body of yours for new ink."

"That's what you've been thinking about?" she called me on my lie and added a sexy smirk to punctuate her point.

"You're skating on very thin ice, baby. You're seconds away from telling our boy, Mommy and Daddy are going upstairs for some alone-time. I figure you're not ready to explain what that means to him but just so *you're* clear about what it means—after I find those tats I'll be having you for breakfast. And if memory serves and I know it does, you're good with your mouth so you'll be returning the favor."

"As long as my tats aren't the only reason you wanna see me naked I'll behave...for now. And it sucks because I'm enjoying this—you and me and teasing. But before Remy gets back please tell me about Kiki."

Teasing? I wasn't teasing about getting my mouth between her legs and I certainly wasn't fucking teasing about getting her mouth wrapped around my dick. But she was right; Remy would be out and I had shit to tell her.

"Brace, baby, it's not good."

Her chest expanded with an inhale and I gritted my teeth when her braless breasts rubbed against my chest. When I had my dick back under control I told her everything Wilson told me, minus the undercover DEA agent inside the Horsemen.

19

If Zeus or Apollo or whatever that idiot biker president called himself didn't kill Kiki I was going to. She was now at an all-time low. How could she lie about Rhode to those assholes? And me? Did she want me dead? Did she want Remy to grow up without me—or worse, get hurt, too?

Had she hated me this much all my life?

"Please tell Wilson I said thank you for taking care of my place. That was cool of him."

"Babe."

I didn't have to look at Rhode to know he was concerned. He'd watched me carefully as he told me about his conversation. He'd been exceedingly gentle when he explained the dilemma we were in. And it was quite the predicament— throw Kiki under the bus and clear our name or keep the target on our backs and let Kiki live.

Honestly, that was what I was most pissed about—the situation she'd put me in was unwinnable. Protect my son— which was a no-brainer. Or protect her—which meant saving the people who took me in after my parents' death a lifetime of hurt.

"I need a few hours to think about it," I told him.

"I can give you that, but while you're thinking about it you need to remember that none of this is your doing."

"But she's lying because she hates me."

Rhode's hand on my back moved lower to my hip and his other went to the back of my neck and both squeezed. I was catching on—he did this when he was going to say something I wasn't going to like. It was a warning to brace, so I did. I gathered up what I had left of my patience for a situation I didn't want to be in, one that was dangerous beyond anything I'd ever experienced, and I waited.

"Straight up, Sugar, I don't give a fuck if she does hate you. Kiki's life choices are Kiki's. If she chooses to allow hate to guide her to making fucked-up decisions that's not on you. She's responsible for her actions. Not you, not Letty, not her parents. Kiki made the choice, and, Brooklyn, you gotta understand this part, it was a cognizant choice, she's been around those bikers long enough to understand the repercussions of lying to them. Not only lying, but starting what's gonna amount to a war because she's an immature, selfish twit. Let me put it this way; if she went to Lawrence and told him that she hates you because she's jealous and thinks you got more attention than her growing up and asked him to fuck with you because of *that* he would've laughed in her face and likely kicked her out of the clubhouse for wasting his time. She's not so stupid to tell him the truth. So she made up a bunch of bullshit. Whatever comes her way because of that is on her. Not you. But saying all of that, as pissed as I am, I'm not fired up about making the Welshes pay for their daughter's fucked-up choices. So we're gonna sit on this, think about it, then make the right plays so everyone walks away unharmed."

Rhode didn't strike me as the sort of man who sat on

information and waited around. He'd been clear from the start his priority was keeping me and Remy safe. He was a good guy so I believed he wouldn't be keen on seeing the Welshes suffer more, especially since he'd already had a front-row seat to their pain. But that was not why he was weighing the options to ensure no harm came to Kiki, who I reckoned he couldn't care less about.

He was doing it for me. He knew what the Welshes meant to me. He knew that as pissed as I was at Kiki, a part of me still loved her. At least I loved the little girl I'd grown up with.

"Thank you."

Dark brown eyes bore into mine and I watched as they gentled and lost some of their anger.

"We're gonna get through this."

"I know."

The rest of the anger slid clear away and he grinned.

"How upset are you gonna be when I take Remy out later on the dirt bike?"

Considering he hadn't known about Remington long enough to purchase a bike small enough to teach Remy to ride I wouldn't be upset at all. And if for some reason he had a bike small enough and wanted to teach him, I'd hold my tongue and let father and son do their thing.

"I'll only be upset if you don't have a bike for me to ride."

"You think you can hang with the boys?"

He had no idea. I'd been riding since I was Remy's age. Which was exactly why everyone gave me shit about not allowing my son to learn. But I was waiting for...something. Call it the romantic in me. But now that Rhode was here I knew what I was waiting for and that I'd made the right decision.

"Eh." I shrugged. "I might be able to keep up."

"Why do I get the feeling you think you can best me?"

"Because I know I can, and even if you could beat me—which you can't—you'll have Remy with you so I know you'll take it slow."

Rhode gave me one of his panty-melting smiles and I fell a little more in love when he teased back.

"Love your confidence, Sugar, but I'll smoke your ass."

"It's cute you think that, honey."

Lucky for me when Rhode tipped his head to the side and roared with laughter he was still holding on to me so I got to hear, feel, and watch his beautiful face alight.

I also got to memorize it.

But I would find out later there was no need to file away the sound of his happiness—he gave it freely and often. Something else to love.

"Can we have SpaghettiOs every morning for breakfast?" Remy asked as he wiped sauce off his face.

I looked over Remy's shoulder to the clock on the wall and noted it was ten to six. Then I tried to remember a morning when my son had been up this early alert, happy, smiling, and ready to tackle the day. It was a fruitless endeavor; I didn't have to waste time thinking about it because I knew the answer was never. Remington was just like me, neither of us morning people. And on a morning that was sure to be shitty—the morning Remy woke up in a bed he'd never been in the day after his home had been destroyed causing us to flee—he was smiling instead. Yet after a hard start, he was sitting at the table alert and happy.

So I was giving great consideration to allowing him to eat SpeghettiOs every morning for the rest of his life if a bowl of empty-calorie-laden noodles made him this happy. Though I figured his happiness had more to do with Rhode and the promise of fishing. Which was good news because my concern for my son's nutritional well-being won out and I had to break the unfortunate news he couldn't eat processed, canned spaghetti for breakfast every morning from here on out.

"Sorry, bud, but the answer is no."

"Bummer."

"Do you know what bummer means?"

"Auntie Letty says bummer. Is it an adult word?"

Remy's gaze lifted and his face showed confusion; a reminder that he was four, not fourteen despite some of the things he said. Nervousness set in, bringing me back to how we were going to tell Remington about Rhode. I didn't even know how to start the conversation.

"No, bud, it's not. I was just wondering where you heard it, that's all."

"How long are we staying here?"

"Um..."

Shit.

"A few days," Rhode smoothly interjected.

"Cool. No school."

Double shit. How could I have forgotten about school?

"Cool? You don't like school?" Rhode asked between bites of his ravioli.

"It's okay. But my teacher makes us take naps."

"Yeah, I don't like naps either."

"I love naps," I told them.

Remington looked at me and scrunched his face. "Naps are boring."

"Agreed," Rhode said.

"Boring? How can sleeping be boring?"

With identical brown eyes staring at me I lost my train of thought. God, they were beautiful, both of them. The only thing that would've made the vision better was if they were smiling their perfect, matching smiles. The icing would've been if I'd had this every morning since Remy was big enough to sit in a high chair. Breakfast with my beautiful boys. I might not have appreciated the extreme beauty in front of me quite as much if I'd had it all along, though I was pretty damn sure I would've.

"Sugar?"

I was beginning to learn not much slipped past Rhode and I was also learning he was quick to call me on it when my mood shifted. Seeing as I was a woman and my mood shifted frequently, he had his work cut out for him.

I ignored Rhode's concern and concentrated on my son, then I went for it.

"Remington, I need to talk to you about something."

"Naps are boring but I don't argue," he rushed out.

Shit. My son thought he was in trouble. I was making a mess out of this and I hadn't even started.

"It's not about naps, bud, and I know you do. It's about your dad."

Remy's tiny body snapped straight and his eyes got round. I'd never brought up this topic with him and I'd artfully avoided it the few times he'd asked.

"I have a dad?"

The guilt that slammed into me stole my breath and shattered my heart.

Not only was I botching what should be a special moment for Rhode and Remington I was irrevocably proven to be the worst mother in the history of motherkind.

"You absolutely have a dad," Rhode told him fiercely.

"Are you my dad?"

Time stood still.

"Yes, Remington, I'm your dad."

Five life-changing words hung in the air and I still couldn't get my lungs to work. I needed to say something but my mind blanked. All I could do was stare at my son staring at Rhode.

No, my son was staring at the man he now knew was his dad and still, I couldn't speak.

"Are you staying?" Remy squeaked.

"Yes!"

"Are you going to live with us?"

Oh, Jesus.

"Your mom and I are going to give you time to adjust, then we'll talk about it."

Good answer.

"What does that mean?"

Rhode smiled at Remington and I finally inhaled.

"That means that for now, I'm gonna spend all the time I can with you and your mom."

"But you're not leaving?"

"No."

"Okay."

Wait? *Okay*? That was it?

I found my voice and asked, "Do you have any questions?"

"When are we going fishing?"

Fishing.

I glanced at Rhode and he gave me a short shake of his head, which I interpreted as *leave it*. So I left it and didn't push Remy on the subject.

"Can I let the SpaghettiOs settle in my belly before I take a boat ride?" I joked.

"How long will that take?"

Kids are as resilient as they are fragile. They'll roll with change as long as their foundation is solid. You've given Remington solid parenting, so he'll roll with this change.

Tally was right.

Remington was rolling with change.

"Ten minutes?"

"Ten minutes," Remy agreed and jumped off the chair. "Do you know what's cool about staying here? I don't even have to get dressed since I'm still wearing clothes from yesterday."

"Yes, Remy, that's cool. I can see how changing clothes is a waste of time when a boat ride and fishing are imminent."

"What does im-men-ent mean?" Remy asked.

"Upcoming. Happening soon," Rhode explained.

"May I be excused?"

Further proof Remy was rolling with his life changing in ways he couldn't begin to understand.

"Please, rinse your bowl and go wash your face."

Remington dashed into the kitchen. I heard the water go on and off. Then he dashed by the table and up the stairs. Through all of this Rhode had his gaze locked with mine. His expression gave nothing away. When the pounding of feet stopped Rhode got out of his chair, plucked me out of mine, and brought his lips to mine.

"Thank you."

I didn't respond.

I couldn't, with Rhode giving me the best kiss of my life.

20

"Can we throw the football?" Remy asked.

I set the cooler with Remy's catch on one of the picnic tables I had at the back of the house and bit back a groan. I knew I wasn't going to say no but damn if I didn't need a break after sitting in the sun all day on the boat.

"Rethinking your view on naps?" Brooklyn chuckled.

Instead of answering either of them, I asked my own question, "Fish on the grill or should we build a fire?"

"Fire!" Remy shouted.

"My thoughts as well," I agreed. "And, yes to tossing the ball but after we gut and fillet."

"And after you shower off the guts and change your clothes," Brooklyn amended.

Shopping with Brooklyn had been as eye-opening as shopping with Remy a couple days ago. The woman was efficient and according to what I'd heard that was unusual. The moment we pulled up to the shopping center Brooklyn declared her hatred for shopping. This elated me. I avoided the mall, big box stores, and the like at all costs. And I only went to the grocery store when I absolutely had to. We were in and out of the clothing store in under thirty minutes with her and Remy fully kitted out for a five-day stay at the cabin.

The grocery store the same. She tackled that like a champ. Brooklyn didn't peruse and only went down the aisles she needed. We were in the checkout line before Remy could utter a complaint. Though like me, he'd trailed behind Brooklyn mechanically bored.

I, however, had offered to help but she declined my offer asking me instead to keep my eye on Remy so she could get what she needed.

It wasn't until we were back in the car and on our way up the mountain that it hit me how exhausting keeping up with a four-year-old was—and how easily she'd done it. I had one full day keeping Remington occupied and I hadn't even had to do it alone and I was seeing why Brooklyn enjoyed napping.

The only thing that kept the guilt from gnawing at my insides was remembering Brooklyn was no longer alone.

"Then can we go for a ride?"

"It's gonna get dark soon," I reminded Remy. "You gotta pick one. The ride or tossing the ball."

"The football. But can we go for a ride tomorrow?"

"Yep."

"And the day after can you show me the barn?"

I didn't need to be an experienced parent to know something wasn't right. But when I glanced at Brooklyn and she was biting her lip I knew my instincts were spot on.

"Come here, Remy."

Without delay, he skipped over and I bent to lift him onto the bench so we were almost eye level.

"Are you worried I'm leaving?"

Silence.

"I'm not leaving, Remington."

More silence.

"I never left *you*, son. *Never*."

It was then I decided to lie to my boy.

A small, white-lie but I figured Brooklyn, even with her philosophy about lying, would understand. And one day I might have to answer for my slight misrepresentation of the past but there was no way in hell I would ever tell my son the truth about how he was conceived and I didn't give a fuck if that was a parenting mistake.

"When I lost touch with your mom we didn't know she was pregnant with you. And when she found out, it was too late for her to tell me. If we'd known, Remington, I would've been here."

"You didn't know?"

"No, son, I didn't know and your mom did everything she could to find me. But I traveled so much with work she didn't know where I was. But she looked for me. And as soon as she found me, she told me about you. And now I'm not going anywhere."

Remington still didn't look convinced.

"What's wrong, bud?"

"Are you going to leave again with work?"

"No. I quit so I could be here with you and your mom."

"You quit?" Brooklyn whispered.

Fuck. I hadn't told her.

"Takeback's headquarters are in Arizona. I told Wilson after this job's complete I wasn't going back. I still need to give him my formal resignation but, yeah, I quit."

That reminded me—I still needed to make arrangements to clean out my place in Arizona and get it ready to sell.

When no one said anything I broke the silence and told

Remy, "We have fish to clean and a ball to toss. Do you have any questions?"

Remy shook his head.

"All right. If you think of something you wanna know, just ask. Sugar, you got anything to add?"

"No." The word sounded like she'd forced it through gritted teeth.

I craned my neck and looked over my shoulder to find her staring at me with blue fire dancing in her eyes.

"What's—"

"I'm gonna get the groceries and let you guys handle the fish."

Before I could stop her Brooklyn strutted her ass to the back door and disappeared into the house. When I turned back to Remy his lips were pinched together.

"You're busted," he announced.

"What?"

"That's momma's mad face. That means you're in trouble."

"Trouble?"

"Totally."

How could I be in trouble?

"What am I in trouble for?"

Remy shrugged his shoulders then passed on valuable information.

"Pop says that women are creatures and us men never know why they get mad. He says that flowers work." He ended with another shrug and I couldn't stop myself from laughing. Though I did it praying Brooklyn didn't hear.

"I think your pop meant women are mysterious creatures."

Again his shoulders went to his ears and he grinned.

"Just try flowers."

"Smart. After we clean up I'll find some flowers."

I glanced around the back of the house and there wasn't a flower in sight.

I was totally fucked.

I was hosing fish guts off the table when Remington came back with an armful of sticks and dropped them into the fire pit.

"This is your house."

"Yep."

"Can we live up here?"

Damn, but I loved Remy was asking.

"Do you like the cabin?"

"Yes."

Damn, I loved that, too.

"What's your favorite part?"

"The backyard."

I didn't have a backyard as such. There was no grass up there to mow, just trees and shrubs I bushhogged every year to keep from encroaching on the cabin. But no grass didn't mean lots of room for Remy to run and play.

"The problem with living up here is, it's far away from your school. And in the winter the road coming up the mountain gets closed when we have a big snow. Which means sometimes I can't leave for days. So I don't know about us living up here but we can come up whenever you want."

"I don't mind being snowed in."

I'm sure he didn't. But he would when he was a teenager and wanted to get down the mountain to hang with his buds. That thought led me to the terrifying thought of Remy being old enough to drive—and before that, Brooklyn having to drive Remy up and down the mountain in ice and snow.

"Snow days are fun but they're more fun when they don't last for weeks at a time."

"Can I call you dad?"

The hose fell from my hand and every muscle in my body stiffened.

"Yes."

"Are you and Momma gonna get married?"

Do four year olds know *about marriage*? Apparently, they did, but what the hell? Where was Brooklyn? How was I supposed to answer that?

"What do you know about marriage?"

"Pop says that marriage is a street with no exits, just lots of bends and twists. I don't know how a road twists but that's what he says when Grams is mad at him."

More wisdom coming from a four-year-old.

Great.

"Your pop sounds smart."

"He is."

Right. What now?

"Hungry?"

"Starving."

"Let's get cleaned up and we'll start dinner."

"Don't forget the flowers, Dad."

Dad.

Jesus Christ.

An emotion I'd never felt before burned through my body, leaving a trail blazing in its wake that hurt so good I wanted it to never end. With my heart in my throat, I watched my son walk into the house.

Then I went in search of flowers.

21

"Whoa there, buckaroo, where are you going?" I shouted after Remington as he bound up the stairs.

"Dad said to clean up so we could start dinner."

Dad?

Wait. What?

Dad?

My legs trembled and my hand shot out to the countertop for balance.

Dad.

My breaths came out choppy, my heart pounded, butterflies erupted and fluttered in my stomach. This was it. This was what I'd wanted. All of it. This was what I was dreaming about as I stood in the kitchen of Rhode's awesome cabin putting away groceries. This was what I hoped Remy and I could have as I watched them throwing the football. Rhode infinitely patient with Remy when he fumbled the ball, helping him arrange his little boy fingers on the giant football, teaching him how to throw. Rhode smiling when Remy got it right.

I thought back to our fishing trip and how Rhode let

Remy help steer the boat. Father and son cutting up, laughing at me when I reeled in a fish so small we had to throw it back. Rhode ruffling Remy's hair when he caught a big one, making a big deal about it, making Remy smile. Rhode holding my hand in front of Remy and my son taking that in with a smile and rolling with the new change.

Rhode's presence rocked our solid foundation in the best of ways. He'd slid in and fit. I was living a fairy tale— well, minus the bullets, the threat of death, and a dirty, felonious MC. But even with the dark pall of Kiki's threats everything was perfect. Too perfect. So perfect I was scared it couldn't possibly be real.

Not since before my parents died had my life been this perfect.

I'd been so lost in thought I hadn't heard Rhode come in so when I felt my hair being moved off my neck I startled but relaxed when warm lips pressed to the now exposed skin, and finally, I smiled when I saw a ragtag bouquet of mostly leafy stems with some budding weeds thrown in for color.

"What's this?"

"Wasn't lost on me you were pissed at me, Sugar. Not sure what I did, but Remington advised when women are pissed a man brings them flowers. Seeing as it would take an hour round trip to go down the mountain and I don't have a green thumb so there're no flowers up here this was the best I could do."

His best was perfect.

And I'd forgotten I was mad when Remy had dropped his verbal bomb but now I remembered.

"You quit your job."

Rhode set the shabby posy of stems on the counter before he gently turned me to face him. Warm brown eyes locked onto mine and his hand came up to cradle my face. I knew this was one of those times he was preparing me so I braced for the onslaught.

But I would find my defenses were no match for the series of velvet blows Rhode landed.

"With everything going on we haven't had much time alone, and the time we have had I used to keep you up to speed about what's going on with Kiki and the Welshes. I know they're important to you and you're up here cut off from them. And it sucks, but that's the way it has to be until we figure out what to do about Kiki. On top of that, and more important, is the reason why you and Remington are up here. My team's split running two operations that are separate but connected. They know getting my family safe is priority one but they're having a mind to what you need, and that's keeping the Welshes protected and that includes Kiki. They're out there not sleeping, busting their asses while I'm here with you and Remy. They know this is where I need to be, where I want to be, and where I'm going to stay. But that doesn't mean that I still don't need to kick in and help. I've got work I gotta do tonight, a few hours of running checks on the victims we rescued.

"I'm telling you that so you'll understand where my head's at. I wasn't keeping quitting my job a secret. I made the decision the day after I saw Remy at the bookstore. It wasn't something I needed to think about. I knew I wasn't going back to Arizona with my team and leaving you and Remington behind."

"You didn't need to think about it?"

"Sugar, you and Remy are in Idaho."

Rhode said that like his statement said it all, which in his mind I guess it did. But quitting a job and moving two states away even if you had a kickass mountaintop cabin you vacationed at in the state you were going to move to, required thought and planning.

"Don't you think this is fast? Shouldn't—"

"Fast? This move is five years overdue."

I loved he thought that. Loved it down to my soul he wanted to be close to me and Remy. I wanted him here. But I didn't want him to give up his job and grow to resent me.

"Do you like your job?"

"I love my job. But I love Remington more."

That was sweet. No, that was perfect. But it sliced to the bone. I wasn't stupid enough to think after two days Rhode would be head over heels in love with me. My heart was just dumb enough to wish for it.

"Sugar, you're looking at me like I just told you I killed puppies for fun."

"I just don't want you to regret giving up your job and your life in Arizona."

"Bullshit," he rapped out. I jerked my head in surprise. "I told you I have one regret and that's letting you walk away. Leaving a job I love for my family won't be a mistake. I said I loved Remington more than my job and that's the damn truth. I have been straight with you and that's from the very beginning back in D.C. I've never lied, I've never pretended to be someone I'm not, and I'd never lead you to believe something was true that wasn't. So believe me now when I tell you I know what I want. I know what I feel. I know where I'm at with you. And, baby, I know where you're at with me. I know what we have and what it will be as we build from here."

Rhode dropped his forehead and I closed my eyes.

"I love my son, Brooklyn, and I'm falling in love with his mom. You need to know that so when I give you those words you'll trust they're real. You'll believe in them and you'll give them back to me knowing I'll want to hear them. Right now, everything's moving fast. You've got enough stress so I don't want you worrying about my job. But I do want you to think about something."

It wasn't something I needed to think about.

You and Remy are in Idaho.

I'm falling in love with his mom.

Dad.

Rhode was right. Everything was moving fast and maybe I should've been worried about that but I wasn't. I was worried about Kiki and gunfire. I was worried about Michael and Tally. I was worried about Letty and I hadn't been able to talk to her. I knew she would be freaking out about Smutties. That bookstore was her baby, her pride and joy, and thinking about someone destroying all of her hard work made my heart hurt. I should've been worried about *my* job and getting back to work but I was ahead of schedule and always had a built-in two-week buffer so I didn't need to start worrying about that for another week. And honestly, if the shooter still wasn't caught by then I'd have more to worry about.

Then I started to wonder if the reason I wasn't worried about how fast things were moving with Rhode was because everything else was taking up headspace. But I knew that wasn't right. I knew I wasn't worried because he was Rhode and he said what he felt and meant what he said. He could've lied and told me he loved me and Remy both but he didn't. He told me the truth.

I'm falling in love.

That was all I needed to know. That was what I had to believe in.

"What do you want me to think about?"

"I'd love to know what goes on in that pretty head of yours when you close your eyes."

"I was thinking that I hadn't talked to Letty since her store was destroyed and she's probably freaking out. I was thinking that if this situation isn't fixed in the next week I need to start thinking about work. I was thinking that I liked how you're always honest with me and it makes me trust what you say. Oh, and I was thinking that I wasn't worried about how fast we were moving and that Remington called you Dad."

Rhode's forehead pressed deeper into mine and now I was thinking about how much I loved how he did the forehead touch when he wanted my attention. And how much I loved that I was learning him—when he wanted me to listen, when he was preparing to soften a blow, and what his eyes said when they warmed.

"Straight up," Rhode murmured. "No games, no hiding. I like that, Sugar."

"What'd you want me to think about?"

"Remington asked if we could live up here."

Rhode hadn't even finished his question when my head jerked back.

"What?"

"I told him we couldn't live up here because it was too far from town," he explained.

"Do you *want* to live up here? Full-time I mean?"

Why did I ask that? Was I inviting myself to live on Rhode's mountain? Did I *want* to live with him?

"No, baby. I love this cabin and I love the mountain. But the drive up in the winter is ass-clenching. And when the snow melts and the roads are mud, no way I want you driving down. Not to mention, this place runs on a generator. It's a two-week-at-a-time getaway, not a full-time residence. Which means I gotta find a place in town."

"Okay."

"I want you to think about helping me find a place. I want a place with land. Lots of space for Remington to play."

"He'd like that."

"And you? Would you like that?"

Who wouldn't like a house sitting on land?

"What exactly are you asking?"

"You've got a nice house, but you said you rented."

I was trying to keep my heart from pounding out of control and my dumb imagination from running wild, and failing miserably at both.

"I do."

"So while you're looking for a house for me I'd like you to find one you'd wanna live in."

It was fast.

Like, catch-your-hair-on-fire, Mach-one—fast.

"How 'bout I look at houses with you and in six months—"

"One month," Rhode cut me off.

"Are you negotiating a timeframe for me and Remy to move in with you?"

"Yes."

"Two months," I countered.

"Three weeks."

Rhode's lips twitched at the same time I felt my lips tip up.

"That's not how negotiating works," I said through a smile.

"Move in with me, Brooklyn."

"Like roommates?" I asked half-teasing.

"You can call it a roommate situation if that's what it takes to get you to move in with me. But just so you know you'll be in my bed."

"Remy—"

"He asked me if I was going to marry you right after he asked if he could call me dad. And let's not forget he brought up all of us living together."

"He what?" I screeched.

"Let's just say your boy's a vat of wisdom."

"Fish!" Remy shouted from the steps. "Time to cook fish!"

"Inside voice!" I yelled back.

"Babe?" Rhode chuckled. "Move in with me."

"Okay."

Rhode looked stunned. Then his handsome face lit and he smiled and kissed me.

Unfortunately, it was quick and closed-mouthed but it was still awesome.

"I told you flowers worked!" Remy shouted.

"Seriously, kid, inside voice."

"It was totally the flowers," Rhode confirmed.

I'd never tell him it actually wasn't the flowers, it was just him—and his smile, and his great laugh, and his warm eyes, and how he was with Remington, and how he treated me gently but still gave it to me straight.

"Don't you guys have a fire to light or something?"

"Yes!" Remy took off toward the door. "Can I light the fire, Dad?"

Whoosh.

That was the sound my breath made as it evacuated my body.

And for the third time in my life, it happened...

Speech*less*.

Breath stolen.

Butterflies swarming.

I felt Rhode's lips next to my ear then I felt them moving when he whispered, "Thank you, Sugar."

Then he was gone.

And with him, he took my soul.

22

A little foot kicking dangerously close to my balls woke me up. Remington was once again between me and Brooklyn and he was doing his best imitation of an alligator's death roll—limbs flailing, body twisting and turning.

Before I lost the ability to give Remington brothers and sisters I tagged him around the middle and hauled him across to the bed and pinned him to my side.

"Are you awake, Dad?"

I was and I was finding it to be a miracle Brooklyn had slept through Remy's thrashing.

"Yes. Why are you awake?"

"It's morning."

I didn't need to look at the alarm clock to know it was *barely* morning. And after another late night, I figured Remy would've slept in. But here he was—bright-eyed and bushy-tailed at the ass-crack of dawn. Apparently, the kid didn't need much sleep. This shouldn't have surprised me. I was a morning person; even after years of late-night ops, it didn't matter what time we rolled back to base—if the sun was up I was awake.

Which meant I was now awake. But Brooklyn wasn't— she was asleep on her stomach, gleaming brown hair splayed over the pillow, lips slightly parted. She was so pretty I couldn't stop myself from staring. I'd been to a lot of places, seen a lot, done a lot, had my fair share of women. Some of them had spent the night, some more than once. But never had I simply slept in a bed next to a woman. And I'd certainly never shared a bed with a child. Yet for the past two nights, I'd slept with Brooklyn with Remy between us, which meant I'd woken up in bed next to them. And both mornings I'd woken up feeling lucky. Both mornings I woke up happier than I'd ever been, even with all of the shit swirling around us. I had Remington and Brooklyn—the rest would be sorted and then life would just be life and I'd still have Remy and Brooklyn under my roof. Brooklyn in my bed—Remy hopefully in his and not sleeping between us.

As much as I loved my son, loved Remy close, loved watching him sleep, I wanted time with Brooklyn. Which meant Remington needed to be in his bed so his daddy could show his mommy how much he missed her. And that needed to happen soon—as in this afternoon when we tested the importance of naps.

"I have to pee, Dad."

Dad.

Since Remy had asked if he could call me 'Dad' he tacked it on to every question and statement. He used it whenever he could and as much I loved hearing it I hoped one day he'd be so used to me being around and secure in the knowledge I wasn't going anywhere that he'd mellow. But for now, I was enjoying hearing it too much to be overly concerned at the frequency he said it or that he was still asking to plan activities days in the future.

"Do you need help?"

Remy scrunched his face and shook his head in disgust. "No."

"Then get to it, boy."

The kid scrambled over me, landing a knee to the gut and another way too close to my crotch before his feet hit the wood floor and he ran to the bathroom, leaving me alone in bed with Brooklyn for the first time. Knowing I didn't have much time I moved to the space Remy had vacated and brushed Brooklyn's hair off her face. With the long strands still gathered in my hand, I bent and kissed her neck. Then because she smelled so fucking good, I needed a taste. So I tasted—up her neck, over her jaw, cheek, and stopped at her temple.

"Rhode."

Throaty. Husky. Breathy.

Fuck, but I liked hearing her call my name like that. Sleepy and sweet.

"Morning, Sugar. Remy's awake. I'm gonna take him downstairs so you can snooze."

"Okay."

"But, baby, today we need to carve out some time for just me and you."

"Everything okay?" she mumbled.

Everything was fucking perfect. Everything but one thing.

"No."

Brooklyn shifted and rolled to her side, her blue eyes still groggy as she tried to focus.

"What's wrong?"

What was wrong was it had been over twenty-four hours since I'd had her heat pressed against my dick and my hand up her shirt while she groaned into my mouth.

"I made a promise to you the other day I've yet to fulfill. Need to do that soon, baby."

A ghost of a smile pulled at her lips and tugged at my heart.

I play this right, I'll get to see that smile every day.

"You did. I seem to remember you made several of them, actually."

Fuck, she was cute.

"Naptime?"

"I thought you said naps were boring."

I only had seconds before Remington would be done in the bathroom, and not wanting to be overheard, I leaned closer and found her ear.

"Brooklyn, Sugar, I know it's been a long time but I know you remember."

Her hand lifted and settled on my bare chest. Then featherlight, she skimmed her palm down over my ribs and back up until she traced the lavender rose. My muscles clenched as I fought for control, doing my best to remember Remy was in the bathroom, but my dick didn't care and that was extremely unfortunate.

"Huh," she mumbled. "I seem to have developed a case of amnesia. I think you're going to need to remind me."

Praying Remington wouldn't pop out of the bathroom—but if he did he wouldn't be able to see what was happening —I grabbed Brooklyn's wrist, moved her hand down, rested it on my hard-on, then covered her hand with mine.

"Remembering yet?"

Over my pants, she slid her hand up and down my erection.

"Mmm. Maybe," she purred on an upward glide. "I think I'm starting to remember." I gritted my teeth as her hand went to my waistband and slowly her fingertip pushed under the material. With a tight fist and long, slow strokes, and a sexy-as-fuck smile, she pumped my dick. "Oh, yeah, *now* I remember."

"That's good, baby. Then you'll also remember how much I love you on your hands and knees with a red ass."

"Haven't forgotten, honey."

I bet she hadn't. Never felt anything as good as Brooklyn's pussy convulsing around my dick every time I smacked her ass. Also, I never had a woman come so many times with just my cock taking her there.

"Naptime," I grunted. "That's first up. You on your knees taking my cock. We got time after that, you're riding me with your tits in my mouth and your hand between your legs."

"Is that a promise?"

It was a motherfucking vow.

"Naptime," I repeated.

"Naptime," she echoed and thankfully released her grip on my dick.

"Rest up, Sugar. I'll make breakfast."

"Kay."

Her hand slid out of my pants and she lifted her head off the pillow. Knowing what she was asking for I met her halfway and gave her what she wanted. Brooklyn's mouth opened, my tongue slid in, and I barely had the wherewithal to stop myself from taking the kiss deeper. The bathroom door opened and with one last taste, I lifted my head.

"Naptime," I whispered.

"Naptime."

"Ready, Dad?" Remy chirped, looking adorable in his little boy pjs.

"Almost. You good going down without me?"

"Yes!"

Christ, he was cute and loud.

"Go on, I'll be right there."

Remy shot across the room, flung the bedroom door open, and was gone.

With one more quick closed-mouth kiss, I rolled out of bed. Once I was on my feet I looked back and Brooklyn was up on her elbow, her eyes on my crotch.

"You seem to have a problem." She giggled and dipped her chin, indicating the tenting in my pants.

"I have a big fucking problem," I agreed and reached into my pants to adjust my now throbbing dick. "And you looking at it isn't helping."

"Oh, I'm sorry, is he shy? Should I look away?"

Sonofabitch. I should've fled. I should've taken my rock-hard dick out of the room but that was not what I did. I pounced. Before I could stop myself I was on top of Brooklyn. My hands went to her waist and my fingers pressed in until she squirmed under me and squealed in a fit of laughter.

"You think you're funny," I rapped out and kept tickling her. "Who's funny now?"

I came up on my knees straddling her hip, keeping her lower half immobile, and glided my hands up over the swells of her perky tits, then over until my fingers dug into her armpits.

"Stop," she wheezed. "Mercy. You win."

Brooklyn bucked her hips and twisted her torso, unsuccessfully attempting to dislodge my hands.

"I won? What's my prize, baby?"

"Anything you want."

"You sure you wanna give me anything I want?" I asked, not letting up.

"Anything!" she shouted through a laugh.

"Oh, Sugar, you have no idea what you're agreeing to."

I barely heard the sound of pounding little boy feet over Brooklyn's squeals and snorts. But I couldn't miss the "Yippy!" Remington shouted as he did a flying leap on the bed.

"Sneak attack!" he roared, negating the sneak in his attack as he landed on my back.

Before he could tighten his legs around my waist I dipped my shoulder and Remy landed on the bed with a bounce. I went after him with tickling fingers.

"I'm gonna pee," Brooklyn croaked.

Remington's high-pitched giggles mingled with Brooklyn's and that feeling of powerlessness came back full force. There in my bed listening to them laugh, watching them smile, both happy, my heart burst wide open and I fell a little deeper—powerless to stop it and liking that state.

"Who wants pancakes?" I asked.

"I do!" That was Remington and you guessed it—he shouted it at the top of his lungs.

I plucked Remy off the mattress, swung him up onto my shoulder, and shifted off the bed leaving Brooklyn lying tangled in the sheets. Hair tousled, face flushed, cheeks pink —not the first time I'd left her in bed looking like that, but the last time she'd looked that way it wasn't because she'd been laughing. It was from multiple orgasms and exertion.

Arguably this time was better—but just barely.

I was almost to the door with a squirming Remington when Brooklyn called my name and I glanced back to the bed.

"Problem solved." She smiled.

"Not even a little bit, Sugar."

"What problem, Dad?"

Brooklyn busted out laughing. I took a moment to enjoy the sight and the sound before I answered Remy.

"Breakfast, son."

"Why is breakfast a problem?"

"Because we haven't eaten it."

Holding my boy, I left the room with my woman laughing herself sick.

I was halfway down the stairs when Brooklyn's words from yesterday hit me.

This mountain is magic.

She was more right than I'd realized.

It was after pancake making which left the kitchen looking like a science experiment gone wrong. Flour dust covered the counter along with baking powder and sugar. Remy had smashed an egg when he'd tried to crack it. The goo mixed with the spilt flour, baking powder, and sugar on the counter. Batter had dripped onto the floor, on Remy's pjs, and again—all over the counter.

Brooklyn had wandered into the kitchen, smiled, shook her head at the mess, and promptly exited the war zone.

We sat and ate and I learned my boy didn't care what was put in front of him; he'd eat it. SpaghettiOs or pancakes smothered in syrup—the kid could eat. I also learned my son liked more than just fishing. He also loved comic book movies. His favorite was Captain America. His favorite color was green and he thought he should be allowed to eat popcorn every day. Remy was also easily distracted which worked in my favor when he once again asked me my nickname. Still not having come up with a good one, I changed the subject to his best friend Serafina and he was all too happy to tell me story after story about her.

He hadn't asked when we were going back to CDA, he hadn't asked about school, or his toys. Remy seemed perfectly happy being with me and his mom. I loved how chill he was—until bedtime that is. Then he was having no part of sleeping on his own.

Little cockblocker.

I was fairly certain calling my kid a cockblocker was frowned upon in a parenting handbook somewhere, but damn if it wasn't true. I was convinced he had a finely tuned radar that pinged every time I got close to Brooklyn. Twice he'd walked in on me kissing his mom and once I'd been copping a feel, which required skill and stealthy maneuvers to get my hand out of Brooklyn's shirt without him seeing.

I left Brooklyn and Remy in the living room playing checkers and went out to the back patio to check in with Wilson. It sucked because I didn't want to leave them alone but I also had to check in and give Wilson the bad news that the internet was so spotty up here I couldn't get a secured connection to run the searches he'd asked me for. And as much as I didn't want to leave the mountain I was wondering if new leads were found and if we should move locations.

The phone rang twice before Wilson picked up.

"I was just getting ready to call you."

"What's up?"

"Coupla things. Shep called." I figured by the tone of Wilson's voice I wasn't going to like what he had to say.

"Yeah?" I prompted when he didn't continue.

"Money that was set up for the reward is gone."

"What do you mean gone? Did Michael close the account?"

"Brother—"

"Where'd it go?"

"As far as Shep could track it, a bank in Canada."

My gaze shot to the huge floor-to-ceiling windows that

looked into the living room. The afternoon sun was already high in the sky and no longer casting rays onto the glass so I could see in. Remy and Brooklyn were both on their knees, elbows to the coffee table. Remy's face lit, with a big smile. I couldn't see Brooklyn's face but I would bet she was smiling at her boy. Bet she wouldn't be smiling when she found out the life savings she'd given to the Welshes to help with Kiki's reward was somewhere in Canada, not in the account Michael had set up with The Bank of Coeur d'Alene.

"Rhode, you there?"

"Please tell me Shep's got a lock on that money."

"Not yet. This morning the local PD got a warrant for the bank records. Wire transfer was a forgery. Michael Welsh has already been in to give his signature and affidavit. Shep'll find the money but it might take some time since his time is limited."

"Brooklyn doesn't have time, Wilson. All her money was tied up in that account."

There was silence, then, "I know you're not gonna like this, brother, but she gave that money for the reward obviously hoping not to get it back. So—"

"Yeah, Wilson, she *gave* her money to the fund. *Gave* it at a time when she was scared Kiki, who's essentially her sister, was missing. Since then that bitch has been found and Brooklyn's not feeling real sisterly toward her. But even if she was, she didn't put up her money to be *stolen*."

"I hear that. What I'm saying is, Brooklyn gave it thinking she wouldn't get it back, so obviously she's not hurting financially. And she *will* get it back. Shep's working on it. But that had to hit the back burner when an anonymous call came in about a shooting. Make and model of the car, where it could be found, and names. Guess where the call originated from?"

Fuck me.

"Canada."

"Bingo. Two suspects are in custody. Thomas Brady and Chet Brown. Guns found in Chet's house. Both are convicted felons, neither is supposed to be in possession of firearms. The PD's running ballistics right now to see if any of the bullets pulled out of your Jeep or from the house match one of the ARs. Once that's a match you'll be able to bring Brooklyn and Remington home."

Home.

Fuck.

"Not all that fired up taking my boy back to the scene of the crime when he's refusing to sleep anywhere but between me and Brooklyn," I told him. "But I need to come down the mountain. The internet up here's extra shitty this week and I've got searches to run."

"Use the safehouse, it's empty."

Shit. I hadn't thought about the house in Spokane Wilson had secured.

"You sure?"

"We're not using it. You'll have internet and if you need I can send Davis—"

"No," I rushed out, not wanting any company on the off chance we could get Remington into his bed.

"I hear that." Wilson chuckled. "Last order of business and I'll let you get back to your family."

Jesus.

Sock to the gut.

"Kiki and Lawrence."

"Kiki and Lawrence," he confirmed. "I think our best play is to have a sit-down with the fucker and lay it all out."

"Kiki'll be dead in less than twenty-four hours."

"Not if we bring in local PD. Detective named Brasco

said he'd sit in, officially put Kiki on the radar. She comes up missing, Lawrence is his prime suspect. He'll also remind him, the cops are watching the Horsemen. One fuck-up and the PD's ready to take 'em all down."

Fuck, that might work.

It also might not.

"Lawrence thinks he's got brass balls," I reminded Wilson. "Men like that are unpredictable. And men like Lawrence like a challenge. He might take her out just to fuck with this detective."

"Thought about that, but you're forgetting we got intel from the inside. Lawrence makes a move, we'll know before he has time to execute it and we'll cover Kiki. This is our best play."

Goddamn, but Wilson was right. Lawrence had to be neutralized, and with an ongoing DEA investigation, our hands were tied. Even if, and there was strong evidence suggesting we could dig up something on Lawrence to get him off the street and behind bars, we'd fuck the DEA's case.

But there was one problem with Wilson's line of thinking. "Kinda hard for the team to cover her from Arizona. So it'll be me covering Kiki's ass."

"Yeah, we'll talk about that, too, when you come down the mountain. Oh, and before I forget, Davis is on the verge of tying up and duct-taping Letty and I'm on the verge of shooting Davis if I have to hear him bitch about Letty one more time. Please, have your woman call her friend before there's bloodshed."

"Cell service sucks up here," I reminded him.

"Yet, you manage to get calls through."

My gaze went back to the windows and I saw Brooklyn walking Remington up the stairs.

Naptime.

Time to get off the phone.

"You got anything else for me?" I asked.

"You're not gonna have your woman call," Wilson correctly surmised.

"She can call her when we're down the mountain tonight."

"I'll get Davis to stock the house. It'll give him something to do besides argue with Letty."

"Hey, real quick, the Welshes doing okay?"

"Michael's pissed. Beyond angry-dad pissed. His daughter's fucked up with a dirty MC, his money's been stolen, his other daughter's hurt and mad, his wife is a mess, and he loves Brooklyn something fierce so he's pissed as fuck Kiki's shit has bled into her and Remington's life. So, no, they're not okay. But once we get Kiki clear of the Horsemen and the money back I reckon he'll go back to being a plain old angry dad and some of the violent tendencies he's feeling right now will subside."

Fuck, Brooklyn had to call Letty.

I'd update her on everything after naptime.

"I'll call you when we're on our way down."

"Talk then."

Wilson disconnected but I didn't move.

I stayed where I was and cast my gaze on the mountains in the distance. Nothing but beauty as far as the eye could see. A different kind of beauty than Arizona had to offer. I couldn't say I'd miss the sweltering Scottsdale heat, but neither was I looking forward to cold, snowy winters. What I was looking forward to was spending the snowy days taking Remy sledding and those cold nights bundled up with Brooklyn.

But while the weather was still nice we'd have more time on the lake. More time playing ball.

We needed a house, and soon. Remington and Brooklyn weren't going back to her old place.

I wasn't worried about a job; that wouldn't be hard. Before I went to work with Takeback I'd kept myself busy as an investigator. Easy work, mostly boring, and totally unrewarding. But I'd have my family.

On that thought, I wondered what the hell I was doing staring at scenery I'd stared at a hundred times before when I had a beautiful woman to take care of.

And hopefully a sleeping son.

23

"Rhode," I gasped.

"Give it."

The vibration of his growl against my clit shot through me and my head fell forward.

Rhode was on his back on the bed in the guest bedroom, my knees on the mattress on either side of his head, my hands on the headboard, and he was eating me.

I knew what he wanted me to give. I just didn't want to.

"More," I begged.

His hands on the back of my thighs tightened and he pulled me down, spearing me with his tongue.

No. I had no choice to give him what he wanted. He was taking it and I couldn't stop the rush of pleasure as my climax washed over me. I tried to pull up but Rhode was of a different mind and held me where he wanted. He stopped fucking me with his tongue and I breathed a sigh of relief. But that was short-lived when his teeth grazed my sensitive clit right before he drew it in his mouth and sucked.

"Too much."

He sucked harder.

"Rhode."

His mouth released and I groaned at the reprieve.

"Don't move."

I didn't move but I shivered at the sex-induced rumble of his voice.

I felt him slide out from underneath me, then I felt a hand on my back glide up my spine gathering my hair as it went. There was more movement behind me, none of which was worth my attention now that Rhode had a fistful of my hair, using it to turn my head. With his big, powerful frame curled over me, his mouth crashed onto mine. But instead of the kiss being wild it was slow. It was also the first time he'd kissed me on the lips since he pulled me into the room, ordered me to take off my clothes, and pulled his off. Oh, he'd kissed me other places. My neck, shoulders, chest, breasts, stomach, thighs. And that was before he'd put me on my knees and kissed me between my legs, though that had quickly turned into other things that required the use of his tongue and lips but it couldn't be described as kissing. He devoured me; he liked what he was doing and it showed by ending spectacularly.

Rhode was good with his mouth; wherever he used it he excelled. But his slow, drugging, languid kisses were my favorite. With every stroke of his tongue he tasted, he savored, he controlled and cherished. I was so lost in the kiss I jolted when I felt the broad head of his dick slip inside me. Slow, so slow like he had all the time in the world and he was determined to use it. He pushed in.

Inch by inch.

God.

Lazy. Gentle. Unhurried.

That was what Rhode was giving me with his mouth and his cock. After our fevered start, he was giving me this.

Sweet. Achingly sweet. Beautiful. So damn beautiful my heart swelled.

My whole body quivered as he sank all the way inside. Fully connected. His chest pressed to my back, our mouths fused, his cock deep.

Slow ins and outs, his tongue matched the pace, driving me crazy for more. This lasted until I groaned and Rhode's hand went from my hip around to my stomach before he dipped lower and cupped my sex.

The kiss broke but not our connection. Rhode stayed bent, his face in my neck, his breath gliding over my heated skin when he said, "Fuck, you feel good."

"I was thinking the same about you."

His hand between my legs started moving and I knew he was feeling himself as he glided out of me.

"Feels like a lifetime," he whispered. "Dreamed of this, wanted it so fucking bad and I could never figure out why. Now I remember."

"What do you remember?" I moaned.

"Never forgot the feel of you wrapped around me. Never forgot what you tasted like. Never forgot the look on your face when I was giving you something you liked. Never forgot your beautiful eyes or your body. I wanted all of that back, I wanted *you* back." Rhode slid out and I pushed back, wanting more. "But I forgot why. Forgot the way you make *me* feel."

I wanted to know how I made him feel but my body's need won out when he drove in hard and my pussy spasmed.

"Tip your ass up, Sugar."

I tipped and his fingers worked their way up to my clit. With no warning, no gentle lead-in, Rhode went to work— hard and fast he rubbed, slow and deep he stroked his cock through my wet until I was panting on the edge of orgasm.

"Christ, that pussy," he groaned, bringing me closer.

"Harder."

"Wanna watch you when you come, Sugar."

"Okay."

He could watch all he wanted if he didn't stop.

But he did stop. He pulled out, I lost his hand, then his warmth when he straightened, then all of him when he moved to the bed beside me.

He patted my hip and ordered, "Get on."

Though Rhode's directions were clear he didn't wait for me to comply; his hands went to my hips and he lifted me up and shifted his body under mine. I would've been impressed he could pull that off if he hadn't continued to prove he had some seriously good moves and perfect aim when he slammed me down on his cock.

"Jesus," he gritted out.

I on the other hand couldn't speak because I was breathless. I couldn't even groan as all the air left my lungs and the orgasm I thought I'd lost sparked back to life.

"Ride, baby."

I could do that so I rocked forward and ground down, but that was as far as I got before Rhode's hand between my shoulder blades kept me still and his head lifted off the pillow and his tongue circled one nipple before it moved to the other. With a minimum amount of space to move since he was holding me where he wanted me, I lifted up the few inches I could and slid back down.

"More'a that, Sugar. If you need your hand, use it."

"I don't," I mewed, telling the truth.

I was so close, a few more strokes and I'd be done.

"Eyes on me when you come."

I lowered my gaze. His dark brown eyes tipped up, I watched him draw my nipple into his mouth, and I couldn't hold back. I'd waited five long years to have him. I'd known from the start who Rhode was. Not his name, not what he did for a living, not where he lived, but I knew he was meant to be mine. I knew I was born to be his. I was so certain I ran scared so I wouldn't know the pain of losing him. Which meant I lost him. It made no sense. I let my fear blind me.

But not this time.

This time, I was holding on.

I wasn't going to ever let go.

With my thighs as tight as I could get them against his hips and my hands on his chest for leverage, I let go. No thoughts, no worries. Just me and him and everything he was making me feel. It was better than perfect. Better than my dream. Way better than my memories.

"Come with me, Brooklyn," he grunted and thrust up.

Try as I might to focus, he was hazy. Try as I might to concentrate on how he looked as his cock pulsed inside of me, I couldn't. I was a ball of nerves and they were unraveling, every part of me sensitized. And when it finally broke, my muscles seized, my back arched, and my mouth opened in a silent scream. Pleasure was still rippling through me when Rhode flipped us over, his mouth came down on mine, and I moaned my orgasm down his throat. This was good, because he repaid the favor and he tasted phenomenal.

But I'd bet mine was better.

It must have been minutes later when Rhode broke the kiss and my eyes opened. It took a few moments before my vision cleared. And when it did I found Rhode smiling down at me.

"God, you're handsome."

His smile widened and I didn't give one single shit I'd blurted that out. Hell, if he smiled at me like that every time I said that I'd tell him fifty times a day.

"Ocean blue," he whispered and my body locked.

He'd said that before.

Right before I walked out the hotel room door.

"What?" I wheezed.

"Never seen more beautiful eyes. The color of the ocean —clear, blue, warm, and welcoming. They haunted my dreams," Rhode finished on a whisper.

Like it was a confession.

And I didn't understand.

"What'd you mean when you said you forgot the way I made you feel?"

"All these years I was thinking about you and how good you felt in my arms and I didn't remember *why* it felt so good. How *I* felt when I was holding you."

"How did you feel?"

"Invincible. At peace. Home. Like I was where I was supposed to be. Like I was yours."

I sucked in a breath and I watched his eyes warm.

"As smart as I think I am I can be pretty damn stupid. I just didn't understand what I was feeling until I watched you walk away and I knew it was wrong. Everything about letting you leave was all kinds of dumb. I regretted closing the door. I regretted getting dressed that morning and leaving the hotel. I need you to get that. This is about Remington but it's also not. I had feelings for *you* first. I started falling in love with you without knowing I was doing it. I regretted you walking away long before I knew about Remy. And when I saw you again, I made the decision not to let you go and that was before I knew about him. He's not the reason I'm staying, he's the icing." Rhode stopped. With his forehead scrunched and his brows pulled tight he said, "Though that's the last we talk about my boy while I'm still hard inside of you."

Rhode looked positively horrified and there was something so cute, so funny seeing his forehead furrowed that way I couldn't stop the laughter that bubbled up. I also couldn't stop all the hope I'd kept bottled up from bursting free.

I was so right.

"Now before I get up so can I toss this condom and get you cleaned up I wanna hear about your new tats. I saw them earlier but I was too distracted to ask what they meant."

He hadn't been too distracted to trace them with his tongue.

"The orchids are for you—rare beauty and strength." Rhode's body went solid above me and I quickly rushed out, "The ancient Greeks believe orchids are a sign of virility and masculinity."

"And the red tulip?" he asked, his voice unusually gruff.

"It's for Remington. It means perfect love."

"And the numbers? One-one-zero." Still his voice was a little hoarse with a sharp edge to it and I was worried he thought it was weird I'd tattooed flowers along my ribs in almost the same spot he had. Only, mine curled around to my back whereas his slanted to the front and ended on his chest.

"Room one-ten," I whispered.

And if it was possible, Rhode stiffened more and I felt the muscles under my palms twitch right before he dropped his head and muttered, "Fuck."

There was a beat of silence then, "Fucking Goddammit. Fucked up so bad letting you walk away. Five fucking years we lost because I was too goddamn weak to ask you to stay. Too fucking scared at the enormity of what I was feeling. All this time, so close. Total fucking waste."

"Maybe we needed—"

Rhode's head shot up. Fire was dancing behind his brown eyes, his big body still hard and pinning me to the bed. What came next burned my soul.

"Don't, Sugar. It was a fucking waste and you know it. You admitted it, you knew. You felt it same as me. You told me you were in deep and asked me to have a mind to that. And that started five fucking years ago and not a day since then has that feeling gone away. Not for you, not for me. I told you; I see you in my dreams, those blue eyes haunting me, begging me not to let you leave. We could've—"

"Stop, honey. You're right; it was a waste. But you know what would be a bigger waste? No, not a waste, a travesty. If we let those five years eat at us. Look where we are, Rhode. We're here, together. We're not wasting any more time. As a matter of fact, we're on the super-speed-highway. Stay on that path with me. The rest of the years, we can't get them back. They're gone but look what's in front of us." I stopped to draw in a breath and with it the courage to finish. "I want this, Rhode. I've waited so long for you, honey. So, so long. Please give this to me. Please don't look back with guilt and regret. That night, for six hours in that room I had you, all of you. You teased me, you laughed with me, you made me feel more beautiful than I'd ever felt."

"Jesus."

I was looking up at him while he was looking down at me and there was still fire burning in his eyes, only now it held more warmth than I'd ever seen.

Then I lost sight of his beautiful eyes.

But I wasn't complaining at the loss because what I gained was his lips on mine.

He gave me more when he whispered "mine" right before he kissed me.

That sent a thrill racing over me.

I was his.

24

We were dressed—*unfortunately*. Cleaned up—*again, unfortunately*. And back in bed. This was good seeing as Brooklyn was on her side with her head resting on my chest, hand resting on my heart, and her leg thrown over my thighs—though not as good as it would've been if Brooklyn still had been naked. But I didn't need my boy waking up to find Daddy naked with Mommy, hence the unfortunate necessity of clothes.

This wasn't the first time I'd felt Brooklyn cuddled close. The first time, she'd been naked with her perky tits pressed to my chest so I could see how I'd missed it then. I wasn't missing it now. Not the way she snuggled deep, seeking closeness. Not where she'd placed her hand, not the way she'd flattened her palm and sought out my heartbeat. And I didn't miss her sigh when my arm closed around her, pinning her body to mine.

Yes, I'd been a dumbfuck because if I'd been paying attention she would have given all of this to me five years ago.

With a great deal of effort, I pushed those thoughts from

my mind. I had a lot to tell her and I wanted it hashed out before Remy woke up.

"I talked to Wilson. Good news is, two suspects are in custody for the shooting."

"Really?"

"He's waiting on a ballistics match, then we can go down the mountain."

Brooklyn went stiff and her fingertips pressed deeper over my heart.

"Hey," I called and waited until her eyes tipped up. "No way in fuck I'd take us down the mountain if I didn't know it was safe."

Brooklyn nodded, unconvinced.

"Wilson's set a meet with Trevor Lawrence. A detective's agreed to go. A show of protection for Kiki. Lawrence will know that truth but it will be made clear Kiki's off-limits. I need to be at that meet."

"Why?"

"Because I need to make sure Lawrence is crystal clear what happens if he fucks with you or Remington."

"You're gonna threaten him in front of a detective?"

I was going to do more than that.

"I'm gonna put the fear of God in him. He's gonna know exactly what happens if he chooses to be a dumbfuck and fuck with my family. By the time the meet's over, he'll see it clear and he'll forget you and Remy exist."

"And Kiki?"

I gritted my teeth in an effort not to say what I wanted to say. Something about Brooklyn I'd learned was that she saw the good in people. She saw what she wanted to see and not what they showed her. Kiki was a selfish, envious, nasty bitch. It was plain to see and from what I'd heard from Letty and her parents they all knew it. That wasn't to say Michael and Tallulah didn't love their daughter. They did. They'd said it themselves—they'd tried for years to save Kiki from her bad choices. Letty sounded like she was plain fed up, which was understandable. But not Brooklyn, it was like she had to believe there was good in Kiki, something to be redeemed.

"I say this cautiously, but, Sugar, not everyone gets a happy ending."

"What?" she breathed and looked up at me with big eyes.

"We're taking precautions to ensure her safety. Part of what I'm going to explain to Lawrence is Kiki's to walk away from the Horsemen physically unharmed. But, Brooklyn, Kiki made a series of bad choices. And from what I've heard they didn't start when she hooked up with Lawrence. They started when she was a kid. I get that you love the Welshes. I understand you want to believe there's some good in Kiki but sometimes there's not. Not everyone sees the error of their ways. And I want you prepared for that."

"I'm not stupid," she mumbled.

"Never thought you were, baby."

With a long-suffering sigh, Brooklyn settled back and nuzzled closer.

"I know who she is. I know all the bad shit she did to Letty and what she put her parents through. But I also saw her act apologetic and loving. When she wasn't being a brat she could be sweet. She'd make up these cute songs when we were kids and sing for me and Letty. She could be funny when she forgot to be jealous. I admit those times were few and far between but they happened. That's what I can't let go of. Not for Kiki, but for Michael, Tally, and Letty. I want them to have the Kiki I saw in those rare moments. And I know what she said about Remington and it hurt so bad to hear her say it, not only because Remy's my son but because after Remy was born, Kiki would light up when she saw him. It was like she was a different person. These last couple of years the only person Kiki's been nice to is Remington. I never would've allowed her around him if she wasn't."

I didn't want to think about that bitch around my son and I didn't give the first fuck if Kiki liked spending time with Remy, that shit was done.

"Love that about you, baby. The way you see the good in people. So it gives me no pleasure to remind you that this might not end with Kiki going home and patching shit up with her parents. She's likely going to be pissed and she's got a history of blaming other people for her mistakes. I want you prepared for that."

"It'll be my fault just like everything else. For Kiki it all boils down to me and what I took from her."

"Sugar—"

"Logically I know I did nothing wrong. But Kiki's right about one thing. It's always been me and Letty. Best friends since we were in diapers. Kiki didn't have all of her sister's attention because I had it. We tried to include her but she's younger than us; by the time we were teenagers we didn't want her tagging along. Maybe we shouldn't have left her out so much."

Fuck no.

"How about this for an alternate scenario; maybe Kiki should've found friends her own age. Maybe Kiki should-n't've been a nasty bitch and she would've been included. You and Letty weren't leaving her out; you were escaping her. You and Letty did nothing wrong. And Michael and Tallulah did everything a parent could do to help their daughter. Kiki chose this. Kiki decided how she behaved. Kiki is still making shitty life choices and she alone is going to have to take responsibility. Not the Welshes. Not Letty. And certainly not you."

That was met with silence, which I hoped meant Brooklyn was thinking about what I'd said. Unfortunately, we had other shit to discuss so I got on with it.

"Two more things," I carried on. "First up is, we're not going back to your place. We're going to a safehouse until we can sort our living situation. We'll come up here whenever we got time, let Remy get used to this place being his. Give me and you our time up here. I like that you get this cabin means something to me but I hope you understand this mountain means something different now. This is *us*. This is where you gave me you. This is where you gave me my son. This is where I became a dad. I want time up here— the three of us, family, bonding, memories. But we need to find a place in CDA to live. I don't want you and Remy going back to your place. Warning, Sugar, you wanna go back there I'm gonna spend a good amount of time talking you out of it. And I'm not gonna let up until I dissuade you from sleeping in a house where you and Remy experienced a trauma."

"I don't want to go back to my place," she admitted.

Thank fuck.

No arguments there, which was good because the next topic was going to piss Brooklyn off and my solution to that problem was going to piss her off more.

"We gotta talk about the reward money you gave Michael," I started, and just as I thought, Brooklyn's shoulders tightened and she started to roll away. "No, baby, just listen. First, you gotta know we've got resources and Wilson deployed the best we got to resolve this situation."

"What situation?"

"Michael's name was forged on a wire transfer. The

money was moved out of the account to a bank in Canada. We'll get the money back but it might take some time."

Brooklyn's whole body sagged right before it bucked and a hiccupped sob echoed in the room.

"How much more?" she whimpered.

"What, Sugar?"

"How much more do they need to go through? This isn't fair. They're good people. The best. How much more shit do they have to go through?"

Of course, she was talking about the Welshes. That was pure Brooklyn, worrying about those she loved before herself. She wasn't crying because she'd lost her life savings; she was crying because Michael and Tallulah had more shit piled on them.

And I didn't have the heart to tell her that life wasn't fair, that all too often bad shit happened to good people.

"The money was moved to a bank, Brooklyn. They left a trail that will be easy to follow and we'll get the money back. It's just gonna take time. In the meantime, you and Remy are covered."

"Covered?"

"Four years you've been going at this alone. I owe you—"

With a mighty heave, Brooklyn pushed off my chest and sat up.

"You don't owe me shit," she spat. "I told you I didn't want your money."

I took in her frown and her squinty eyes and read what they said but unfortunately didn't take the time to contemplate her reaction before I went on.

"You might not want it but that doesn't mean it's not yours. And at this juncture, sucks, Brooklyn, but you're gonna need it."

Wrong thing to say.

Brooklyn scrambled off the bed, blue fire blazing from her eyes. If that hadn't clued me in to just how pissed she was, when her hands went to her hips and she leaned in deep, bending at the waist, giving me the woman's universal sign that her man's an idiot—*that* was a clear indication.

"I don't need shit. We've been doing just fine without you, Rhode. I have a job, it pays well, and Remy's never gone without. So, no, I don't *need* your money."

No, *that* was the wrong thing to say.

I clenched my jaw trying to keep the anger burning in my gut from exploding all over the room. To keep the anguish at the reminder she and my son had been fine without me from igniting. And to prevent all the bitterness I'd been ignoring from detonating.

"Don't need the reminder, Brooklyn." I tossed my legs over the bed and stood. And instead of taking a moment to compose myself, I faced the mother of my child and the bomb ignited. "Trust me, baby, not a second's gone by that I don't remember you and Remington didn't *need* me. You and my boy living your lives happy and content. The two of you building a life, you giving my boy good. *Without me*. Now here I am wondering how I can fit myself into the family you've given him. My son sharing wisdom with me that another man taught him. My son sharing with me stories about his life that don't include me. Four goddamn years, Brooklyn. Four. I missed those. *Me*. Not you. Not Michael or Tallulah or Letty. Me. So while I'm remembering all that I missed I haven't forgotten all that you don't need from me because, baby, they go hand in hand. You wanna take more from me, I can't stop you. You wanna throw the one fucking thing I can give you to make up for missing out on those years, I can't stop that either. And it fucking kills I can't get those years back. I can't make it up to my son in any real, meaningful way because those years are gone. They're lost to me."

"You don't get it," Brooklyn whispered.

I couldn't miss the hurt in her voice. But with fury still burning through me I ignored what I heard and carried on.

"No, Brooklyn. It's you who doesn't get it."

And with that, I rounded the bed and left.

It wasn't until I was standing out back looking over the majesty of the mountains did the guilt start to gnaw.

Fuck.

"Fuck," I grunted into the warm breeze.

Unable to look at the beauty around me, I dropped my head and focused on my feet. My bare feet. Which led me to remember why I wasn't wearing my boots. How not even thirty minutes ago I'd reconnected with Brooklyn. How all the emotions I'd buried had rushed to the surface. How I finally remembered why I couldn't forget her. Now I was standing alone, contemplating my bare feet, wondering if I would ever be able to get past losing what I'd lost.

25

And the pendulum swings.

That was what I was thinking as Rhode drove us down the mountain.

In the two hours since our blow-up, I'd given Rhode a wide berth. Which hadn't been difficult since Remy had woken up not long after Rhode had stormed out of the room. Then he'd spent time on the back patio, one of the two places on the mountain there was cell reception.

Leaving Rhode to his call I took Remy out front to keep him occupied. And if I was being honest with myself— which I didn't want to be because I was supremely pissed— it hurt to see Rhode. Even the back of him while he stood with his phone up to his ear. Physically he was there, so close, just on the other side of a wall of windows. Emotionally, he'd put miles between us, and since I was hurt I put up my defenses and added to the distance. Then I'd put more physical distance between us and took Remy out front to play so I wouldn't have to see him. That had lasted all of five minutes before Rhode prowled out the front door. His eyes came to mine and sheer panic shone. Then his gaze went to Remington and he relaxed.

What'd he think, that I'd take Remy and run down the mountain? I didn't ask, but then his panic said it all. And that further pissed me off that he thought I was that kind of woman. Something else we needed to address because if he thought I was capable of sneaking out the door and taking Remington away from him I was going to punch him in his throat.

That led to more anger on my part. Onward from that—hurt. Which meant our last few hours at the cabin were uncomfortable for me. But not for Remington. Rhode acted no differently toward his boy. He was the same patient, loving, attention-giving dad he'd been. And that irked me as much as I was relieved. Totally irrational and I knew it. But my emotions were all over the place. I'd gone from the highest of highs lying next to Rhode after finally having him again to being slapped in the face with all the ugliness Rhode was bottling up. Guilt I wasn't sure he'd be able to let go of.

The mindfuck of it was, he was right; I hadn't missed a single day of my son's life and I felt no remorse about this. I did feel horrible Rhode had missed those years but I couldn't change that. Neither could he. And I was being stubborn about the money and I knew it. But I didn't want Rhode to think I wanted him in our lives because I needed him. It was important to me that he knew I *wanted* him in our lives. Wanted, not needed. It was important to me that he knew I could provide for Remington, that I'd worked hard, I'd given his son a good life.

"Dad?" Remy called from the back seat and my heart lurched as it did every time I heard my son call Rhode Dad.

"Yeah?"

"What's your nickname?"

"Did we decide what yours is gonna be? Popsicle or Bulldog?"

"Bulldog," Remy huffed.

"Then Bulldog it is. Have you ever thought about what you'd name your bulldog?"

Interesting. Rhode was changing the subject again.

"Hector."

"Hector?" Rhode laughed.

God, he had a beautiful laugh.

"Hector protects Tweety Bird from Sylvester."

"Right. Looney Tunes. What other kinds of dogs do you like?"

And the topic was successfully changed as Remy blathered on about all of the dog breeds he knew.

In all the Kiki drama, drive-by shooting drama, finding Remy's long-lost dad drama I realized there hadn't been much getting-to-know-you conversation. He'd started but never finished telling me what he did in the military and he never fully explained what Takeback did. He didn't talk about or tell me about his friends. I knew his parents were currently traveling but I didn't know where or how he grew up or if he went to college. No, scratch that, I did know he didn't go to college because I'd learned that five years ago. When we were whispering secrets in the dark.

"Where'd you go to college?" I asked.

"Didn't. You?"

"ASU."

"How old are you?" he volleyed.

"Thirty. You?"

"Thirty-three. Best childhood memory?"

"Easy, any time spent with my mom and dad." I tamped down the pain of loss and continued our game. "Yours?"

"Being on the back of my dad's Harley." He said that with sadness. *"Worst memory."*

My parents dying, but I didn't say that out loud.

"Pass. Yours?"

It was unfair of me to ask him when I wouldn't tell him mine and I figured he'd pass as well but to my shock, he answered.

"Watching my dad leave on some wild adventure, leaving me and my mom behind. He'd say 'the road's callin', gotta chase the wind.' What he meant was, he was leaving his family for sometimes months. My mom would shrug it off and tell me she knew the man she married wasn't a man you tied down and wave him out the door. I guess that life worked for them, they're still married. But for me, watching him leave us knowing we weren't important enough to make him want to stay was a gut punch. The fuck of it was, he was a good dad when he was home. But the truth is, he was also a shit dad. A part-time dad who smothered me when he was around to try to make up for when he was gone."

That memory morphed into a recent one.

Straight up, I'm gonna be in Remington's life. I want him to know me. I want to be his dad—not part-time, not a once-a-month dad, not a holiday-dad.

Then another.

I'm not gonna be a part-time dad. I'm also not going to take a boy away from his mom and family. I'm gonna stay in Idaho and be present in his life and in yours.

Part-time.

Make him stay.

The guilt.

"Sugar?"

I jolted and slowly turned to look at Rhode.

So much becoming clearer.

"What?"

"You okay?"

"Yeah."

Lie. I wasn't okay. But with Remington in the back of the car, now was not the time to address what was burning a hole in my heart.

"Dad, do I still need a booster seat?"

"Yes," Rhode and I said in unison.

"But I'm not in one now," he proudly declared.

"Extenuating circumstances," Rhode returned.

"I don't know what that means."

"Special occasion," Rhode clarified.

"Will you teach me to be a soldier, Dad?"

And there was further proof Remington had the attention span of a gnat.

"Yep."

"Will you teach me how to paint my face and sneak up on bad guys?"

"Yep."

Great. Just what every mother wanted—her four-year-old learning how to be sneak*ier* and the *er* was important because Remy could be as quiet as a church mouse when sneaking an ice pop.

"Favorite dessert?" he asked.

"Slurpee. You?"

"Mint chip ice cream. Beach or mountains?" he went on.

"Mountains, I hate the sand. You?"

"Same. Oral or shower sex?"

I stopped looking at his muscled stomach and cast my eyes up and saw his were already aimed down. There was just enough light in the dimly lit room to see his dark brown irises. But I didn't miss his beautiful smile.

"Oral."

"Good answer. Want your mouth around my cock while I eat you."

I shivered. He smiled.

"Hurry, Sugar. I'm hungry."

Sugar.

He'd called me Sugar then, too.

At the time I figured it was a necessity since he didn't know my name. Just a throwaway endearment he called the women he took to his bed.

"Why are you in D.C.?" I asked.

"Work. You?"

"Same."

"Do you live within a hundred miles of here?" I inquired.

"Nope. You?"

"No."

"Scary movies or comedy?" he asked.

"Comedy. You?"

"Same."

"Really? I'd take you for a scary movie or action man," I told him.

"Action man, huh?" His hand left my hip where he'd been slowly grazing my skin with his fingertips. He wrapped them around my wrist and pulled my palm off his heart. I didn't move my head off his chest but I watched as he moved our hands down and shoved them under the sheet resting below the last row of his muscled abs. "You all rested up, Sugar?"

"Again?" I smiled against his warm skin as he placed my hand on his hardening dick. I tipped my chin to see the sheet jostling over his lap as he stroked himself using my hand under his.

"Sweetest pussy I've ever tasted. Best head I've gotten. Nicest ass, tightest cunt. Baby, if all that I have is tonight, I'm not wasting a second of it. So, hell yeah, again. That is if you're up for it."

I was up for forever. But I wouldn't tell him that.

"If you think you got it in you for another round, I'm game."

I tightened my fist and he groaned.

Then I wasn't on my side cuddled close to a stranger who no longer felt like he was a stranger. I was on my back, he was between my legs, and the sound of foil tearing had me smiling.

Only something was different. His eyes were soft and he was smiling back. That wasn't the weird or different part; he'd smiled a lot. He'd given me plenty of sweet, soft looks. It was the way he entered me. Slow. Gentle. Like he wanted me to feel every inch of him as he came inside. But it didn't stop there—his strokes were deep and powerful but they weren't pounding.

He made love to me.

With one hand tangled in my hair, the other gripping the back of my thigh even though my legs were wrapped around him —he was holding me close. And he did all of this with our eyes locked.

He made love to me.

The revelation was so startling I jolted in the seat.

"Brooklyn," Rhode growled. "Now you're freaking me out, Sugar. What's wrong?"

"Nothing," I squeaked out.

I hadn't lied, I remembered everything about that night. But I'd never closely examined the hours we'd spent together. I remembered them. I'd thought about them. I even scrutinized how easily I'd given him my heart. But never, not one time, did I think he'd given me his.

He made *love* to me.

The last time we were together was not hurried and frantic, and not just because there had been four times before that, not including the times he'd gone down on me. He'd been generous with orgasms—seriously generous.

I knew why I'd blocked that out, that last time. It made

the scene at the door when we were saying goodbye all that more painful to remember.

God, I'd been such a coward.

So damn stupid.

"You jumping in your seat isn't nothing, Brooklyn."

"Sorry. I was just thinking."

"About?"

"You."

"And that made you jump in your seat and snap your seat belt?"

"I was remembering something you told me about your dad."

I wasn't sure this was the best time to have this conversation but I also knew that we'd procrastinated enough. If I didn't tell him now what I remembered the phone could ring with a new drama. So it was now.

"My dad?"

His voice sounded funny, like it had years ago when he'd told me his worst memory.

"You told me your best memory was being on the back of your dad's Harley."

The air around me turned stale and my skin started tingling.

"Cool. Your dad has a Harley?" Remy rambled from behind me.

"He does," Rhode confirmed, his voice still gruff and not right.

And it was the gruffness and waves of unfriendly energy rolling off of Rhode that made me lose my nerve to go on. I didn't even have the courage to look at him. So I kept my gaze averted, clamped my mouth shut, and watched the nothingness of trees pass by.

It happened a few minutes after I'd fallen quiet. The

unfriendliness turned into hostility when Rhode broke the silence.

"And my worst memory."

He let that hang in the air.

Though that said it all because he knew if I was thinking about his best, I was also thinking about his worst.

"And yours," he went on. "Your parents dying."

I sucked in a breath as the sadness tore through me.

"Yes."

"I never told anyone what he did."

I assumed he was talking about his father taking off for sometimes months to chase the wind. Whatever the hell that meant.

"He's still living his life for his next adventure. Only now, he at least takes his wife."

Translation: he still leaves me.

So much was becoming clearer.

"It's not the same, Rhode. Not even close."

"It's not?" he snarled.

"No, honey, it's not. You didn't have a choice. He did and he still does. There's a big difference."

The heaviness lingered and the quiet was damn near suffocating. Not even Remington uttered a peep as Rhode drove.

I was lost in my head wondering what in the world I was thinking bringing up a topic that I knew wasn't pleasant in front of Remy when Rhode's hand picked up mine off my lap. He brought our combined hands up to his mouth, kissed my palm, then rested them on his thigh.

"I shouldn't've snapped at you," Rhode started. I glanced back and saw Remy's eyes were closed and his head lulled to the side in that way only a kid could sleep without waking up with severe neck pain. "He fell out about ten minutes ago."

"I should've waited or maybe not brought it up at all."

"No, Brooklyn, you should never hold back asking or telling me something. But I was talking more about up at the cabin. I shouldn't've lost it."

"Back atcha, Rhode. I need to trust that when something's heavy on your mind, you'll tell me. And you need to trust me enough to tell me."

There was a stretch of silence—not comfortable but not uncomfortable. I just didn't feel the need to fill it.

"I don't want you to think I'm staying because I got issues with my dad."

"But you do have issues with your dad."

"How can I not? He was great when he was around but he had no problem taking off whenever the spirit moved him. My mom's been making excuses for his behavior for as long as I can remember. And maybe, she truly didn't mind her husband taking off, but not once did either of them ask me how I felt about it. And neither cared when I left to join the Navy. It was like I lived in their house, they provided everything I needed, but we weren't a family, we just lived together. And when I left, they packed up and hit the road. I feel no connection to them. Months pass with no communication and I don't feel the loss. Years go by and I don't see them and I don't long for a visit. That's screwed up. But what's more, I didn't have a bad childhood. Really, I had it better than most. So I've got nothing to complain about, yet here I am approaching forty wondering why my dad didn't love me enough to stay home. You know something else that's screwed up? I found out I had a son and reaching out to my parents to tell them they had a grandchild was an afterthought. My first call wasn't to them to share my happy news. My first thought wasn't that I couldn't wait for them to meet Remington. It was a passing thought that I should email. And I never want to be a passing thought to my son. I want to be his first call when he has good news. I want to be in the forefront of my son's mind."

My son sharing wisdom with me that another man taught him.

Shattered.

Horrified.

Crushed.

That was what I felt hearing Rhode tell me about his parents. It was also what I felt when I realized how badly I'd screwed up.

"I asked you to be careful with my heart and I'm seeing I haven't been careful with yours and I'm sorry. I was so hell-bent on showing you what I thought I wanted you to know I didn't think about what I was saying and how that might make you feel. I didn't want you to think I wanted you around for money."

"Brook—"

"Please, honey, listen for a second. It's important to me that you know that I've wanted you in my life—in Remy's life—not because I needed your financial support. But it came across as us not needing you at all and that's not the truth.

"I've needed you since the day I saw the plus sign on the pregnancy test. I needed you when I was craving mac and cheese but I was too tired to get out of bed to make it. I needed you when I was so scared of being a single mom I balled up on my bed and cried. I needed you badly when I was in labor and in pain and depressed because you weren't there. And I love Letty but part of me was so mad she was there holding my hand because you weren't. I've needed you every second of every day and so has Remington. But in all those times I needed you and didn't have you, I learned how strong I was. I learned to be a good mom. I did the best I could."

I stopped to take a breath then rushed out the rest of what he needed to know.

"You said something about making up for the lost time in a meaningful way. Honey, you're not seeing it but just you being here is meaningful."

"Brooklyn," he rasped.

"And you fit into our lives because you're the missing piece we've been waiting for."

"Baby, please stop talking."

"Rhode—"

"I'm begging you. Right now, while I'm driving and the two most important people are in the car with me, please, baby, give me this and stop talking."

"Okay," I stammered, not understanding.

"I lied to you," he rapped out and my body stilled.

"What?"

"I told you I was falling in love with you. But that's a lie, Brooklyn. And I think since you were thinking back on the night we shared you know exactly when it stopped being one thing and turned into something else."

"I remember," I confirmed on a whisper.

Rhode picked up my hand, kissed my palm, and settled our hands back on his lap. I didn't feel his lips touch my skin, though I knew they had. I was too busy trying not to hyperventilate.

"Now, I'm seeing we did a few things right that night."

We did a lot of things right that night including making Remington. But I didn't say that.

"What'd we do right?"

"Chicken or steak?"

I felt my lips curve into a smile and scooted in my seat so I could face him.

"Steak. You?"

"Same. Football or baseball?"

"Neither. You?"

"Both."

I internally sighed, hoping I wasn't in for a lifetime of sports on the television. Then I wondered if I'd give a shit a game was on the TV if it meant he and Remy were planted on the couch together watching. I found I didn't give a shit.

"The Navy?" I prompted.

"Did twelve years, ten of those as a SEAL. When I met you I'd been out a few years and was living in Virginia. I was pretty much aimless, working as an investigator mostly for law firms. It was boring as shit but it paid well and kept me busy. I was working on something that brought me to D.C. and I ran into Wilson. He was working at Homeland then but getting ready to make a move. He needed men for an off-the-books taskforce that would work with the feds on human trafficking cases. He asked if I was interested and I jumped on that."

A SEAL.

I couldn't stop the bubble of laughter from bursting from my chest.

"What's funny?"

"Let me tell you a little story about this time when I was sitting in a bar enjoying a cheeseburger and the hottest guy I'd ever laid eyes on walked in. So there I was sitting in a booth after spending all day at a book signing. A romantic suspense book signing. Now, see, I read a lot of romance so my imagination runs wild, I can make up stories in my head about everyone I see and meet. Which of course I did that night. My first thought was you were law enforcement, then I thought military, fed, or marshal."

"Seriously?" He chuckled.

"Yep. It was the way you moved—confident and alert."

"Let's get back to this book signing."

"I was there to support some of the authors I narrate for. Letty was upstairs in our hotel room sleeping. I was messaging her on my laptop after you sat down begging her to bring me my phone so I could take one of those covert snapshots. You know, where I find a shiny surface to take a picture of your reflection so you wouldn't catch me. But being the good friend she is she refused to allow me to turn into a stalker and wouldn't come down. The end."

"Hardly the end. Smutties?"

I glanced back to check that Remington was still asleep and when I found him still snoozing I answered.

"Smutties is all about romance. Mostly indie-published books."

"Smut romance?"

"You can call it that as long as you're calling it smut as a compliment. Sexy romance."

"I gathered that when I walked in on you reading."

Gah. That was embarrassing. Which made no sense because thousands of people listen to me. But they don't get to hear me practice.

"Do you like what you do?" he asked.

"Love it. Couldn't think of a better job. My hours are flexible. I love the authors I work with. And I get to read books for a living. It's my dream job." That got me thinking about Letty and her dream. "Did Wilson update you on the bookstore?"

"No, Sugar. But when we get to the house you can call Letty and ask her yourself."

Thank God.

I missed her.

"Favorite number?" I asked.

"One-ten. You?"

I gave him a smirk and answered, "Same."

"Dog or cat?" he inquired.

"Dog."

And that was how we spent the next thirty minutes.

Back and forth. Getting to know the most trivial facts about each other.

It was everything.

26

Davis and Letty were waiting for us when I pulled into the driveway of the safehouse. This wasn't a surprise though it was a bummer. My time alone with Brooklyn and Remy had officially come to an end and I wasn't happy about it.

Though Remington's shriek of excitement reminded me I was being a selfish prick.

"Letty looks peeved," Brooklyn noted.

"Davis looks the same."

Brooklyn's lips twitched and she smiled huge.

"Maybe Davis is just who she needs."

"Come again?"

"I'll explain later. But if me being hung up on a man for five years is a little strange Letty's got me beat by about nine years. She's going on fourteen years pining after a man she doesn't know. It's time she woke up."

"Doesn't know?"

"She's coming, don't tell her I told you. It's not a secret—everyone knows—but she gets pissy when I tease her about it."

It was safe to say I wouldn't say anything because I didn't

know what the fuck Brooklyn was talking about. I also wasn't going to tell her I was mighty pleased she'd been 'hung up' on me for five years. Did that make me an asshole knowing she hadn't had a man since me? Probably. Did I give a fuck? Hell no. I wouldn't have had a damn thing to say if she had been in a relationship since me. I had no call to be upset with her if she had. But that didn't change the fact that I liked it.

Letty pulled Brooklyn's door open, shoved her upper body in, and pointed at me.

"You're not allowed to take them and run to a remote locale with no cell reception ever again. You hear me, Dulles? I require constant contact or I get grumpy. And tell your friend Davis over there that if he wants children of his own in the future he needs to stop making fun of me."

"Um, Lets, you're acting crazy." That came from Brooklyn and I had to agree.

Letty was a woman undone and I was unclear what her tizzy was about. Not talking to Brooklyn, or Davis ribbing her, or both. Or the stress of everything going on.

"Woman, you need to learn how to take a joke," Davis called out.

Letty's body disappeared out of the car and Brooklyn glanced at me and smiled.

"I better calm her down."

"You better do more than calm her down; she's kicking Davis." I gestured to the scene playing out in the front yard.

Davis on the defensive backing up, Letty on the offensive attempting to nail him in the balls.

"What?" Brooklyn unbuckled and jumped from the car.

I turned back to look at Remy who was laughing.

"Auntie Letty's dramatic. Pop says she should've moved to Hollyweird."

"Again, your pop sounds smart."

"He says that if it wasn't for Mommy, Auntie Letty would be in jail."

"Oh, yeah?"

"Yep. Pop says Mommy's the brains and Auntie Letty's the fun."

I glanced out the window, happy to see Brooklyn and Letty hugging and Davis standing tall, balls intact.

But this time I had to disagree with Michael Welsh. Brooklyn was the brains and she was also the fun. But I wouldn't be sharing that with my son.

"I think it's safe to get out now," I told Remy but he didn't move. "Remy?"

"You're gonna stay, right, Dad?"

I fucking hated my boy needed me to reassure him. No, I hated the reasons why he needed me to reassure him. But I'd do it as many times as he needed.

"I am absolutely staying."

"Are we going home?"

"No, son. We're going to stay here while we look for a new house—for all of us. Is that okay with you?"

"With you, too?"

"Yes. Me, you, and your mom. All of us."

"Will I get new toys?"

Toys.

Shit. I totally had to get my act together with this parenting stuff.

"All of your stuff from your old house will be moved into the new house. All your toys and clothes."

"And my baby seat," he grumbled.

"Booster seat," I corrected. "And yes, your booster, too."

Remy gave me a disgruntled look and I swear he rolled his eyes before he opened his door. I bit back a laugh that would probably be misconstrued as encouragement and got out of the car.

Remy and I slammed our doors and I held out my hand.

Remy's little hand fit perfectly in my palm and we started walking. I was man enough to admit emotion clogged my throat and I had to swallow the lump in order to control the tears.

Only thing better than my son's hand in mine was the feel of Brooklyn when she nuzzled in, wanting closeness.

"Yo. Little man," Davis called out.

"Hey, Davis."

I felt no jealousy when Davis ruffled Remington's dark mop of hair.

I felt pride.

Immense pride.

Brooklyn and Letty pulled apart, I heard a gasp, and my attention immediately went to Letty.

"Oh my God," she breathed and started fanning her face. "Oh my God."

Remington tugged my hand and I looked down at him.

"Told you she was dramatic, Dad."

"Dad," Letty blubbered.

"Letty," Brooklyn warned.

"So, *so* long, Brook. So long," Letty weirdly said.

But Brooklyn seemed to understand when she returned, "I know."

Then Letty turned back to us, jutted out her chin, and put a hand to her hip. "What? No love for your Auntie Letty?"

Remington looked back up and this time I clearly saw the eye roll before he let go of my hand and ran to Letty. She picked him up, swung him around, and peppered his face with kisses.

Again, no jealousy.

"Happy for you," Davis muttered from beside me.

"Happy for me, too, brother. What's up with Letty?"

"The woman is a pain in the ass. When she's not bossing she's bitching. She's lucky she's funny as fuck and gorgeous or I would've cuffed her and taped her mouth shut days ago."

"Gorgeous, huh?" I prodded.

"Just because you got a woman and a son when a month ago you had neither don't mean you don't got eyes. And there's no denying Letty is smoking hot. High maintenance ain't my thing. And trust me, with her wicked smart mouth, if there were ever a woman to make me a believer I could handle high maintenance without losing my mind it would be her. And I know I'd lose my mind. But she's fun to look at."

This was true, both accounts. Letty was a beautiful woman and Davis didn't like high maintenance. He was chill and he liked his women shy and retiring. The shier the better. Davis Wright liked a challenge.

"Ballistic match come back?" I asked.

"Yeah, about ten minutes ago. It's a match. There's been a change; Jack and Asher are on their way to Canada. Shep's looking into the money...Wilson filled you in on that, right?"

"Yeah."

"Wilson wants to be ready with an apprehension team when Shep makes the connection. The money that Desi had in her account was drained and put in the same account as the reward money. The woman's not smart and not hiding her tracks. I don't know why the teller at the local bank agreed to help Desi because she isn't smart and left a paper trail pointing right back to her. It's so sloppy, I don't know if I want to laugh or if I'm thinking someone is yanking our chain and this is one big cover-up for something bigger."

"What do you mean something bigger?"

"Desi's flush with cash in her own account but she steals the reward money. And she's not smart enough not to transfer both accounts to the same one in Canada. No one's that stupid. And the teller at CDA National. A man comes in to wire fifty K to Canada and the teller doesn't check the signature card on file. Really?"

"He came into the branch? So there's surveillance."

"Yeah, of a man fitting Michael Welsh's build wearing a ball cap, knowing where not to look and how to avoid the cameras."

"What's the teller's name?"

"Jordan Pearson."

"Jordan have any connections to the Welshes, Desi, or Brooklyn?"

"None that we could find. Letty saw a picture of her and said she'd never seen her before and she's never heard the name."

"She give an excuse why she didn't check the signature card?"

"Jordan says wires up to Canada aren't unusual. The manager confirmed that. Though he was mighty pissed Jordan failed to comply with bank procedure."

Something wasn't sitting right.

"Simple and stupid, brother. If you couldn't find a connection between Jordan Pearson and any of the other players—trust that. This is about Desi."

"Hell yeah, it's about Desi. But now I'm wondering who she's running from. Us or someone else."

"Me, too." I looked back at Letty and Remington then turned back to Davis. "You staying?"

"You cooking dinner?"

"It's three o'clock."

"And?"

"Did you stock the house with groceries?"

"Is my name Davis?"

"No, it's Fat Bastard."

"Six percent body fat, brother. Far from fat but I'll give you the bastard since I ain't got a daddy."

I shook my head at his ridiculousness and moved to get my family inside.

"Not bit...*complaining* now, are you?" Davis caught his curse and corrected it at the last minute.

"Nope."

I looked up from the steaks I was grilling to Davis tossing the football with Remy and smiled.

I was going to miss the guys when they went back to Arizona. With everything going on I hadn't thought about that, what it truly meant to quit Takeback. No more all-night strategy and planning sessions, no more operations, no more sitting around hotel rooms bullshitting, no more throwing back beers decompressing.

The flip side to that was they wouldn't be around to get to know Remy and Brooklyn. They'd be gone as soon as they ensured my family was safe. A twinge of pain traveled through me at the thought of my boy not having these men around. Good, strong, honest men. I wouldn't have Wilson's wisdom at the ready. Davis's humor. Cole citing some obscure poet or philosopher none of us had ever heard of. Reese's optimism. Jack's strength. Asher's intelligence. All of that would be lost to me and my boy. Their loyalty would remain but they'd be gone more than not. Off saving the world like the men they were.

I pushed those depressing thoughts away and went back to thinking about Desi Cunns. Nothing about the woman made sense. Criminal mastermind she was not. The cash deposits into her bank account were a dead giveaway.

Victim or accomplice?

Or both.

Something in my gut told me she was an unwilling accomplice.

"Say what?" Letty's screech from the kitchen snapped my attention to the house.

"Inside voice!" Remy shouted.

Damn, the kid's funny.

With my shoulders shaking with humor I turned to my boy and smiled.

"Your Aunt Letty doesn't have an inside voice, pal," Davis told Remy.

I watched Remy fumble a catch and run after the ball. The screen door slid open and out walked Letty followed by Brooklyn. Letty's eyes were narrowed on Remy, Brooklyn was fighting a smile.

"Cheeky boy!" Letty yelled across the yard.

I stopped paying attention to Letty teasing Remington as Brooklyn made her way to me. There was a lot left hanging between us. Things I needed to apologize for, things I couldn't tell her while Remy was sleeping in the car. Explanations she deserved. But right then, walking toward me, smiling, she looked like she'd put the blow-up at the cabin behind her. But I couldn't get her sad blue eyes out of my head. I'd been so lost in my own insecurities I'd ignored her pain.

As soon as she was close I took my shot and tagged her

around the waist, bringing her body flush with mine, and buried my face in her neck.

"I'm so fuckin' sorry, Sugar."

"What?"

"The cabin—"

"Stop, honey." Her arms went around me and damn if they didn't feel good. "High emotions and lots of drama swirling around us."

"Don't make excuses for me being a dick. I never should've snapped at you."

"Maybe not, but you did. And you've already apologized. If you make a habit out of it I'll call you on it, trust me. But we're both under stress, trying to navigate our way through something that's important to both of us. And I started the argument by being stubborn. We'll talk about the money tonight. I've been thinking on it, and I need to let you do what you feel you need to do. The same as I'm asking you to let me be the woman I am."

I dropped a kiss below Brooklyn's ear then pulled my face out of her neck. Staring up at me was a woman who was too damn good for me. But I wasn't stupid enough to tell her so.

"I won't make a habit out of it," I promised.

"Potatoes will be done in ten minutes." She deftly changed the subject.

Yeah, I'd done nothing good enough in my life to deserve her.

"What was Letty yelling about?"

Brooklyn's eyes rolled skyward and I knew where my son had learned that particular trait.

"I told her we were moving in with you."

My body stilled and my blood ran hot.

"You told her?"

"Was it a secret?"

"Hell no."

"Then why do you look so surprised?"

"Not surprised. Just happy you told her, I guess."

Though I was a little surprised Brooklyn had told Letty. I suppose a part of me was worried Brooklyn wasn't serious about moving in with me, or maybe she'd think on it and back out.

"For the record, Rhode, when you forget to mask it, you wear your thoughts on your face, too. I'm excited about us living together. I'm happy you asked. I knew Letty would be thrilled for all of us. But even if I didn't think she would be, I still would've told her. I'm in charge of my life. I know what I want. I know what's gonna make me happy. And I love Letty, I value her opinion, and I'm smart enough to seek her wisdom when I'm unsure of something. But I didn't tell her because I was asking what she thought. I told her so she could share in my excitement."

"Beautiful and smart. I'm screwed."

"Handsome and a sweet-talker. I'm screwed."

Uncaring we had guests and our son was in attendance I dropped my mouth onto hers and kissed the fuck out of my woman. I did this while she giggled herself stupid.

And she tasted sweet like sugar.

"Honey," Brooklyn groaned.

I pounded deeper.

"So close. Please don't stop."

Like I would.

I shifted my weight to my elbow planted on the mattress above her shoulder and slipped my free hand under her ass and ground down while she lifted her hips to meet my driving cock.

"Oh, God," she moaned again against my neck right before she sank her teeth in.

Fuck, that felt good. All of her felt good. Her tits pressed against my chest, her long legs wrapped around my waist, her heels digging in, her nails raking down my back, her pussy hugging my cock, her tongue now gliding over her mark.

All of it so goddamn good, I was close. Thankfully she was closer.

Brooklyn's back arched, taking with it her neck, giving me her pretty eyes.

"Ocean blue."

As soon as the words rolled off my tongue she smiled.

Christ.

Beautiful.

"I missed everything about you but I especially missed the way you looked at me."

And it hit me—why all those years ago I'd felt invincible. Why her eyes had haunted me. She'd been telling me everything without words. She couldn't hide the love she felt; it shone brightly in the way she'd looked at me.

The way she was staring at me now.

Window to the soul.

"Every day for the rest of my life I wanna look into those eyes, Sugar."

"Please," she purred. "More."

She wanted more.

I'd give her anything she wanted.

I took her mouth and gave her more.

Until her orgasm broke, then I swallowed her moans and followed her over the edge.

27

I had a bodyguard.

I wasn't sure how I felt about this.

Rhode called Reese being at the house while he was working 'a precaution.'

I called it a reminder I wasn't safe.

Letty called it entertainment and told me to shut up and not complain in fear Reese would leave. But she also called Reese eye candy and she wasn't wrong—the guy was good-looking. I just didn't want entertainment or a bodyguard even if it came in the form of eye candy. I wanted one day—just one—where I didn't have to think about Kiki, money, Desi, the Horsemen, or any of the emotional fallout.

Just one.

And so far we'd been in the safehouse for three days and every day there'd been a reminder. Some small, some bigger. Today being the biggest. Reese was here to babysit...*er*...bodyguard because Rhode was meeting with Davis, Wilson, and a local detective, then they were going to the Horsemen's clubhouse to have a chat.

A chat.

Like Rhode, Davis, Wilson, and a detective were going to meet a bud at a bar and chew the fat—or was it cut the fat? Have a gab, shoot the breeze, whatever men did when they communed.

I was nervous. Not because I might or might not be in danger. I was nervous because Rhode was walking into danger. The Horsemen were bad guys, not your everyday, run-of-the-mill bad, *really* bad. Everyone knew to stay away from them. I didn't want Rhode anywhere near the clubhouse.

"Brook, if you're gonna pace at least do it in the other room," Letty complained from her spot on the couch.

"How are you calm?" I asked.

"Who says I am?"

"You're scrolling on your laptop," I reminded her.

"Ordering new bookshelves. You know, to replace the ones I had to throw away because there were *bullet holes* in them is hardly scrolling."

Damn.

Properly chastised, I grumbled, "Sorry."

"I hate this for you," Letty whispered.

Was she nuts?

"For me? I'm not the one—"

"This should be a happy time for you and Remy."

What was she talking about?

I didn't ask but Letty being my best friend didn't need me to verbalize my question.

"Rhode coming back. He and Remy bonding. You and him reconnecting."

Oh, that.

"You know what's strange? It feels like he's always been here. That's weird, right? He just so naturally fits into our lives that I forget last month I was wondering where he was and what he was doing."

"Yeah, Brook, that's weird. It should be exciting and new and the sex—"

"Shh," I cut her off and jerked my head in the direction of the kitchen.

"And the sex should be what?" Reese asked, sauntering into the living room with a huge sandwich in his hand. "Please don't tell me my boy's falling down on the job."

Someone kill me now.

"No, he's not falling down on the job," I snapped.

"I hope he's at least going down on the—"

"Letty!"

"Jeez, lighten up. The five-year dry spell's over, I figured you'd be in a good mood."

My face blazed hot and I knew my damn cheeks were turning red.

Damn Letty.

"No shit? Five years?" Reese asked around a bite of roast beef so his words came out mumbled.

"She was into Rhode," Letty helpfully supplied.

"Rare."

Rare?

"What's rare?"

"You," he said after he swallowed.

"Why am I rare?"

"Hard to find a woman who's loyal. A beautiful woman who's loyal, harder. A woman who's got it going on the way you do, and is so into her man that she doesn't see him for five years but stays true to her heart, rarest of the rare."

I didn't bother explaining to Reese there were extenuating circumstances, like I was pregnant for nine months and having sex with a man who was not the father of the baby growing in my belly was icky. And after the pregnancy came a baby and I'd been busy learning how to be a new mom. And after that I was busy raising the baby, working, and I'd been exhausted. But even if all of that had been absent, I wasn't sure if I would've gone in search of another man when my heart belonged to Rhode.

"Someone cheat on you, big guy?"

"Letty! Jesus."

"Yep. First deployment. My bitch wife found herself a play toy."

Letty gave me big eyes and I gave her a narrowed look that I hoped conveyed my reprimand.

"You two are too much." Reese chuckled. "You do remember I'm standing here so I can see the conversation."

I was sure he could.

"I'm sorry your wife cheated on you," I told him.

"I'm not. Better to learn the bitch was a cheat out the gate rather than wasting more years on her lying ass."

He was right, but still.

"Letty shouldn't have asked."

"Why not? Friends ask questions," Reese countered. "And besides, I don't give a shit who knows. I wasn't the one fucking someone outside my marriage, the bitch was."

It was safe to say I was really happy Remington was taking a nap.

Letty's phone chimed, she picked it up off the couch, and her face lit when she looked at the screen.

Interesting.

"Who's that?" Reese inquired.

Obviously he, too, saw the way Letty's mouth had curved into a smile.

"Nosy much?"

"Woman, you just asked me a personal question. I answered. And was clear I didn't mind you asked."

Letty went into a staredown. This didn't bode well for Reese. Letty was stubborn with a capital S. And she had the patience of a saint. It was annoying as hell.

"This is when you say, touché," I told her.

"Touché," she parroted but didn't answer.

"Davis know you have a man?"

Whoa. Whoa. Whoa.

"Davis?" I squeaked.

"I don't have a man. And trust me, if I did, Davis wouldn't care."

I wasn't sure if she was right. Davis had been flirting with her all night. And she'd flirted back. They were actually fun to watch.

Letty's head bent and she went back to her phone. Another thing Letty was good at was ignoring you if she was done with a conversation.

Reese looked mildly irritated and I didn't need a best friend/bodyguard throwdown so I started babbling.

"Thank you for coming over today. I hope you didn't have plans that needed to be canceled."

Reese's gaze came to mine and male beauty hit me full on.

Rhode was the sexiest man I'd ever clapped eyes on. There was something about him that exuded confidence and coupled with his good looks, his appeal was off the charts.

But Reese was classically beautiful. I doubted he'd appreciate it if I told him so out loud and I doubted he'd take it as a compliment. But he was a magazine-cover pretty boy. Complete with green eyes that had striations of brown. They weren't hazel, they weren't completely green. What they were was cool. His ex-wife was an idiot. God, I hoped she was his ex, though he called her his wife. Was he still married to her? No way, he called her a bitch. No man calls his wife a bitch. At least not a good man, and Reese struck me as a good guy.

"Are you married?"

"No."

Phew. He'd divorced her. That was good.

"Girlfriend?"

"No."

"Seeing someone?"

Reese's head tilted to the side and his lips twitched.

"Nosy much?" he quipped.

"Friends ask questions."

"Right." He chuckled. "No. And so we're clear, that's a no to any and all questions about me dating or shacking up. Though I'm not lonely if that's what you're worried about."

Actually, I wasn't worried if he was lonely.

"Happy to hear that."

"But if you've got any girlfriends that need company for a night I'd be happy to provide entertainment."

There was that word—entertainment.

Eek.

"I'll keep that in mind."

Not that I had any real friends besides Letty.

"Remy's a cool kid."

"Yeah, he is."

My heart soared thinking about my boy.

"Lots of shit changing. He adjusting okay?"

"Kind of you to ask, Reese. Remington's happy his dad's here. He and Rhode are good together."

Reese looked like he wanted to say something but was interrupted by his phone ringing.

"Gotta take this," he said before he even pulled the phone out and walked out of the room.

As soon as Reese was out of sight I turned back to Letty.

"Who texted you?"

"Pen Pal."

Pen Pal was Letty's texting buddy and had been for years.

"He's back?"

"Yeah, he texted me last night."

Some might think Letty having a texting buddy for fourteen years was strange. Some might think it stranger they'd promised never to look the other person up on the internet or social media. Which Letty had never done and she'd never let me look him up either. Something I wanted to do really, really badly. But I respected the boundaries they'd set on their friendship.

"I told him about Kiki. He was pissed."

"Pissed?"

"Yeah, he said I should've called him."

"Called him? He told you he was unavailable."

This was something that happened from time to time. Pen Pal would go radio silent. This would've been a red flag if he was say, a boyfriend. But Pen Pal was just that, a pal. Letty had dated, he'd dated, and they shared their dating mishaps.

She was my best friend, I wanted good things for her, and part of that was having good friends. But in the last couple of years, I was beginning to think she was in love with Pen Pal. When I broached the subject she'd shut me down then go on a date. But the guys she dated were duds, like she picked them on purpose because she knew they were boring.

"He said I should've known that he would've become available for me."

"Obviously, he's not mad anymore. You're smiling," I noted.

"Oh, no, he's pissed. Super pissed. I was smiling because apparently his sister got engaged while he was away so he's busy giving her shit. But he texted to let me know he hasn't forgotten he's pissed at me, too."

"You're a strange bird, Letty. Only you would smile because someone's pissed at you."

She shrugged. "He's a good friend."

My eyes got squinty when I reminded her for the five millionth time, "I'm the BFF."

"That you are." She patted the cushion next to her. "Now help me pick out the new bookshelves. The insurance company's paying through the nose so we're getting the good stuff. And the new windows were put in yesterday so we can reopen Smutties next week."

"I'm a shit friend, Letty. I should've asked you earlier but are you doing—"

"I'm so fucking angry with my sister I can't see straight. Dad is livid. And Mom is madder than I've ever seen her. I mean, we knew Kiki could be a pain in the ass. But this is beyond the beyond. There are no words for the shit she's pulled. And I don't want to talk about the drive-by. I'm grateful I wasn't at the store when it happened but you and Remy *were* home. I mean, what the fuck? Why the fuck would someone shoot at you? Or me for that matter? And Desi? I should've throat punched that chick when I caught her with the phone. I knew something wasn't right. Knew it. Then when she happily hightailed her ass back to Seattle I knew that wasn't right. She hates her parents. Then when her friend *Peaches* came around the store asking how Desi was and if I had a number for her I should've kicked that chick in the ass just for being friends with Desi."

"Wait. What? Peaches came to the store asking about Desi?"

Incidentally Peaches was a nickname Letty gave a girl named Marsha because the chick always wore way too much body spray. She was friends with both Desi and Kiki.

"Yeah, I didn't tell you? Right after you left to pick up Remy. Peaches and Flavor of the Week came in. She said she heard what happened and Desi was staying with Mom and Dad and she was worried...*oh, fuck*."

Oh, fuck was right.

"How'd she know Desi was staying at your parents?"

"The phone?"

"Did you tell one of the guys Peaches came by?"

Letty slowly shook her head. "I didn't think anything of it but—"

"But your store and my house got riddled with bullets a few hours later..."

"Oh, fuck."

Again, oh fuck, was right.

28

"Right. Thanks, Reese, got it." Wilson disconnected and tossed his phone onto the table. "I'm tired of running this operation out of a goddamn hotel room."

My eyes went from my laptop where I'd been running a background check on Marsha Peters to my boss—soon to be former boss—and guilt set in. Takeback was still in Idaho and not back in Scottsdale in the cushy office because they were helping me.

"I can—"

Wilson's fiery look shut me up.

"Was gonna wait until this shitshow was over but damn if the shit doesn't just keep piling on. I don't accept your resignation."

"What?"

"The team's not losing you. We can't lose you. We also get you need to be here in Idaho for your boy. I'm not willing to break up the team or your family so we talked about it and everyone's on board moving the office here. The new space won't be ready for a few weeks. And I've got feelers out. I'll hire someone to rotate in, but there will be a

time when I'll need you in the field. Won't be every operation. But, Rhode, there are times when we need your skills
and you know it."

By skills Wilson meant: up-close-and-personal.

As I'd told Remy, a nickname is earned and I'd earned
mine—repeatedly.

"Wilson." That was all I could get past the lump that had
formed in my throat.

"We save lives," he told me. "You save lives. You do
important work and we need you and you know we do."

He was correct, we did save lives. We did important work
and I didn't want to turn my back on it but I'd told Brooklyn
I'd quit.

"You need to talk to your woman?" Wilson surmised.

"I told her I quit. We haven't discussed what I planned
on doing for work but I'm thinkin' she thinks I'll be home
for dinner. And with this job, that won't always be the case.
So, yes, I love my work and it's important and I appreciate
the sacrifice y'all are willing to make but, brother, my son
has to come first."

Wilson blew out a frustrated sigh but immediately
relented. "Loud and clear."

"What'd Reese give you?" Davis asked.

"Letty gave him access to her security feed. She only has
one camera near the register and she doesn't remember if
Marsha and the guy walked that far into the store."

This was good news. Letty didn't know who the man was
who came in with Marsha. And I hadn't found a spouse or
even a roommate on Marsha's lease agreement but I did find
a rap sheet. Various narcotics violations and petty thefts that
are typical of addicts.

"Deeper we go down this rabbit hole the less anything
makes sense," I bitched.

There was a knock at the hotel door and Wilson moved to answer it while muttering his agreement. "No shit. Welcome to the clusterfuck."

After checking the peephole Wilson opened the door and stepped to the side.

"Brasco, appreciate you joining us."

I put my laptop on the coffee table and stood.

"Should be thanking you for inviting me," the man returned. "Anytime I get to deliver bad news to the Horsemen is a good day."

"Rhode Daley." I offered my hand to the detective.

He took it in a firm shake and introduced himself. "Jethro Brasco. My friends call me Jet."

"Jet it is." I dropped his hand and Davis took a step closer.

"Davis Wright. Good to meet you."

"You, too."

"Hate to throw you straight into the fire but we got some new intel from Letty Welsh," Wilson started. "A few hours before her bookstore and Brooklyn Saunders' house were hit she got a visit from Marsha Peters. Marsha was accompanied by an unknown male—"

"That'd be Tug Anderson. And yes, his mamma named him Tug," Brasco interjected.

"What makes you sure Tug was with Marsha?"

That was Davis and he was moving to the table to pick up a notepad. The guy loved to draw mind maps of suspects; he said the diagrams helped him find connections faster and I couldn't say he wasn't right. If there was a connection to be found Davis could find it.

"Marsha is Tug's newest moneymaker."

"Moneymaker? He pimps her?" I asked the detective.

"He's got a small stable that we know is his but we can't

directly tie him to it. We pick up one of his girls on solicitation, offer her a deal to flip, and she closes up tight. Not a single one will give him up."

"The cash," I muttered. "Desi was turning tricks."

"That I can't confirm. Desi Cunns was never picked up and I've never seen her on the street."

"Expanding operations," Wilson theorized. "Desi had more money in her account than a garden variety hooker. She wasn't making that kind of cash walking the streets. She was also clean. Could be Tug Anderson's fishing in bigger ponds that pay more. High class."

There was nothing high class about Desi but she wasn't a junkie and she wasn't hard to look at.

"What about Thomas Brady and Chet Brown? Are they tied to Tug?"

The detective's jaw clenched, his nostrils flared, his right eye twitched.

"Rumor on the street, nothing concrete or proven," he started. "But word is, Brady supplies the girls with drugs and Brown's the enforcer. One of the girls steps out of line, either not performing or skims, they get a visit from Brown. Again, not proven because not a single one of the women will flip."

"What stops a junkie from snatching up a get out of jail free card?" Davis asked.

"He's got something over them or they're more scared of him than they are of doing time."

"My guess is they're more scared of Tug," Brasco answered. "They come in tweaked they've been arrested but the second Tug's name is mentioned they start quaking. The guy's a crazy motherfucker. Crazy but slippery."

"Now Desi's running scared," I added. "What's the draw to Canada?"

"Don't know why she'd go there," Brasco started but

stopped and shook his head. "Tug Anderson's Canadian. Or I should say, he's got dual citizenship."

"Farther down the fuckin' rabbit hole," I muttered.

"Shep's got a lock on the money," Wilson announced and my gaze sliced to him.

"What the fuck?"

"The account was opened the day before the transfers happened," he continued like he hadn't just dropped a bomb. "Mark Twain."

"For the love of God, please tell me you aren't serious," Davis asked incredulously. "That's the stupidest fuckin' thing I've ever heard."

"Dead serious. Shep's got eyes on the local branches in Abbotsford and Jack and Asher are in place. I don't want that money moved until someone makes a grab for it."

I clenched my molars and prayed for patience.

"The money's gone if that withdraw happens," I ground out.

"Jack and Asher are in place," Wilson repeated. "If it's transferred, Shep's on that. We'll get the money back but for now, we need it where it is."

Goddamn, logically and tactically Wilson was right. But right then I wasn't thinking tactics and apprehension. I didn't want my woman's money being used as bait.

"We'll pick this back up after our meet with Lawrence," Wilson carried on. "At least this is one loose end we can wrap up quickly."

I hoped like fuck Lawrence got our message. If he didn't, Kiki would be missing for real this time.

"Confirm you get me, motherfucker."

"Said I did," Lawrence sneered. "Bitch ain't worth it."

"Glad you think that."

Lawrence and his pissant MC buddy who was more of a pissant than Lawrence stood in identical poses—arms crossed, boots planted shoulder-width apart, ugly scowls that I was sure were meant to intimidate but missed the mark by a mile.

Their Harleys were behind them and if it wasn't sacrilege I would've loved to have seen the looks on their ugly mugs when I backed over them. But seeing as they were Harleys I'd have to be happy with what I came for and that was their assurance Brooklyn and Remington were off-limits, and even though Kiki Welsh was a lying, grasping bitch she was untouchable, too.

Lawrence agreed.

Time to move on.

"You want the bitch now, feel free to go in and get her."

I glanced at the clubhouse behind them, and while there were only a few bikes in the forecourt, I wasn't dumb enough to waltz into a biker hangout with an unconfirmed number of tangos. And I certainly wouldn't do that with a police detective watching.

"I'll pass."

"That an open invitation, Lawrence?" Brasco smiled.

"Fuck you."

"Yeah, didn't think so." Brasco chuckled. "Just to be safe, I think I'll do a wellness check on Kiki Welsh tomorrow morning."

"The bitch won't be here. Good luck finding her."

"As I mentioned, I don't find her untouched and healthy you'll find yourself in an uncomfortable position," Brasco unnecessarily reminded Lawrence.

"Told you, the bitch ain't worth it."

"Great, then we're done," I announced.

"Though, that bitch Desi comes around again," Lawrence whistled low. "Now she's worth keeping for her mouth alone. World-class head and she likes spreading the love so don't think you get that bitch on the cheap."

Motherfucker.

He played us.

I glanced at Wilson and waited for his volley.

"Noted." Wilson jerked his chin and we started to move out.

"You don't wanna know the last time the bitch had her mouth on my dick?" Lawrence called out.

"Not especially," Wilson returned.

Not fucking at all.

Doors were opened, we piled into the SUV, doors were slammed, and I backed out of the lot. Wilson had his phone to his ear before I had the Tahoe out of reverse.

"Cole?" Wilson barked. "Need you at the Horsemen's clubhouse. Desi's in Idaho. Reese will relieve you later." There was a pause then, "Yeah. Thanks."

"The Horsemen have beef with Tug Anderson?" Davis asked.

"Everyone's got beef with the Horsemen," Brasco confirmed.

"Fuckin' great," I muttered.

"Desi's bank account was cleaned out. She's got no means. She went to Lawrence for protection," Wilson declared.

"Fuckin' great," I repeated.

"Those two in a war means bad shit," Brasco griped. "I gotta call this in."

"We get the reward money back and we're officially done," Wilson told Brasco. "Brooklyn and Remington Saunders are clear of the Horsemen, Kiki Welsh has the opportunity to walk out of the mess she created breathing. Those were our goals. They're accomplished. We're done."

Once we had the money we were indeed finally fucking done.

Life would be life.

Except Wilson calling Brooklyn and Remington—Saunders. That shit wasn't done. That needed to be rectified and fast.

29

"Dad!"

Every time. My heart squeezed and my breath caught.

Dad.

Remy ran past me with the football tucked under his arm. My gaze followed boy and ball to find Rhode walking out the back door.

"You need a dog," Letty said from beside me.

"What?"

"The only thing cuter than a boy running across the backyard to his dad is if a puppy is chasing the boy."

She had that right.

"Sugar. Letty." Rhode called his greeting from where Remington had stopped him.

My boy's arms wrapped tight around his dad's waist. Rhode was ruffling Remy's hair with one hand while the other was on Remy's shoulder.

Father and son.

"Hey, Dulles. How was your day?" Letty asked.

"Productive."

Remy stepped to the side and I took in Rhode. My eyes raked the length of him. Same tan cargos, same navy blue t-shit, no blood stains, no injuries. I let out a breath I didn't know I was holding.

He was home safe.

"Well, that's awesome because Mom and Dad are on their way over. They said not to cook because they're bringing dinner."

Rhode's eyes cut to me and I was happy I was sitting down because the look on his face made my body tingle. From my toes all the way to my scalp. I could only describe it as peaceful. There was a tinge of happiness but mostly everything about him screamed at ease. Like he liked coming home from work, finding his boy in the backyard playing ball with one of his friends, then abandoning the game to run to him calling his name.

Yes, that was exactly what Rhode looked like.

And that made me tingle from top to toe.

"Sounds good," he answered Letty but didn't take his eyes off of me. "Did you look at the listings?"

The house listings. That was one of the few bright moments when the drama surrounding us fell away. And now seeing that look, knowing that was my future—Rhode coming home to us after work and finding what he needed to let his day fall away I was more excited than I had been. And I was pretty damn excited about us moving in with Rhode.

"I like the one on twenty acres."

"It's outside of town aways," he reminded me.

It was twenty minutes south of downtown CDA where Smutties was. But it was perfect. Without seeing the pictures of the house, just the property and backyard, I knew it was exactly where Remy and Rhode needed to be. Seeing the house had sealed it for me.

"It has a room in the basement that would be perfect for a booth," I told him. "I could work part-time from home."

Something passed over his face but he masked it before I could get a lock on it.

"I'll call the realtor, get us a tour."

"Okay."

"No one wants my opinion?" Letty cut in.

I knew her opinion; she'd expressed it—repeatedly.

"No guest house."

"But it's twenty acres. You can have a mini compound. All I need is a tiny house," she argued.

"No."

"Sure."

The "no" was me. The "sure" was Rhode.

"What?"

"Sweet. Told you Dulles would see the benefit of a built-in babysitter."

I looked over at Letty to see her smug smile.

"Rhode's not building you a tiny house."

"Of course he's not. I'm building myself a tiny house."

"Cool!" Remy shouted. "I want to help build a tiny house."

Reese's laugh boomed like it had done many times over the hours. He liked Remy and he openly showed it. I loved that the big, tall, often scowly man could light up and laugh at a four-year-old.

"Do you know what a tiny house is, pal?"

"No, but my dad will teach me."

As if Remy's statement flipped a switch, Rhode beamed.

"Indeed I will, bud."

"Awe-some. Now that we've worked that out. And I've ordered all the new bookshelves and furniture for Smutties. *And* you've had a productive day which I'm assuming means life can get back to regularly scheduled programming, it's time to celebrate." Letty stood and scooted around the ugly wicker patio table. "Apple juice and double-decker sundaes for my good-looking nephew and margaritas for the adults."

"Adults disqualified from the sundaes?" Reese inquired.

"Aww, do you want apple juice, too?" Letty teased.

"Prefer it actually."

"Over a margarita?" Letty gasped in mock horror.

"Don't drink."

"Like at all or just not to-*kill*-ya?"

"Not a drop."

I looked from Reese to Rhode and found him clenching his jaw listening to the exchange. And I really, really wished Letty would learn when to let conversations drop. But in true Letty fashion, she pushed.

"Would you rather we not—"

"Just because I don't drink doesn't mean I can't be around people who do."

"We can—"

"Letty," I hissed. "My son's lookin' parched. How about you get him some apple juice?"

"Right." She waved her hand like she was brushing away the very uncomfortable topic of conversation and moved to the door. "C'mon, Remy, let's start this party."

I groaned and dropped my head. I heard the back door open, then a hand hit my shoulder and when I looked up Rhode was smiling.

"He's not an alcoholic. And he really doesn't care if other people drink. It's just when he drinks he can't control the memories so he doesn't give them an opportunity to creep in."

"Memories? The ex-wife?"

"He told you about her?" Rhode asked as he lowered his big frame into the wicker loveseat.

"He didn't get into details, just that she was a cheating bitch."

"Then he told you the whole story. But no, not memories of her. Memories of his time in service, the men who didn't come home. The things he saw and did."

Oh, no. I hated that for Reese.

Wait.

"Do you have those same memories?"

Rhode swept the hair off my neck and let his fingers glide down to the collar of my t-shirt and back up to my ear. Just a whisper of a touch but he was watching his fingers as they grazed my skin, and for some reason I seriously liked him watching himself touch me.

"I do, but not the same as him. When I fall into my thoughts I replay the situation and what I could've done differently. How my actions impacted or my inaction affected the men around me. The battlefield's like life; it's the test. Only, the lesson comes *after* in the form of blood, despair, and death. If you're lucky, you live. If you're smart, you learn. And if you're both, you're sent back out and the cycle continues."

"Did you—"

"Yes," he interjected.

"I didn't finish."

"You don't need to. Yes, I lost friends. Yes, I saw death. Yes, I've taken a life. Yes, I'm happy I'm out. Yes, I miss it. Yes, I wish I'd done things differently. Yes, to all of your questions."

"You miss it?"

"Yep."

"But you're happy you're out?"

Rhode's gaze lifted to mine and he grinned.

"Never been happier in my whole life, Sugar."

Sigh.

"When you say stuff like that you make me want to melt into a puddle of goo," I blurted out.

"How about we settle on a kiss? A puddle of goo sounds messy."

That I could do.

I tipped my chin and leaned close but I didn't get a chance to kiss Rhode. He kissed me. No, rewind, scratch that. He tasted and he took. He did this deep and wet but unfortunately, he did it quick. Rhode broke the kiss, slid his lips to my jaw, then straightened.

I blinked away the haze his smooch left behind and the contemplative look on his face gave me pause.

"What's on your mind?"

"Wilson offered me a job."

Now I was blinking for a different reason—confusion.

"A job?"

"He and the guys talked—without asking me my opinion—and they've decided to move Takeback's office to Idaho."

"That's fantastic!" Rhode's jaw clenched at my outburst. *Maybe it wasn't.* "Isn't it? I thought you loved your job."

"I do."

Okay, now I was more than confused. I was totally baffled by his strange reaction.

"I thought you only quit to stay in Idaho."

Rhode let out a sigh—not an irritated one, a painful one.

"My job requires field work. Sometimes we're wheels up

and in the air on a moment's notice. Sometimes we have weeks or months when we're working a case before we get a lock on where a trafficking ring is located before we go in. Notice or no notice, the bottom line is with this job comes traveling."

Now I understood. He was thinking about his dad leaving on a whim to follow the wind or whatever bullshit phrase the man used to go off on his own and leave his wife and child behind. It wasn't something I'd given a lot of contemplation—why Rhode's dad would just take off. And I didn't give it headspace because I knew I'd never understand why a parent would willfully, happily, eagerly leave their family to chase an adventure. In my humble opinion if Rhode's father was the adventurous type that couldn't get the wanderlust out of his veins he should've included his family in these ventures.

"It's not the same thing," I told Rhode.

"Isn't it?"

"No. Not even a little bit. Not even in the same ballpark. You wouldn't begrudge a soldier for his duty. You won't resent a long-haul trucker for putting food on his table. You leaving to go to work is very, extremely, absolutely, vastly different."

"Part-time—"

"I love you want to spend every minute with Remington. I love that you are committed to your son and to being a good father. But, Rhode, part of being a good father is teaching your son how to be a good man. How to be happy. How to make sacrifices. You can't be everything you want to be for him if you're miserable working a job that you don't like that's empty, that doesn't challenge you even if it means you'll be home for dinner every night."

"Brooklyn—"

"One more thing," I cut him off. "I want you to be happy. Period. You're changing your life to be here with us. I know you don't see that as a sacrifice but I do. In the sense that you're leaving your life behind to start one with us. I will support whatever decision you make. But my vote, even if it takes you away from us, is take the job. But even if you don't take the job I'm happy Wilson moved the company to Idaho. I'm happy Remington will have the guys around to—"

I didn't get to finish.

Suddenly Rhode's mouth was on mine.

If all of the other kisses Rhode and I had shared were described as hot, this one was scorching. Mind-bending. Fantasy-inducing. Toe-curling. Soul-locking.

"Damn, I love you," he murmured against my lips.

Four words lingered in the air.

Speech*less*.

Breath stolen.

Butterflies swarming.

My heart pounded so hard in my chest I was worried I'd crack a rib.

"You love me?"

"So damn much."

My eyes drifted closed and I let it wash over me—the warmth of the sun on my skin, the beauty of the day, the sound of the birds chirping, the feel of his lips on mine, the fresh spring air in my lungs.

Blessings.

Then I smiled.

"I knew you'd find me," I whispered. "I knew all I had to do was wait and you'd come back."

"I will always come back to you."

"I know you will. Take the job, honey."

"Baby."

"I love you, Rhode. Take the job."

"Okay."

"Pure drama, that one," Michael grunted.

He was talking about Letty squaring off with Reese. But he was doing it with a smile on his face.

"Dramatic," Remington agreed.

Rhode swung Remy over his shoulder and laughed.

"Reese!" Rhode shouted. "Game time."

Thankfully Rhode's bellow broke up the bickering duo and Letty huffed and walked into the house. Reese joined Remy and Rhode in the grass and ball-throwing commenced.

"That girl could argue with a brick wall," Michael continued.

I pinched my lips and said nothing. I mean, really, there was nothing to say—Michael was correct. Letty loved to argue. Of course, Letty called it debating but it was simply good ol' fashion arguing, though she'd argue that it wasn't.

Michael grew silent. Then he grew stiff and finally, his face turned to granite.

"I'll never understand why my girl does what she does," he stated.

Oh, crap.

Fucking Kiki.

"Raised 'em both the same. Not one got more than the other. Gave 'em both the tools they needed but I guess some people aren't happy with the tools; they want it done for 'em."

Again I said nothing because he was right.

"Can't take the selfish out of someone no matter how hard you try."

"No, Michael, you can't."

"Can't tell you how sorry I am."

I hated that Michael thought he needed to apologize to me.

"You have nothing to be sorry for. Kiki's an adult. She makes her own choices. Sometimes she lets her jealousy get the best of her and she lashes out. But what she did to you and Tally is unimaginable and I'm sorry she did that to you."

"Always finding the good in people," Michael muttered. "You get that from your mother. She never had an unkind thing to say. I'm glad Rhode's here."

So was I but I didn't get what Rhode had to do with anything.

"Not that I'm disagreeing but why are you glad he's here?"

"Soft-hearted woman," he oddly started. "Strong in all the important ways but too kind for your own good in others. Your mom, she found herself a husband that appreciated that soft spot but protected it. No one, not anyone, was gonna hurt Diane, Ron saw to that. And after you were born he protected you the same. Now Rhode, he'll see to you."

"You're forgetting you saw to me, too. After I lost them. I had you and Tally. And like my dad, you looked after me."

"Your dad was the best friend I ever had. Best man I knew. Damn fine father and husband. Him and your mother asking me and Tally to look after you if something should happen to them, no greater honor. If your father was here and he could pick the man you were going to spend your life with he'd have picked Rhode Daley."

My throat burned and tears pooled in my eyes.

I loved that!

Loved it so much that Michael thought that way.

God, Kiki was so stupid. Two great parents who were alive and would do anything for her.

And for the second time in the last hour, I counted my blessings.

They were bountiful...and beautiful.

30

"Rhode."

Fuck.

Breathy. Needy. Hot. Close.

I took her mouth and her pussy until she mewed down my throat and clenched around my cock. Only then, with her sex still spasming, I slammed deep and let her tight, wet, heat milk me.

I wrenched my mouth free and looked down at the beautiful woman under me. Big ocean blue eyes full of rapture stared back at me.

~

The phone ringing woke me up.

Careful not to disturb a sleeping Brooklyn, I rolled her off my chest and reached for the phone.

"Lo?"

"Desi's in custody."

It had been a week since our meeting with Lawrence and nothing had happened. The money was still sitting in an account in Canada. No further threats were made. Kiki had walked out of the Horsemen clubhouse without a scratch on her. She hadn't done the smart thing and contacted her parents; instead, she was sleeping on some new scumbag's couch with no money to her name. Tug Anderson and the Horsemen were giving each other a wide berth. Letty reopened her store. Brooklyn had gone back to work. Remington back to preschool. We moved into our new office. The Welshes were trying to get back to normal. Brooklyn and I had looked at the house on twenty acres, she declared her love for the house, we made an offer, it was accepted, and we were fifteen days to closing.

Nothing had happened but life.

Normal life.

"You there?" Wilson asked.

"Yeah. I was just thinking about how we've had nothing but smooth for the last seven days."

"Something was bound to fuck that up," he returned.

"Station or office?"

"Station."

"Be there in ten."

I disconnected and looked over my shoulder to find pretty blue eyes looking at me.

Every night. Every morning.

For the rest of my life.

Ocean blue.

"Everything okay?"

Sleepy and sweet. My life was damn good.

"Yeah. I gotta meet the team at the station, Desi's in custody."

Her eyes widened comically before she brought her hand up to cover a yawn. The movement allowed the sheet to slip down, giving me a perfect view of her cleavage.

Brooklyn's gaze dropped to her chest then flicked back up to mine.

Smug.

"Last night went fast," I told her. "Tonight I get to take my time."

That got me more smug.

"I see you're pleased with yourself," I said.

"What can I say? Any time I can make you lose your mind and you jump me I'm pleased with myself."

"Baby, you had your sweet mouth wrapped around my cock while you had your hand between your legs. Torture watching you get yourself off and suck me off at the same time."

"You weren't complaining last night," she reminded me.

"And I'm not complaining now. Just pointing out that tonight's your turn."

I watched a tremor rush over Brooklyn and her lids went half-mast.

"Stop turning me on when you have to leave."

Christ, she was right.

With a hard, brief kiss, I got out of bed.

"That's all I get?" she asked to my back.

I turned to face the bed figuring this was one of those times it was better to show rather than explain.

Brooklyn's gaze dropped and smiled at what she saw.

I didn't need to look down to know my cock was hard and standing at attention.

"Careful with that thing. You might poke someone's eye out."

Smug and cute.

Yeah, my life was damn good.

"About goddamn time," Cole grumbled.

"No shit," Reese agreed.

"Impressed she held out so long," Wilson added.

It was nearing on eleven a.m. and Brasco had had Desi in interrogation since six a.m.. That was an hour after Cole had picked her up leaving the Horsemen clubhouse.

I wasn't impressed. I was annoyed. Desi had started playing dumb. She was the victim. She had no idea what Brasco was talking about. Then her story changed with only a slight variation. Hours and hours of telling, retelling, screwing up the story, Brasco calling her on it, her trying to fix and remember her lies. Finally with a huff of indignation did she fucking *finally* break.

Now we were getting somewhere.

"Tug didn't want me on the street."

Desi sat back in the chair and crossed her arms. Even through the one-way glass, I could see the worry etched on her face. The woman looked like she hadn't showered in a month—her hair was a tangled, matted mess and her clothes filthy. She looked nothing like the woman we'd found at the abandoned lumber mill.

"What'd he want you for?" Brasco asked.

"High-paying clients. There were three of us. He drug tested us, gave us nice clothes to wear, and we got a bigger cut."

"I need the names of the other girls."

"Fine, whatever. I'm dead anyway so it doesn't matter."

Desi's face crumbled and for the first time since I started watching this shitshow of a performance, she gave an honest reaction. Desi wasn't scared. She was terrified of Tug Anderson.

"Do you have any idea why Tug would hire Thomas

Brady and Chet Brown to shoot Brooklyn Saunders and Letty Welsh?"

"I don't know what—"

"You called it in, Desi. Don't deny it. You made the call from the hotel you were staying at. The call was easy to trace and you checked in under your name."

Desi's gaze darted around the room before it settled back on Brasco.

"A warning."

"Warning? What kind of warning?"

Desi shrugged like the bitch didn't care that my family had almost been murdered.

"Marsha called and said that Tug was pissed I disappeared. He wanted me back." Desi paused and with small, jerky shakes of her head she continued. "I didn't want to do it anymore. I couldn't do it anymore. Being a whore, I just...I needed to leave but somehow my bank account was emptied. Marsha said Tug was mad that Brooklyn and Kiki's family had showed up that night, then helped me, and he was going to make sure that they didn't do it again."

"So, you're telling me you went to Canada with no money?" Brasco pushed.

"I confessed everything to my dad. He gave me money and let me use his car. He told me to go to Canada and wait until he could come up with a plan."

"Shit," Wilson rumbled. "Desi better pray Tug doesn't find that out or her parents are fucked."

Wilson wasn't wrong. If a drive-by that could've resulted in murder was a warning I shuddered to think what Tug would do if he found out Desi had told her parents he'd been pimping her out.

"How'd you enter Canada?"

"What do you mean? I drove."

"Did you have your passport? Birth certificate?" Brasco inquired.

"I used my NEXUS card."

NEXUS was a trusted traveler program that allowed someone to travel between the US and Canada without a passport. Probably not unusual for someone who lives in North Idaho to have.

"Tell me about the night the old lumber mill was raided. The night you were found with forty missing people on the verge of being sold."

Desi's eyes closed and she dropped her chin to her chest and shook her head violently.

"I had nothing to do with that. Nothing. I didn't know."

The detective opened a file and images of the victims spilled onto the table.

"Look at them, Desi, and tell me again that you didn't know what was getting ready to happen to them. Look at the little boy who was snatched away from his parents. You were there!" Brasco shouted his last sentence and Desi jolted.

"I want protection," Desi murmured. "I'll tell you everything but I need to disappear after I tell you."

"That's not the way this works. You need to give me something to take to the feds. Something that will warrant them expending the time and money it will take to set you up with a new life."

"Anderson's operation is bigger than Brasco imagined," I muttered.

"Agreed."

"Yep."

"Absolutely."

With all of us in concurrence, we listened to a new story. This one the truth.

Thirty minutes later Brasco left the interrogation room

with a legal-sized pad of paper. On it a list of names and dates.

The door opened to the small room where we'd been watching him work Desi, and in walked the detective, his face full of thunder.

"She won't give up more until she's offered witness protection," Brasco told Wilson.

"I heard."

"You think that's something you can arrange?"

"Already called my contact. He wants Desi moved to Montana for further questioning. You arrange it with your captain and Cole and Reese will go with you."

"Appreciate it."

Brasco let out a breath that punctuated his gratitude.

"Now that we know the players and the game I'm bringing my guys home and having the money moved. The Welshes and Brooklyn get theirs back and we'll turn Desi's account over to you."

"That'll work." Brasco's chin lift turned into a shake of his head. "Right fucking here, under our noses and we missed it."

They *had* missed it. But it'd be easy to miss.

Tug Anderson had moved up the fucktard tree—way up. He went from a street pimp, to call girl pimp, then all the way up to the top rung—human trafficker. His error was to trust Desi to watch over his cargo until he moved it. She freaked when we'd shown up, gave Kiki's name since she knew Kiki was in California and she didn't want Tug to find her. How she thought giving a fake name would throw Tug off her trail is beyond me but stupid people make stupid mistakes. And Desi proved she was stupid getting wrapped up with Tug Anderson in the first place.

My phone vibrated in my back pocket. I glanced at my

watch seeing it was just after noon, I knew it was Brooklyn calling to tell me she'd picked up Remington. I pulled out my phone, saw I was right, and stepped away from the huddle to answer.

"Hey, Sugar, I'm almost—"

"Remington's gone."

Time stood still and while it did that snake in my gut that since I'd left the Navy I'd worked hard to keep at bay, uncoiled and grew into a fiery serpent.

"Repeat that."

"I'm at Remy's school. He's not here. Kiki picked him up."

Kiki.

"I'm on my way, Brooklyn. Stay there. Fifteen minutes, Sugar."

"Okay, Rhode."

I disconnected and looked around the room. Wilson already had the door open. Davis and Reese were alert and ready.

Thank fuck they were here.

"Kiki Welsh kidnapped my son."

And Jesus fuck those words blistered my throat.

"I'll get it to dispatch. Which school?" Brasco asked.

"Little Tikes on Dalton."

"Got it. Meet you there."

Brasco was out of the room.

"We'll get him back." Wilson's promise jolted me from my stupor.

I didn't say a word as I ran out of the police station.

But I did it making my own promises.

The bitch was dead if one hair on my son's head was out of place.

31

"I'm so sorry, Brooklyn. So sorry. I didn't know," Ellie said for the one-thousandth time.

"It's my fault."

And it was. All of this was my fault.

I hadn't thought about it. With everything going on I didn't think to take Kiki off Remington's pick-up list.

It never occurred to me Kiki would kidnap my son.

Jesus.

Remington was kidnapped.

My hand went to the wall for balance but my legs still buckled. But at least I landed on my knees and not flat on my face.

"Brooklyn! Oh my God!" Ellie screamed and I closed my eyes against the sound.

Too loud.

Everything was too loud.

Blood was whooshing in my ears, my heart was pounding, and I was so dizzy I thought I was going to vomit.

Why wasn't Kiki answering her phone?

Why did she take Remy?

Where did she take Remy?

Yep. I was going to puke. On my ass in the director's office of my son's preschool, I was going to vomit.

"Trash can," I groaned.

The pail appeared in front of me and without caring that Ellie was standing there, I lost my breakfast.

And while that fun thing was happening a commotion happened all around me. I heard Rhode. I heard Wilson. I heard Letty. And my stomach revolted at the sound of their voices. Why? Their voices were carrying down the hall of Remy's preschool on a Thursday afternoon when my son should've been buckled in his booster seat in the back of my car, and Rhode, Wilson, and Letty should've been at work.

But they were here and Remy was not. And I was on my ass on the floor puking my guts up.

Some mother I am.

"Jesus Christ," Rhode growled.

Then I felt him behind me, his thighs bracketing my shoulders. One hand gathered my hair, the other brought the trash can closer.

"I got you, Sugar, get it all out," he cooed.

Raging mad to gentle in a split second.

He did that for me. Seeing me losing my shit, Rhode was giving me what I needed. I would've been elated if I wasn't so scared.

"Let's give them privacy." I heard Wilson's voice boom. "I'd like to see the footage of Kiki picking up Remington and the sign-out sheet."

Feet shuffled and the door closed.

"I think I'm done."

Rhode pushed the can away and stood. Then I was up in his arms like a groom would carry his bride. Only, I wasn't a bride; I was a horrible mother.

"Bathroom?"

"Down the hall on the right. Yellow door."

The next thing I knew Rhode was setting me on my feet and I heard water running. My mind was so cluttered with other thoughts that Rhode wiping my mouth barely registered.

"Hey, Brooklyn, what are you doing here?" Ellie smiled.

"Picking up Remy."

"But Kiki already got him. She said you were running late."

Kiki already got him.

Got him.

And no matter how many times I tried to tell myself that Kiki Welsh, the little girl I rode bikes with, camped with, the girl whose hair I braided, and knees I'd helped clean up after a fall would never hurt Remington, I couldn't quite believe it.

That girl might not hurt my son but the woman she'd become might. The woman who'd come to my house and spewed nasty hate that night. The woman who'd lost her hold on the anger she felt for me might.

"Baby, I need you to tell me what happened."

My head jerked back as I pulled back into the present.

"It's my fault," I admitted. "All my fault. Kiki's on Remington's emergency card and pick-up list. I never took her off."

I watched Rhode close his eyes, the movement slow and pain-filled, like that small task of lowering his lids hurt him deeply.

When they opened the pain was still there. So was the anger, and I wondered if he'd ever forgive me. Not that I'd ever forgive myself.

"Listen to me." His biting tone sounded like a snarl. It boomed and ricocheted around the small bathroom then hit me with the force of a slap to the face. "This is not your fault. You're not responsible for Kiki's actions."

"But I—"

"I don't give the first fuck Kiki was on his pick-up list. That doesn't give her the right to pick him up without permission. Don't take this on. Don't make this about you when it's about her. An APB has been put out but since we don't know what kind of car she's driving that's incomplete. And an Amber Alert has been initiated. Detective Brasco says it takes about thirty minutes to get those pushed through the proper channels and sent to cell phones. Letty, Michael, and Tallulah are giving the police the names of everyone they can think of that knows her and would let her stay with them. We've got the ball rolling; we're gonna find him."

I nodded because I couldn't speak.

"Okay, Brooklyn. Here's what happens next. We're leaving. Tallulah's staying at her house, Michael's going to your old house, Letty's going back to the bookstore. If Kiki shows up in one of those places someone has to be there. You're coming with me to the office."

I didn't want to go to Rhode's office.

"I want to go out and look for him."

"Where?"

"What?"

"Where are you gonna look?"

"I don't know."

Somewhere. Anywhere. *Everywhere.*

"Right. Driving around aimlessly gets us nowhere. That's not how this works. We plan, we investigate, then we recover. I don't want you out of my sight so you're coming with me."

Recover.

Sweet Jesus.

My son needed to be recovered.

"Breathe, Brooklyn."

I inhaled. Then I did it again. After that, I pulled my shit together. Remington didn't need me puking my guts up or hyperventilating. He needed me strong, so Rhode could concentrate on finding him and not taking care of me.

"There she is," Rhode whispered.

"Who?"

"That fierce woman I love so much. Let's get out of here and find our boy."

Yes! Let's do that.

"I'm ready."

Rhode tossed the paper towels in the trash and grabbed my hand. With our fingers laced together and both of us squeezing, looking for strength, he pulled me out of the bathroom.

By the time we made it to the front of the preschool, Michael and Letty were gone. Davis was pacing, Reese looked murderous, and Wilson looked impatient.

"Let's go," Wilson barked.

"Got the footage?" Rhode inquired.

"Yes."

The ferocity of Wilson's answer slammed into my chest.

White-hot anger was rolling off these men and in my current state that gave me the strength I needed.

My phone ringing on the desk sounded like an atomic bomb going off in the room. The percussion of the blaring noise sent a shockwave through me, the force of it leaving me immobile.

Kiki's name lit up the screen and I still couldn't get my heart to beat.

"Brooklyn!" Davis snapped—literally snapped his fingers in front of my face. I blinked. "I'm gonna put this on speaker. Keep her on the line as long as possible."

I nodded, Davis answered the call then I croaked, "Kiki," my voice pained and tortured to my own ears.

Where was Rhode?

As if my heart conjured him up, he strode into the room, eyes wild, lips two white lines.

"Where's Remy?" I managed to get out.

"No cops, Brook. Find Desi. Tug wants back what she took. She'll know what he wants. When you have it, call me back."

Find Desi?

No cops?

Call her back?

"Where's my son, Kiki?"

"You'll get him back when you get what Desi took."

"Kiki—"

"Shut up and listen to me," she hissed. "Hurry the fuck up and find Desi. He said not to call again unless you have it."

"Kiki?"

Nothing.

"Kiki?"

"Baby, she hung up," Rhode told me softly.

No! No, *no*, no.

"Does Tug know Desi's in custody?" Davis asked.

"Who's Tug?" I probed.

No one answered.

There was commotion all around me.

Rhode gave my shoulder a squeeze, his mouth pressed

against the top of my head, then I felt his presence move away.

There was more talking.

I didn't hear what was said.

Too kind for your own good.

Michael was right. For years and years, I'd given Kiki the benefit of the doubt. I never wanted to believe she was a bad person. I'd loved her, I'd trusted her, I'd fucking made excuses for her shitty, selfish bullshit.

I'd been wrong. So wrong. Deadly wrong.

The bitch was the fucking Devil.

Hate unfurled inside me. It invaded, it saturated, it infused itself in my heart. And for the first time in my entire life, I wished death on another human.

32

"If I tell you then I'm dead," Desi announced.

"If you don't, and something happens to Remington Saunders, you're as good as dead," Brasco returned.

That was the Goddamn truth. If this bitch didn't start talking and something happened to my son I would choke the life out of her.

"God, Kiki!" Desi complained and I felt my blood pressure rise.

"That's another minute wasted, Desi."

Desi's chin lifted, her eyes steady on the one-way glass, and it looked like she almost looked remorseful.

And for the next ten minutes, we were treated to yet another story. The more she talked the more agitated the detective became. The bitch knew more, a lot more about Tug's operation. She'd also stolen a flash drive that contained a client list complete with booking records. For a complete jackass Tug was smart enough to keep a computer completely offline—no internet connection, no network, no cloud, no online backup. But he was stupid enough to leave the flash drive—his only means of backup—on his desk where Desi could swipe it.

It was her insurance policy.

"The drive's at the Welshes'. In the basement bathroom. Wrapped up in a washcloth under the sink in the back."

No sooner were the words out of the bitch's mouth than I was out the door. Brooklyn was sitting where I'd left her in the hallway. Reese stood next to her—no, stood sentry *over* her. The difference between the two was startling. Brooklyn was the picture of fear and heartbreak. Shoulders slumped, hands clasped, eyes glazed with panic. Reese was at attention, watchful, guarded, and furious.

Perversely, my friends' anger was the only thing holding me together. Knowing I had them at my back and they wouldn't stop until my son was found had kept my mind clear. I needed to think, not only for Remy but for Brooklyn. Wandering around without purpose wouldn't bring my boy home.

"Did she tell?" Brooklyn shot from her seat.

"Yeah, baby. Let's go."

The unshed tears that had been lingering fell but otherwise Brooklyn held her composure.

Reese remained quiet on the way to the SUV, waiting until we all got in with Wilson behind the wheel and Davis riding shotgun before he asked for a SITREP.

Wilson gave a short, succinct account as he drove. Davis made his call, filling in Cole who'd stayed behind at the office.

"Cole will meet us at the Welshes'."

"I'll be gone before he'll make it," I told Davis.

"Brother—"

"We're five minutes out. Cole's thirty. I'm not waiting," I cut off Reese.

"Rhode—"

"Leave it," Wilson ordered.

Brooklyn's hand wrapped around mine and in a moment of weakness my eyes drifted closed. I brought our hands up, twisted them, and pressed my lips to the back of her hand.

Unbearable fear took root.

I pulled my shoulders free and sat back, ass to heels, and unrolled the washcloth.

There it was.

The flash drive.

Before I could stand I was hit with a flashback.

On my knees on the bathroom floor. Remy beside me.

"Do we need this?" he asked, holding up Brooklyn's screwdriver.

Big, bright smile. Dark brown eyes excited to help fix the sink.

"Rhode?" Reese called, pulling me from my thoughts.

Without further delay, I got to my feet but neither Wilson nor Reese moved.

"Why are we standing here?"

"I need to know where your head's at."

My eyes cut to Wilson.

Whatever he read there caused him to hiss then mutter, "Fuck." He held out his hand for the thumb drive, I dropped it in his open palm, and with his head bowed he left the bathroom. I followed him up the stairs and found Tallulah and Brooklyn huddled on the couch. As soon as Brooklyn saw me she was up and rushing across the room.

"Was it there?"

"Yeah, baby. I need you to call Kiki, tell her you have it, and ask her where to pick up Remy. Don't bother keeping her on the phone. All you want to know is when and where to make the exchange."

Brooklyn nodded and I pulled her phone out of my back pocket and handed it over. I watched as her hands shook when she unlocked the screen and her torso swayed when she pulled up her recent call list.

"Sugar. Take a breath." Her eyes lifted and my heart shattered.

"I'm so fucking terrified I can't stop shaking."

I reached for the phone but stopped short of taking it. Instead, my hand went to her elbow and I turned her so her back was to my chest. One arm went low, the other went high, and I locked her body against mine.

"I got you, Brooklyn. Make the call."

"Mrs. Welsh, if you'll please come with me to the kitchen," Reese gently asked.

"I will not say a word."

"Ma'am."

"I also will not leave my girl when she needs me."

Brooklyn's body bucked against mine and I heard her whimper.

I was going to murder Tug Anderson in cold blood and Kiki Welsh would be lucky if I left her breathing.

"Sugar?"

With much steadier hands, Brooklyn made the call.

"Do you have it?" Kiki snapped impatiently.

"I have it. Where are you?"

"Where'd you find Desi?"

Fuck!

Brooklyn's body went solid and with more disdain than I'd ever heard her use she sneered, "It doesn't matter where I found her, Kiki, I have the damn thumb drive. Where is my son?"

"Did you look at what's on it?"

"Of course not," Brooklyn growled. "I don't give a shit what's on it. I want Remington. Where are you?"

"North Crystal Spring. Off the second switchback, there's a logging road. Follow that to the end."

Brooklyn was silent a minute then asked, "By the creek?"

"Not that far."

"Kiki, that's crazy. There's no cell service up there and nothing but woods."

"If you want him, come and get him. But you better hurry your ass up. Tug's pissed it's taking so long."

Kiki ended the call and Brooklyn exhaled.

"Do you know where that's at?"

"Yeah, it's paper mill property. Nothing but hundreds of acres of woods."

I could work with that.

"I got it on the map," Wilson announced. "Rhode, you'll head in from the switchback Kiki mentioned. Davis, you'll follow the road the rest of the way up the mountain and double back through the woods. Reese, you're here with Brooklyn and Mrs. Welsh."

"You did good, Brooklyn." I kissed her temple and pulled back. "I'm gonna go get Remington now."

Brooklyn twisted in my arms and looked up at me. I was taken aback by the trust I saw.

"Please bring him home."

"I will."

She was silent for a beat and immeasurable sadness hit her blue eyes.

"No matter what it takes, Rhode, just bring him home."

Fucking hell.

I knew what she was saying.

I knew she'd given me permission to let Kiki swing.

"Swear it, Brooklyn."

I leaned down and gave her a brief, hard kiss.

"Reese."

My brother was across the room in a flash. I turned Brooklyn into Reese's waiting arms.

No instructions given.

No words needed.

My brother would take my woman's back.

33

We were five minutes into the drive when Wilson broke the silence.

"You snatch Remy and let me take care of clean-up."

No fucking way.

"Wilson—"

"You're gonna snatch and go, Rhode. Remington's been away from you and his mother for three hours. The kid's gotta be scared. Onward from that, you don't want him seeing any more than what he's seen."

"Fuck!"

Fuck.

Sheer force of control stopped me from slamming my fist against the back of the seat in front of me.

No matter what it takes, Rhode, just bring him home.

With no choice, I agreed.

Fifteen minutes later my assent meant nothing when all hell broke loose.

∾

I was counting down the seconds.

Wilson was hoofing it up the heavy terrain and Davis was coming down. I needed to give them time to get close to the end of the trail Kiki had given directions to.

When their five minutes was up I started down the logging road and shoved all thoughts of Remington and Brooklyn out of my mind.

Uncluttered.

Cold.

Calculated.

I couldn't afford to remember a smile, a giggle, a 'hey dad' to cloud my mind. I couldn't remember the nights my son had asked me to read to him, or the mornings we'd made breakfast together, or the games of football we'd played.

Detached.

But detachment felt so fucking wrong when all I wanted was my boy close.

The slight weight of my Sig felt right, natural, familiar.

Just another day at work.

But I couldn't get myself to believe the lie as I scanned the dirt for fresh tire tracks. So far there were none. No shoe prints, no disruption, and the hair on the back of my neck started to tingle. No car parked near the switchback.

There was no sign anyone had recently walked this path. If this wasn't an exchange and Wilson hadn't verified the files on the drive I would've turned back.

Something wasn't right. Which made my trigger finger twitchy.

A twig snapped. My focus zeroed and I caught movement out of the corner of my eye. Muscle memory kicked in and I raised my gun.

Tug Anderson stepped out from behind the thick brush

and trees with his gun pointed at my chest. Kiki and Remington followed behind.

"Stupid fucking bitch!" Tug snarled.

He could've been talking about Kiki, Brooklyn, his mother, or the Virgin Mary and I wouldn't have been able to give it a millisecond of thought when all my concentration was on my son and the silver strip of duct tape over his mouth.

Deadly intent crept into my veins.

Remy was on his feet frozen solid, Kiki was standing next to him with her bitch-ass hand on his shoulder.

No blood visible.

Big, wide, scared-as-fuck eyes staring at me.

"Where's my drive?"

"Let Remington come to me and I'll toss it to you."

Tug swung his arm and pointed the gun at Remy. "Not on his life."

I saw red and my vision blurred.

Somewhere in a faraway part of my brain that wasn't determining where I was going to place my bullet—brain or heart—I heard a small whimper and Kiki moved closer to Remy.

"This isn't going to go your way, Anderson, as long as you're pointing a gun at my son. Swing that back my way and—"

"Your *son*? What the fuck, Kiki?"

Kiki didn't answer and gave zero fucks what Tug was bitching about.

"I got your drive. Give me my son and we all walk away."

"Where's Desi?"

"Far's I know on her way to Montana."

Remington jerked away from Kiki. I saw the surprise in Tug's eyes and his hand dropped, intent clear.

Kiki lunged.

I squeezed the trigger and three loud gunshots rang out.

Then utter silence.

In that moment I died a thousand deaths as red plumed from the gaping chest wound right before Kiki fell to her knees. I was jerked out of my stupor and sprinted. Without stopping I scooped up Remington, swung him up into my arms, and ran.

Three gunshots.

Mine. Tug's. And the other had to be from Wilson or Davis.

"I got you, son."

He didn't answer.

"You're safe, bud."

He said nothing. Not that he could with motherfucking tape over his mouth.

I continued running.

I ran until blue and red lights flashed in the distance. The first car sped by, the second didn't stop either. The third pulled to the side and Brasco was behind the wheel. The SUV barely rolled to a stop when I opened the passenger door and jumped in.

My gun dug into the small of my back where I'd mindlessly shoved it on my way to Remy.

"Hospital?"

"Welshes'," I huffed.

"Rhode—"

"Welshes'." I growled the two syllables and Remy jumped.

Fucking shit.

Brasco executed a three-point turn while I gently pulled the tape from Remy's mouth.

"Daddy!" he shouted and twisted his body with more force than I thought possible.

"Whoa, son. I got you."

Remington didn't stop until his knees were in my lap, his little boy chest was pressed to mine, and his face was shoved into my throat.

Then his body rocked with violent sobs. His whimpers filled the car and tears wet my skin.

Only then did I take a breath.

Remy was safe.

Tug was dead—my bullet pierced his skull.

Kiki was...

Fuck.

The woman had stepped in front of a bullet for my son and I didn't know what to feel about that. So I settled on grateful and put her out of my mind.

"You're safe, Remy."

I tightened my arms around my son.

"Safe, son."

He nodded his head but he pushed deeper.

"Love you, bud. Love you so much, son."

Remy was silent.

34

I quietly tiptoed into the bedroom, careful not to wake up Rhode and Remington.

Father and son.

They were both on their sides, Remy tucked close into the curve of Rhode's big body. I knew the comfort those arms offered. I knew what his warmth felt like. Even before Remington was taken I knew—now it was tattooed on my soul.

But it'd been a week and I needed to talk to Rhode. The child psychologist Remy saw said we needed to take our cues from Remington and be patient. It wasn't the patience part I was worried about—Rhode had all the time in the world for his son. All of the time, which translated into Remy never being more than a few feet from Rhode. His protectiveness knew no bounds which I was grateful for. But unlike Rhode, I had talked to a counselor, so I knew my irrational fear Remy would be taken again was just that—irrational. Rhode didn't think it was unreasonable and was glued to his son.

But that talk wouldn't happen today.

Today we were burying Kiki.

I hadn't wanted Remington there. Rhode insisted Remy join us. Kiki's last gesture on this earth was to shield Remy. She'd taken a bullet to the chest and had died before paramedics arrived despite Davis's best attempt to save her life. Rhode's opinion was Kiki died a hero and Remington should know that and honor it.

At four I didn't think he'd understand. But I gave in. Michael and Tally needed to see my family whole and healing after what Kiki did. They needed to see us there to support them.

And Letty. My sweet, stubborn, best friend was running herself ragged. She was at my house every day. She visited her parents every day. She'd helped her mom plan the funeral, she'd spent hours talking with her dad. She'd been to Smutties to accept her deliveries. Hell, she'd even opened the bookstore part-time. What she wasn't doing was grieving, so I needed to talk to her, too.

I snagged my phone off the nightstand and quietly tiptoed back out to the living room.

I sat down on the couch and looked around the room. Plain. Boring. Sterile. One more week and we'd be in our house and I was hoping that would help. Normalcy—a home, a new beginning, our family settled.

"Everything okay?"

I craned my neck and watched Rhode saunter across the room. Bare chest, chiseled abs, sleep pants riding low on his hips, smooth tanned skin, hair messy from sleep, eyes gentle.

Boy, had I been right all those years ago.

Dark and delicious.

"Yeah, honey. Sorry if I woke you."

"You didn't. I was being lazy."

There was nothing lazy about Rhode. He was always in motion, always doing something.

Rhode stopped by the end table, tagged my mug, and took two swallows of piping hot coffee.

"Sugar," he grumbled.

That was not him calling me my nickname. That was him complaining about the four scoops of sweetener I used in my coffee.

I smiled at him as he sat next to me.

"What can I say? I don't like the taste of coffee."

"Yet you drink a pot a day."

He had me there so I said nothing.

"Later, do you think you'll be up to go with me to the dealership?"

I blinked at his bizarre question.

"Dealership?"

"Need a new ride. My Jeep's totaled and Wilson hasn't said anything about my using the company SUV but I can't use it indefinitely. Though, I like the Tahoe, plus it's safer than a Jeep so I was thinking that's what I'm gonna get."

I could see Rhode driving a Tahoe and not just because that was what he'd been driving recently. He was a big guy and needed a big vehicle.

"Maybe Tally and Michael—"

"Sugar," he warned.

Low and rough and unyielding.

Time to talk was nigh.

I shifted and threw a leg over Rhode's lap to straddle him. His hands immediately went to my behind and mine went to cup his face.

If the last week's proved anything to me it was how much I loved him.

"We have to let Remy get back to his life." Rhode stiffened under me and I rushed on. "He's safe, honey. You got to him and made him safe. Nothing's going to happen to him."

Still rock hard.

"Please tell me what's bothering you."

"The tape."

"Rhode."

His name was nothing more than a whisper as I felt his pain and fought to keep my body still and my eyes open even though I wanted to block out the knowledge my son's mouth had been duct-taped.

"Seeing him standing there scared. But it's the tape. My boy gagged—that I can't get out of my head. I can't stop seeing it. Just give me some more time, Brooklyn."

"Okay, honey," I quickly agreed because really, what else could I do?

Rhode was there. Rhode saw things I didn't. Remy did, too.

Patience.

We were giving that to Remington and I had to give it to Rhode, too.

"The house is ready next week and I still need to sort my condo in Scottsdale."

Topic change.

"One last thing before we talk about Arizona," I told him. "I love the way you love me and Remy. I love how protective you are. I even love the way the guys come around all the time to spend time with us. I love that you and Remy have them—"

"You do, too," Rhode interjected. "Circumstances being what they were, Jack and Asher up to Canada, dividing the team, you didn't get to know them well, so they're making up for lost time. But other than that, this is just them. We're tight, all of us. They're brothers. They're gonna want to know my family and be involved. I hope that's not an issue for you."

No way. I loved Rhode's friends.

"No problem. I like having them around and so does Remy. He's got five new uncles to play with. But just to say, Letty's on the verge of physical violence."

Rhode's lips twitched before he smiled wide. "She's found herself six big brothers with protective streaks a mile wide."

True story!

"Well, maybe you can remind Reese she's never had a big brother and tell him to let up on Pen Pal."

"That shit's strange, Sugar. They've been texting for fourteen years. That's a long-ass time not knowing who someone is. All sorts of red flags are waving."

He wasn't wrong. It *was* strange, but strange in a sweet way.

"I would agree if this were new, and in the beginning, I was totally against her texting some random guy, but it's been fourteen years. If he was a bad guy and wanted to hurt her, he would've done it by now."

"The dude could be lying and he's really married with kids."

"So? They're not in a relationship. They're friends and if he has a wife and kids that'd suck only in the sense that would make him a liar. But Pen Pal doesn't scam her for money, doesn't pretend to love her. They're friends. And he's special to her. Letty calls him her MBF. That's Male Best Friend. And he totally is. They tell each other everything and right now Letty needs all the good she can get."

"I'll have a word with Reese," Rhode sighed.

"Okay, back to Arizona. I want to go with you. We'll make it a family vacation. You can show me and Remy all your favorite places. I haven't been back to Arizona since I graduated ASU."

I noticed that Rhode had started to relax but as soon as I said 'family vacation' the remaining tightness vanished.

"Damn, I love you."

Damn. I loved to hear him tell me he loved me.

"Wanna make out?" I blurted.

Rhode's body started vibrating under me right before he boomed a laugh. His first since Remy had been taken.

"All this time I thought I fell in love with you when I first saw you. I was wrong. I didn't *fall*, I was *falling,* and every day since you found me, I've been falling deeper and deeper in love with you, Rhode Daley. Love at first sight isn't real, it's the *beginning* of real. The real love inches its way in. The real love grows a little more every day. Real love isn't a moment in time—it's *all* the moments. As they happen, as they collect, as they continue."

"Ocean blue," he groaned while tipping his chin and tilting his head.

Rhode didn't make out with me.

Though his tongue glided against mine lazily, his lips moved over mine gently, his hands roamed over my rear end and up my back slowly.

He was taking and giving and doing both really well.

I leaned in deeper, moaning into his mouth. He unfortunately broke the kiss but not our connection.

"I want more kids," he muttered against my lips.

"Yeah?"

"As many as you'll give me, Sugar. I want Remy to have brothers and sisters. I want to see you carry our child. I want to hold your hand, I want to hear their first breaths. And not because I missed those things with Remington. I just plain want them."

I fought back the need to strip him naked and get a jump start on making those babies right then.

"Okay."

"I want us to settle into our home, give Remy what he needs to heal. After that, I want to give you and my son my last name."

"As they happen," I whispered.

"Collecting all the moments as they come, Sugar. But I'm telling you now so you're not disappointed—can't fall any more in love with you, can't give you more of my heart, and you can't dig any deeper. It's yours, everything, the blood in my veins, the beat in my heart, the air I breathe. All for you, Sugar."

Perhaps I couldn't fall more in love with Rhode.

"And you say I'm the sweet one."

"No, I said you *taste* sweet."

Little feet pounded on the hardwood floors, then a flying leap had Rhode and I separating just in the nick of time. Remington landed between us with a humph.

"Pancakes!" he demanded.

"Inside voice," I half-heartedly scolded.

"Pancakes," Remy whispered.

"Cheeky boy."

I ruffled my son's thick brown hair at the same time Rhode's hand went to Remy's belly, making our son twist and kick.

"Uncle. Uncle!"

Rhode's gaze lifted to mine, and as it happened so many times before when I saw the happiness dancing in his eyes, my lungs seized.

Speech*less*.

Breath stolen.

Butterflies swarming.

"Nap time?" Rhode smiled.

Oh, yeah!

"To be continued," I agreed and climbed off my man, leaving him to tickle his son.

I was halfway to the kitchen when Rhode called my name.

"Brooklyn?"

I glanced over my shoulder—father and son, hair messy, identical smiles, same sweet look in their eyes.

"Infinitely," he said.

"What?"

"To be continued, *infinitely*."

Yes, breath*less*.

Funny thing about love, the magnificence of it, the reality of it, the moments that start collecting, the beginning that's a forever, and an ending that's a never.

35

Letty Welsh

For the first time in three—no scratch that, four months—I felt normal.

I'd rolled out of bed with a pep in my step and was ready to take on the day. It was the first morning since my sister died that I hadn't felt the crushing weight of guilt. I thought this was a good sign.

A healthy sign.

A sign I was ready to accept my sister was gone and having a loving, normal relationship with her was no longer an option for me.

That was the tricky part, where the guilt and near-constant regret came from. I'd never had a good relationship with Kiki. It was like she was incapable of being a nice person for more than an hour. And it sucked to think ill of the dead but it was the truth. Now she was gone and she'd died with me being furious with her, prepared to tell her she was figuratively dead to me. Then she became very literally dead.

But this morning, I'd woken up for the first time since

she'd died and remembered she'd saved Remington's life. The last breath she took had been for my nephew and I could no longer be angry with her.

However, my good day shit the bed when I opened up my kickass bookstore, Smutties, and Reese and Jack were waiting for me in the store—*in it*—when the door had been locked and the alarm had been set.

"Why me?" I muttered as I walked across the store.

"Why not you?" Jack returned and I narrowed my eyes on him.

"You need better coffee, woman," Reese complained.

"You know who has awesome coffee? Treats Bakery two doors down."

A wide, lecherous smile formed on Reese's stupidly handsome face and at the same time, he wagged his eyebrows.

"Don't I know it?"

"Please tell me you're not banging Sadie," I groaned. "She's one of the few people I really like."

"He wishes he was banging Sadie." Jack laughed. "He only knows how good the coffee is there because the last time he went in, Sadie dumped a very large caramel iced coffee with extra whip over his head."

"Noooo!" I chuckled. "Sadie did that?"

"Yup."

"It's called foreplay." Reese waved his hand like he was swiping the words out of the air. "She wants me. She's just not ready to admit it yet."

"You're lucky you're hot, friend, because you don't have much going on between your ears."

"You think I'm hot?"

Reese smirked and even that was hot.

"Please, you know you're hot. Too bad you're a pain in the ass and you have serious commitment issues."

Jack tossed his head back and laughed.

It must be said, Jack was good-looking, too, with the coolest coal-black eyes I'd ever seen. He was also a pain-in-my-ass big-brother-type and too tall and big for my liking. I liked my men strong but lean, not giants that towered over me and looked like they could crush me with one hand. Besides, I'd sworn off men. At least until I got over the stupid crush I'd been nursing for fourteen years on a man I'd never met in person. It was so insanely ridiculous, I was sick of thinking about it.

Time to move on.

Without telling my hand to do it, I rubbed the ache in my chest.

"You okay?" Reese asked.

"No. You're in my bookstore bothering me," I huffed.

"You love us."

It was a sad truth but I totally loved them all.

"I have work to do," I declared haughtily.

"By all means, don't let us stop you."

A light bulb moment struck.

"As long as you're here, put your muscles to work and help me sort the boxes of books I got in yesterday."

Two   grown-assed-too-big-for-their-own-good   men groaned like five year olds and stood.

The chime over the door rang and I turned to see the finest, hottest, sexiest man I'd ever seen in my life walk in my bookstore.

Well, hello, handsome.

"Can I help you?" Reese boomed and I wanted to kick him in the shins.

"Yeah, I'm looking for Letty."

Yes, today was going to be an awesome day if this man was looking for me.

But before I could speak, Jack got in there first.

"And you are?"

"A friend."

It was then my insides froze and my heart slammed into my ribs like a freight train.

I knew that voice.

I just didn't know the man.

"River?"

His icy blue eyes locked onto mine and he scowled.

Letty Welsh and River Kent are up next in Dangerous Rescue

ALSO BY RILEY EDWARDS

Riley Edwards

www.RileyEdwardsRomance.com

Takeback

Dangerous Love

Dangerous Rescue

Gemini Group

Nixon's Promise

Jameson's Salvation

Weston's Treasure

Alec's Dream

Chasin's Surrender

Holden's Resurrection

Jonny's Redemption

Red Team - Susan Stoker Universe

Nightstalker

Protecting Olivia

Redeeming Violet

Recovering Ivy

Rescuing Erin

The Gold Team - Susan Stoker Universe

Brooks

Thaddeus

Kyle

Standalone

Romancing Rayne

Falling for the Delta Co-written with Susan Stoker

BE A REBEL

Riley Edwards is a USA Today and WSJ bestselling author, wife, and military mom. Riley was born and raised in Los Angeles but now resides on the east coast with her fantastic husband and children.

Riley writes heart-stopping romance with sexy alpha heroes and even stronger heroines. Riley's favorite genres to write are romantic suspense and military romance.

Don't forget to sign up for Riley's newsletter and never miss another release, sale, or exclusive bonus material.

Rebels Newsletter

Facebook Fan Group

www.rileyedwardsromance.com

facebook.com/Novelist.Riley.Edwards

instagram.com/rileyedwardsromance

bookbub.com/authors/riley-edwards

amazon.com/author/rileyedwards

ACKNOWLEDGMENTS

To all of you – the readers: Thank you for picking up this book and giving me a few hours of your time. Whether this is the first book of mine you've read or you've been with me from the beginning, thank you for your support. It is because of you I have the coolest job in the world.

Made in the USA
Monee, IL
10 December 2022

20676899R00203